Ride Proud, Rebel!

BY ANDRE NORTON

Storm Over Warlock
Galactic Derelict
The Time Traders
Star Born
Yankee Privateer
The Stars Are Ours!

EDITED BY ANDRE NORTON

Space Pioneers
Space Service

ANDRE NORTON [pseud]

Alice Mary Norton
III

RIDE PROUD, REBEL!

THE WORLD PUBLISHING COMPANY

CLEVELAND AND NEW YORK

To those Reconstructed Rebels
ERNESTINE and WILLIAM DONALDY
with no apologies from a damnyankee

The author wishes to express appreciation to Mrs. Gertrude Morton Parsley, Reference Librarian, Tennessee State Library and Archives, for her aid in obtaining use of the unpublished memoirs of trooper John Johnson, concerning the escape of the Morgan company after Cynthiana.

Cop. 2

Published by The World Publishing Company
2231 West 110th Street, Cleveland 2, Ohio

Published simultaneously in Canada by
Nelson, Foster & Scott Ltd.

Library of Congress Catalog Card Number: 61-6657

First Edition

HC361

Contents

The cause for which you have so long and so manfully struggled, and for which you have braved dangers, endured privations and sufferings, and made so many sacrifices, is today hopeless. . . .

Civil war, such as you have passed through naturally engenders feelings of animosity, hatred and revenge. It is our duty to divest ourselves of all such feelings; and, as far as in our power to do so, to cultivate friendly feelings toward those with whom we have so long contended, and heretofore so widely, but honestly, differed . . .

. . . In bidding you farewell, rest assured that you carry with you my best wishes for your future welfare and happiness. Without, in any way, referring to the merits of the cause in which we have been engaged, your courage and determination, as exhibited on many hard-fought fields, have elicited the respect and admiration of friend and foe. And I now cheerfully and gratefully acknowledge my indebtedness to the officers and men of my command, whose zeal, fidelity and unflinching bravery have been the great source of my success in arms.

I have never, on the field of battle, sent you where I was unwilling to go myself; nor would I now advise you to a course which I felt myself unwilling to pursue. You have been good soldiers; you can be good citizens. Obey the laws, preserve your honor, and the Government to which you have surrendered can afford to be, and will be, magnanimous.   N. B. FORREST, *Lieutenant General*

1

Ride with Morgan

THE stocky roan switched tail angrily against a persistent fly and lipped water, dripping big drops back to the surface of the brook. His rider moved swiftly, with an economy of action, to unsaddle, wipe the besweated back with a wisp of last year's dried grass, and wash down each mud-spattered leg with stream water. Always care for the mount first—when a man's life, as well as the safety of his mission, depended on four subordinate legs more than on his own two.

Though he had little claim to a thoroughbred's points, the roan was as much a veteran of the forces as his groom, with all a veteran's ability to accept and enjoy small favors of the immediate present without speculating too much concerning the future. He blew gustily in pleasure under the attention and began to sample a convenient stand of spring green.

His mount cared for, Drew Rennie swung up saddle, blanket, and the meager possessions which he had brought out of Virginia two weeks ago, to the platform in a crooked tree overhanging the brook. He settled beside them on the well-seasoned timbers of the old tree house to rummage through his saddlebags.

The platform had been there a long time—before Chickamauga and the Ohio Raid, before the first roll of drums in '61. Drew pulled a creased shirt out of the bags and sat with it draped over one knee, remembering. . . .

Sheldon Barrett and he—they had built it together one hot week in summer—had named it Boone's Fort. And it was the only thing at Red Springs Drew had really ever owned. His dark eyes were fixed now on something more than the branches about him, and his mouth tightened until his face was not quite sullen, only shuttered.

Five years ago—only five years? Yes, five years next month! But the past two years of his own personal freedom —and war—those seemed to equal ten. Now there was no one left to remember the fort's existence, which made it perfect for his present purpose.

The warmth of the sun, beating down through yet young leaves, made Drew brush his battered slouch hat to the flooring and luxuriate in the heat. Sometimes he didn't think he'd ever get the bite of last winter's cold out of his bones. The light pointed up every angle of jaw and cheekbone, making it clear that experience—hard experience— and not years had melted away boyish roundness of chin line, narrowed the watchful eyes ever alert to his surroundings. A cavalry scout was wary, or he ceased to be a scout, or maybe even alive.

Shirt in hand, Drew dropped lightly to the ground and with the same dispatch as he had cared for his horse, made his own toilet, scrubbing his too-thin body with a sigh of content as heartfelt as that the roan had earlier voiced.

The fresh shirt was a dark brown-gray, but the patched breeches were Yankee blue, and the boots he pulled on when he had bathed were also the enemy's gift, good stout leather he'd been lucky enough to find in a supply wagon they had captured a month ago. Butternut shirt, Union pants and boots—the unofficial standard uniform of most any trooper of the Army of the Tennessee in this month of May, 1864. And he had garments which were practically intact. What was one patch on the seat nowadays?

For the first time Drew grinned at his reflection in the small mirror he had been using, when he scraped a half week's accumulation of soft beard from his face. Sure, he was all spruced up now, ready to make a polite courtesy call at the big house. The grin did not fade, but was gone in a flash, leaving no hint of softness now about his gaunt features, no light in the intent, measuring depths of his dark gray eyes.

A call at Red Springs was certainly the last thing in the world for him to consider seriously. His last interview within its walls could still make him wince when he recalled it, word by scalding word. No, there was no place for a Rennie —and a Rebel Rennie to make matters blacker—under the righteous roof of Alexander Mattock!

Hatred could be a red-hot burning to choke a man's throat, leaving him speechless and hurting inside. Since he had ridden out of Red Springs he had often been cold, very often hungry—and under orders willingly, which would have surprised his grandfather—but in another way he had been free as never before in all his life. In the army, the past did not matter at all if one did one's job well. And in the army, the civilian world was as far away as if it were conducted in the cold chasms of the moon.

Drew leaned back against the tree trunk, wanting to

yield to the soft wind and the swinging privacy of the em-
bowered tree house, wanting to forget everything and just
lie there for a while in the only part of the past he remembered happily.

But he had his orders—horses for General Morgan, horses
and information to feed back to that long column of men
riding or trudging westward on booted, footsore feet up
the trail through the Virginia mountains on the way home
to Kentucky. These were men who carried memories of
the Ohio defeat last year which they were determined to
wipe out this season, just as a lot of them had to flush with
gunsmoke the stench of a Northern prison barracks from
their nostrils.

And there were horses at Red Springs. To mount Morgan's men on Alexander Mattock's best stock was a prospect which had its appeal. Drew tossed his haversack back
to the platform and added his carbine to it. The army Colts in
his belt holsters would not be much hindrance while crawl-
ing through cover, but the larger weapon might be.

He thumped a measure of dust from his hat, settled it
over hair as black as that felt had once been, and crossed
the brook with a running leap. The roan lifted his head to
watch Drew go and then settled back to grazing. This, too,
followed a pattern both man and horse had practiced for
a long time.

Drew could almost imagine that he was again hunting
Sheldon as a "Shawnee" on the warpath while he dodged
from one bush to the next. Only Chickamauga stood between the past and now—and Sheldon Barrett would never
again range ahead, in play or earnest.

The scout came out on a small rise where the rails of the

fence were cloaked on his side by brush. Drew lay flat, his chin propped upon his crooked arm to look down the gradual incline of the pasture to the training paddock. Beyond that stood the big house, its native brick settling back slowly into the same earth from which it had been molded in 1795.

In the pasture were the brood mares, five of them, each with an attendant foal, all long legs and broom tail, still young enough to be bewildered by so large and new a world. In the paddock . . . Drew's head raised an inch or so, and he pressed forward until his hat was pushed back by the rail. The two-year-old being schooled in the paddock was enough to excite any horseman.

Red Springs' stock right enough, of the Gray Eagle-Ariel breed, which was Alexander Mattock's pride. Born almost black, this colt had shed his baby fur two seasons ago for a dark iron-gray hide which would grow lighter with the years. He had Eclipse's heritage, but he was more than a racing machine. He was—Drew's forehead rasped against the weathered wood of the rail—he was the kind of horse a man could dream about all his days and perhaps find once in a lifetime, if he were lucky! Give that colt three or four more years and there wouldn't be any horse that could touch him. Not in Kentucky, or anywhere else!

He was circling on a leading strap now, throwing his feet in a steady, rhythmic pattern around the hub of a Negro groom who was holding the strap and admiring the action. Mounted on another gray—a mare with a dainty, high-held head—was a woman, her figure trim in a habit almost the same shade of green as the fields.

Drew pulled back. Then he smiled wryly at his instinctive

retreat. His aunt, Marianna Forbes, had abilities to be respected, but he very much doubted if she could either sense his presence or see through the leafy wall of his present spy hole. Yet caution dictated that he get about his real business and inspect the fields where the horses he sought should be grazing.

He halted several times during his perimeter march to survey the countryside. And the bits of activity he spied upon began to puzzle him. Aunt Marianna's supervision of the colt's schooling had been the beginning. And he had seen her later, riding out with Rafe, the overseer, to make the daily rounds, a duty which had never been undertaken at Red Springs by any one other than his grandfather.

Aunt Marianna had every right to be at Red Springs. She had been born under its roof, having left it only as a bride to live in Lexington. The war had brought her back when her husband became an officer in the Second Kentucky Cavalry—Union. But now—riding with Rafe, watching in the paddock—where was Alexander Mattock?

Red Springs was his grandfather. Drew found it impossible to think of the house and the estate without the man, though in the past two years he had discovered very few things could be dismissed as impossible. Curiosity made him want to investigate the present mystery. But the memory of his last exit from that house curbed such a desire.

Drew had never been welcome there from the day of his birth within those walls. And the motive for his final flight from there had only provided an added aggravation for his grandfather. A staunch Union supporter wanted no part of a stubborn-willed and defiant grandson who rode with John Hunt Morgan. Drew clung to his somewhat black thoughts as he made his way to the pasture. The escape he had found in the army was no longer so complete when he skulked through these familiar fields.

But there were only two horses grazing peacefully in the field dedicated by custom to the four- and five-year-olds, and neither was of the best stock. One could imagine that Red Springs had already contributed to the service.

Of course, Morgan's men were not the only riders aiming to sweep good horseflesh out of Kentucky blue grass this season, and here the Union cavalry would be favored.

There was a slim chance that a few horses might be in the stables. He debated the chance of that against the risk of discovery and continued debating it as he started back to the tree house.

Drew had known short rations and slim foraging for a long time, but the present pinch in his middle sharpened when he sighted the big house, with its attendant summer kitchen showing a trail of chimney smoke.

Alexander Mattock might have considered his grandson an interloper at Red Springs; certainly the old man never concealed the state of his feelings on that subject. But neither had he, in any way, slighted what he deemed to be his duty toward Drew.

There had been plenty of good clothing—the right sort for a Mattock grandson—and the usual bounteous table set by hospitable Kentucky standards. Just as there had been education, sometimes enforced by the use of a switch when the tutor—imported from Lexington—thought it necessary to impress learning on a rebellious young mind by a painful application in another portion of the body. Education, as well as a blooded horse in the stables, and all the other prerequisites of a young blue-grass grandee. But never any understanding, affection, or sympathy.

That cold behavior—the cutting, weighing, and judgment of every act of childish mischief and boyish recklessness— might have crushed some into a colorless obedience. But it had made of Drew a rebel long before he tugged on the short gray shell jacket of a Confederate cavalryman.

Drew had forgotten the feel of linen next to his now sel- dom clean skin, the set of broadcloth across the shoulders. And he depended upon the roan's services with appreciation which had nothing to do with boasted bloodlines, having dis- covered in the army that a cold-blooded horse could keep going on rough forage when a finer bred hunter broke down. But today the famed dinner table at Red Springs was a pain- ful memory to one facing only cold hoecake and stone-hard dried beef.

He had circled back to the brush screening the brook and the tree house. Now he stood very still, his hand sliding one of the heavy Colts out of its holster. The roan was still grazing, paying no attention to a figure who was kneeling on the limb-supported platform and turning over the gear Drew had left piled there.

The scout flitted about a bush, choosing a path which would bring him out at the stranger's back. That same warm sun, now striking from a different angle into the tree house, was bright on a thick tangle of yellow hair, curly enough to provide its owner with a combing problem.

Drew straightened to his full height. The sense of the past which had dogged him all day now struck like a blow. He couldn't help calling aloud that name, even though the soberer part of his brain knew there could be no answer.

"Shelly!"

The blond head turned, and blue eyes looked at him, startled, across a bowed shoulder. Drew's puzzlement was complete. Not Sheldon, of course, but who? The other's open surprise changed to wide-eyed recognition first.

"Drew!" The hail came in the cracked voice of an adolescent as the other jumped down to face the scout. They stood at almost eye-to-eye level, but the stranger was still all boy, awkwardly unsure of strength or muscle control.

"You must be Boyd—" Drew blinked, something in him still clinging to the memory of Sheldon, Sheldon who had helped to build the tree house. Why, Boyd was only a small boy, usually tagging his impatient elders, not this tall, almost exact copy of his dead brother.

"Sure, I'm Boyd. And it's true then, ain't it, Drew? General Morgan's coming back here? Where?" He glanced over his shoulder once more as if expecting to see a troop prance up through the bushes along the stream.

Drew holstered the revolver. "Rumors of that around?" he asked casually.

"Some," Boyd answered. "The Yankee-lovers called out the Home Guard yesterday. What sort of a chance do they think they'll have against *General Morgan*?"

Drew moved toward the roan's picket rope. As his fingers closed on that he thought fast. Just as the Mattocks and the Forbeses were Union, the Barretts were, or had been, Southern in sympathy. Most of Kentucky was divided that way now. But what might have been true two years ago was not necessarily a fact today. One took no chances.

"You come back to see your grandfather, Drew?"

"Any reason why I should?" The whole countryside must

know very well the state of affairs between Alexander Mattock and Drew Rennie.

"Well, he's been sick for so long . . . Didn't you know about that?" Boyd must have read Drew's answer in his face, for he spilled out the news quickly. "He had some kind of a fit when he heard Murray was killed——"

Drew dropped the picket rope. "Uncle Murray . . . dead?"

Boyd nodded. "Killed at Murfreesboro in sixty-two, but the news didn't come till about a week after the battle. Mr. Mattock was in town when Judge Hagerstorm told him . . . just turned red in the face and fell down in the middle of the street. They brought him home, and sometimes he sits outdoors. But he can't walk too good and he talks thick; you can hardly understand him."

"So that's why Aunt Marianna's in charge." Drew thought of Uncle Murray swept away by time and the chances of war as so many others—and no emotion stirred within him. Murray Mattock had firmly agreed with his father concerning the child who was the result of a runaway match between his sister Melanie and a despised Texan. But Uncle Murray's death must indeed have been a paralyzing blow for the old man at Red Springs, with all his pride and his plans for his only son.

"Yes, Cousin Marianna runs Red Springs," Boyd assented, "she and Rafe. They sell horses to the army—the blue bellies." He used the term with the concentration of one determined to say the right thing at the right time.

Drew laughed. And with that spontaneous outburst, years fell away from his somber face. "I take it that you do not approve of blue bellies, Boyd?"

" 'Course not! Me, I'm goin' to join General Morgan now.

Ain't nobody goin' to keep me from doin' that!" Again his voice scaled up out of control, and he flushed.

"You're rather young——" Drew began, when the other interrupted him with something close to desperation in his voice.

"No, I ain't too young! That's all I ever hear—too young to do this, too young to be thinkin' about things like that! Well, I ain't much younger than you were, Drew Rennie, when you joined up with Captain Castleman and rode south to join General Morgan—you and Shelly. And you know that, too! I'll be sixteen on the fifteenth of this July. And this time I'm goin'! Where's the General now, Drew?"

The scout shrugged. "Movin' fast. Your rumors probably know as much as I do. They plant him half a dozen places at once. He might be in any one of them or fifty miles away; that's how Morgan rides."

"But you're goin' to join him, and you'll take me with you, won't you, Drew?"

The lightness was gone from the older boy's eyes, his mouth set in controlled anger. "I am not goin' to do anything of the kind, Boyd Barrett." He spoke the words slowly, in an even tone, with a fraction of pause between each. Men of the command had once or twice heard young Rennie speak that way. Although difficult to know well, he had the general reputation of being easy to get along with. But a few times he had erupted into action as might a spring uncoiling from tight pressure, and that action was usually preceded by just such quiet statements as the one he had just made to Boyd.

Boyd, however, was never one to be defeated in a first skirmish of wills. "Why not?" he demanded now.

"Because," Drew offered the first argument he could think of which might be acceptable to the other, "I'm on scout in enemy-held territory. If I'm taken, it's not good. I have to ride light and fast, and this is duty I've been trained to do. So I can't afford to be hampered by a green kid——"

"I can ride just as fast and hard as you can, Drew Rennie, and I have Whirlaway for my own now. He's certainly better than that nag!" With an arrogant lift of the chin, Boyd indicated the roan, who had raised his head and was chewing rather noisily, regarding the two by the tree house with mild interest.

"Don't underrate Shawnee." For an instant Drew rose to the roan's defense and then found himself irritated at being so drawn from the main argument. "And I wouldn't care if you had Gray Eagle, himself, under you, boy—I'm not taking you with me. Let us be snapped up by the Yankees, and you'd be in bigger trouble than I would." He gestured to his shirt and breeches. "I'm in uniform; you ain't."

"No blue bellies could drop on us," Boyd pushed. "I know where all the garrisons are round here—all about their patrols. I could get us through quicker'n you can, yourself. I ain't no green kid!"

Drew slapped the blanket down on Shawnee's back, smoothed it flat with a palm stroke, and jerked his saddle from the platform. He could not stay right here now that Boyd had smoked him out—maybe nowhere in the neighborhood with this excitable boy dogging him.

The scout was driven to his second line of defense. "What about Cousin Merry?" he asked as he tightened the cinch. "Have you talked this over with her—enlistin', I mean?"

Boyd's lower lip protruded in a child's pout. His eyes shifted away from Drew's direct gaze.

"She never said No——"

"Did you ask her?" Drew challenged.

"Did you ask your grandfather when you left?" Boyd tried a counterattack.

This time Drew's laughter was harsh, without humor. "You know I didn't, and you also know why. But I didn't leave a mother!"

He was being purposefully brutal now, for a good reason. Sheldon had ridden away before; Boyd must not go now. In Drew's childhood, his father's cousin, Meredith Barrett, had been the only one who had really cared about him. His only escape from the cold bleakness of Red Springs had been Barrett's Oak Hill. There was a big debt he owed Cousin Merry; he could not add to it the burden of taking away her second son.

Sure, he had been only a few months older than this boy when he had run away to war, but he had not left anyone behind who would worry about him. And Alexander Mattock's cold discipline had tempered his grandson into someone far more able to take hard knocks than Boyd Barrett might be for years to come. Drew had met those knocks, thick and fast, enduring them as the price of his freedom.

"You were mad at your grandfather, and you ran away. Well, I ain't mad at Mother, but I ain't goin' to sit at home with General Morgan comin'! He needs men. They've been recruitin' for him on the quiet; you know they have. And I've got to make up for Sheldon——"

Drew swung around and caught Boyd's wrist in a grip

tight enough to bring a reflex backward jerk from the boy. "That's no way to make up for Sheldon's death—runnin' away from home to fight. Don't give me any nonsense about goin' to kill Yankees because they killed him! When a man goes to war . . . well, he takes his chances. Shelly did at Chickamauga. War ain't a private fight, just one man up against another—"

But he was making no impression; he couldn't. At Boyd's age you could not imagine death as coming to you; nor were you able to visualize the horrors of an ill-equipped field hospital. Any more than you could picture all the rest of it—the filth, hunger, cold, and boredom with now and then a flash of whirling horses and men clashing on some road or field, or the crazy stampede of other men, yelling their throats raw as they charged into a hell of Minié balls and canister shot.

"I'm goin' to ride with General Morgan, like Shelly did," Boyd repeated doggedly, with that stubbornness which seasons ago had kept him eternally tagging his impatient elders.

"That's up to you." Suddenly Drew was tired, tired of trying to find words to pierce to Boyd's thinking brain—if one had a thinking brain at his age. Slinging his carbine, Drew mounted Shawnee. "But I do know one thing—you're not goin' with me."

"Drew—Drew, just listen once . . ."

Shawnee answered to the pressure of his rider's knees and leaped the brook. Drew bowed his head to escape the lash of a low branch. There was no going back ever, he thought bitterly, shutting his ears to Boyd's cry. He'd been a fool to ride this way at all.

2

Guns in the Night

THERE were sounds enough in the middle of the night to tell the initiated that a troop was on the march—creak of saddle leather, click of shod hoof, now and then the smothered exclamation of a man shaken out of a cavalryman's mounted doze. To Drew's trained ears all this was loud enough to send any Union picket calling out the guard. Yet there was no indication that the enemy ahead was alert.

Near two o'clock he made it, and the advance were walking their horses into the fringe of Lexington—this was homecoming for a good many of the men sagging in the saddles. Morgan's old magic was working again. Escaping from the Ohio prison, he had managed to gather up the remnants of a badly shattered command, weld them together, and lead them up from Georgia to their old fighting fields—the country which they considered rightfully theirs and in which during other years they had piled one humiliating defeat for the blue coats on another. General Morgan could *not* lose in Kentucky!

And they already had one minor victory to taste sweet: Mount Sterling had fallen into their hold as easily as it had before. Now Lexington—with the horses they needed—friends and families waiting to greet them.

Captain Tom Quirk's Irish brogue, unmistakable even in a half whisper, came out of the dark: "Pull up, boys!"

Drew came to a halt with his flanking scout. There was a faint drum of hoofs from behind as three horsemen caught up with the first wave of Quirk's Scouts.

"Taking the flag in . . ." Drew caught a snatch of sentence passed between the leader of the newcomers and his own officer. He recognized the voice of John Castleman, his former company commander.

". . . worth a try . . ." that was Quirk.

But when the three had cantered on into the mouth of the street the scout captain turned his head to the waiting shadows. "Rennie, Bruce, Croxton . . . give them cover!"

Drew sent Shawnee on, his carbine resting ready across his saddle. The streets were quiet enough, too quiet. These dark houses showed no signs of life, but surely the Yankees were not so confident that they would not have any pickets posted. And Fort Clay had its garrison . . .

Then that ominous silence was broken by Castleman's call: "Bearer of flag of truce!"

". . . Morgan's men?" A woman called from a window up ahead, her voice so low pitched Drew heard only a word or two. Castleman answered her before he gave the warning:

"Battery down the street, boys. Take to the sidewalks!"

A lantern bobbed along in their direction. Drew had a glimpse of a blue-uniformed arm above it. A moment later Castleman rode back. One of his companions swerved close-by, and Drew recognized Key Morgan, the General's brother.

"They say, 'No surrender.'"

Perhaps that was what they said. But the skirmishers were now drifting into town. Orders snapped from man to man through the dark. The crackle of small-arms fire came sporadically, to be followed by the heavier *boom-boom* as cannon balls from Fort Clay ricocheted through the streets, the Yankees being forced back into the protection of that stronghold. Riders threaded through alleys and cross streets; lamps flared up in house windows. There was a pounding on doors, and shouted greetings. Fire made a splash of angry color at the depot, to be answered with similar blazes at the warehouses.

"Spur up those crowbaits of yours, boys!" Quirk rounded up the scouts. "We're out for horses—only the best, remember that!"

Out of the now aroused Lexington just as daylight was gray overhead, they were on the road to Ashland. If Red Springs might have proved poor picking, John Clay's stables did not. One sleek thoroughbred after another was led from the stalls while Quirk fairly purred.

"Skedaddle! Would you believe it? Here's Skedaddle, himself, just aching to show heels to the blue bellies, ain't you?" He greeted the great racer. "Now that's the sort of stuff we need! Give us another chase across the Ohio clean up to Canada with a few like him under us. Sweep 'em clean and get going! The General wants to see the catch before noon."

Drew watched the mounts being led down the lane. Beautiful, yes, but to his mind not one of them was the equal of the gray colt he had seen at Red Springs. Now that was a horse! And he was not tempted now to strip his saddle off Shawnee and transfer to any one of the princes of equine blood passing him by. He knew the roan, and Shawnee knew his job. Knows more about the work than I do sometimes, Drew thought.

"You, Rennie!"

Drew swung Shawnee to the left as Quirk hailed him.

"Take point out on the road. Just like some stubborn Yankee to try and cut away a nice little catch like this."

"Yes, sir." Drew merely sketched a salute; discipline was always free and easy in the Scouts.

The day was warm. He was glad he had managed to find a lightweight shirt back at the warehouse in town. If they didn't win Lexington to keep, at least all of the raiders were going to ride out well-mounted, with boots on their feet and whole clothing on their backs. The Union quartermasters did just fine by Morgan's boys, as always.

Shawnee's ears went forward alertly, but Drew did not need that signal of someone's approaching. He backed into the shadow-shade of a tree and sat tense, with Colt in hand.

A horse nickered. There was the whirr of wheels. Drew edged Shawnee out of cover and then quickly holstered his weapon, riding out to bring to a halt the carriage horse between the shafts of an English dogcart.

He pulled off his dust-grayed hat. "Good mornin', Aunt Marianna."

Such a polite greeting—the same words he would have used three years ago had they met in the hall of Red Springs on their way to breakfast. He wanted to laugh, or was it really laughter which lumped in his throat?

Her momentary expression of outrage faded as she leaned forward to study his face, and she relaxed her first half-threatening grip on her whip. Though Aunt Marianna had never been a beauty, her present air of assurance and authority became her, just as the smart riding habit was better suited to her somewhat angular frame than the ruffles and bows of the drawing room.

"Drew!" Her recognition of his identity had come more slowly than Boyd's, and it sounded almost wary.

"At your service, ma'am." He found himself again using the graces of another way of life, far removed from his sweat-stained shirt and patched breeches. He shot a glance over his shoulder, making sure they were safely alone on that stretch of highway. After all, one horse among so many would be no great loss to his commander. "You'd better turn around. The boys'll have Lady Jane out of the shaft before you get into Lexington if you keep on. And the Yankees are still pepperin' the place with round shot." He wondered why she was driving without a groom, but did not quite dare to ask.

"Drew, is Boyd here with you?"

"Boyd?"

"Don't be evasive with me, boy!" She rapped that out with an officer's snap. "He left a note for Merry—two words misspelled and a big blot—all foolishness about joining Morgan. Said you had been to Red Springs, and he was going along. Why did you do it, Drew? Cousin Merry . . . after Sheldon, she can't lose Boyd, too! To put such a wild idea into that child's head!"

Drew's lips thinned into a half grimace. He was still cast in the role of culprit, it seemed. "I didn't influence Boyd to do anything, Aunt Marianna. I told him I wouldn't take him with me, and I meant it. If he ran away, it was his own doin'."

She was still measuring him with that intent look as if he were a slightly unsatisfactory colt being put through his paces in the training paddock.

"Then you'll help me get him back home?" That was more a statement than a question, delivered in a voice which was all Mattock, enough to awaken by the mere sound all the old resistance in him.

He nodded at the Lexington road. "There are several thousand men ahead there, ma'am. Hunting Boyd out if he wants to hide from me—and he will—is impossible. He's big enough to pass a recruiter; they ain't too particular about age these days. And he'll stay just as far from me as he can until he is sworn in. He already knows how I feel about his enlistin'."

Her gloved hands tightened on the reins. "If I could see John Morgan himself—"

"*If* you could get to Lexington and find him—"

"But Boyd's just a child. He hasn't the slightest idea of war except the stories he hears . . . no idea of what could happen to him, or what this means to Merry. All this criminal nonsense about being a soldier—sabers and spurs, and dashing around behind a flag, the wrong flag, too—" She caught her breath in an unusual betrayal of emotion. And now she studied Drew with some deliberation, noting his thinness, itemizing his shabbiness.

He smiled tiredly. "No, I ain't Boyd's idea of a returnin' hero, am I?" he agreed with her unspoken comment. "Also, we Rebs don't use sabers; they ain't worth much in a real skirmish."

She flushed. "Drew, why did you go? Was it all because of Father? I know he made it hard for you."

"You know—" Drew regarded a circling bird in the section of sky above her head—"some day I hope I'll discover just what kind of a no-account Hunt Rennie was, to make his son so unacceptable. Most of the Texans I've ridden with in the army haven't been so bad; some of them are downright respectable."

"I don't know." Again she flushed. "It was a long time ago when it all happened. I was just a little girl. And Father, well, he has very strong prejudices. But, Drew, for you to go against everything you'd been taught, to turn Rebel— that added to his bitterness. And now Boyd is trying to go the same way. Isn't there something you can do? I can't stand to see that look in Merry's eyes. If we can just get Boyd home again——"

"Don't hope too much." Drew was certain that nothing Marianna Forbes could do was going to lead Boyd Barrett back home again. On the other hand, if the boy had not formally enlisted, perhaps the rigors of one of the General's usual cross-country scrambles might be disillusioning. But, having tasted the quality of Boyd's stubbornness in the past, Drew doubted that. For long months he had been able to cut right out of his life Red Springs and all it stood for; now it was trying to put reins on him again. He shifted his weight in the saddle.

"He's been restless all spring," his aunt continued. "We might have known that, given an opportunity like this, the boy would do something wild. Only the waste, the sinful waste! I can't go back and face Merry without trying something—anything! Can't you . . . Drew?"

"I don't know." He couldn't harden himself to tell her the truth. "I'll try," he promised vaguely.

"Drew—" A change in tone brought his attention back to her. She looked disturbed, almost embarrassed. "Have you had a hard time? You look so . . . so thin and tired. Is there anything you need?"

He flinched from any such attack on the shell he had built against the intrusion of Red Springs, for a second or two feeling once more the rasp across raw nerves. "We don't get much time for sleep when the General's on the prod. Horse stealin' and such keeps us a mite busy, accordin' to your Yankee friends. And we have to pay our respects to them, just to keep them reminded that this is Morgan country. I'll warn you again, Aunt Marianna, keep Lady Jane out of Lexington today—if you want to keep *her*." He gathered up his reins. "Boyd told me about Grandfather," he added in a rush. "I'm sorry." And he was, he told himself, sorry for Aunt Marianna, who had to stay at Red Springs now, and even a little in an impersonal way for the old man, who must find inactivity a worse prison than any stone-walled room. But it was being polite about a stranger. "Major Forbes . . . he's all right?"

"Yes. Only, Drew—" Again the urgency in her voice held him against his will, "Boyd . . ."

He was saved further evasion by a carrying whistle from down the road, the signal to pull in pickets. Pursing his own lips, he answered.

"I have to go. I'll do what I can." He set Shawnee pounding along the pike, and he did not look back.

If he were ever to fulfill his promise to locate Boyd, that would have to come later. Quirk's horse catch delivered, the scouts were on the move again, on the Georgetown road, riding at a pace which suggested they must keep ahead of a boiling wasp's nest of Yankees. There was an embarrassment of blue-coat prisoners on the march between two lines of gray uniforms, and pockets of the enemy such as that at Fort Clay were left behind. The strike northward took on a feverish drive.

Georgetown with its streets full of women and cheering males, too old or too young to be riding with the columns. Mid-afternoon, Friday, and the heat rising from the pavement as only June heat could. Then they reached the Frankfort road, and the main command halted. The scouts ate in the saddle as they fanned out along the Frankfort pike, pushing toward Cynthiana. Sam Croxton strode back from filling his canteen at a farmyard well and scowled at Drew, who had dismounted and loosened cinch to cool Shawnee's back.

"Cynthiana, now. I'm beginnin' to wonder, Rennie, if we know just which way we are goin'."

Drew shrugged. "Might be a warm reception waitin' us there. Drake figures about five hundred Yankees on the spot, and trains comin' in with more all the time."

Sighing, Croxton rubbed his hand across his freckled face, smearing road dust and sweat into a gritty mask. "Me—I could do with four or five hours' sleep, right down here in the road. Always providin' no blue belly'd trot along to stir me up. Seems like I ain't had a ten minutes' straight nap since we joined up with the main column. Scoutin' ahead a couple weeks ago you could at least fill your belly and rest up at some farm. Them boys pushin' the prisoners back there sure has it tough. Bet some of 'em been eatin' dust most all day—"

"Be glad you're not ridin' in one of the wagons nursin' a hole in your middle." Drew wet his handkerchief, or the sad gray rag which served that purpose, and carefully washed out Shawnee's nostrils, rubbing the horse gently down the nose and around his pricked ears.

Croxton spat and a splotch of brown tobacco juice pocked the roadside gravel. "Now ain't you cheerful!" he observed. "No, I've no hole in my middle, or my top, or my bottom— and I don't want none, neither. All I want is about an hour's sleep without Quirk or Drake breathin' down my back wantin' to know why I'm playin' wagon dog. The which I ain't gonna have very soon by the looks of it. So . . ." He mounted, spat again with accuracy enough to stun a grasshopper off a nodding weed top, which feat seemed to restore a measure of his usual good nature. "Got him! You comin', Rennie?"

The hours of Friday afternoon, evening, night, crawled by —leadenly, as far as the men in the straggling column were concerned. That dash which had carried them through from the Virginia border, through the old-time whirling attack on Mount Sterling only days earlier, and which had brought them into and beyond Lexington, was seeping from tired men who slept in the saddle or fell out, too drugged with fatigue to know that they slumped down along country fences, unconscious gifts for the enemy doggedly drawing in from three sides. There was the core of veterans who had seen this before, been a part of such punishing riding in Illinois, Ohio, and Kentucky. The signs could be read, and as Drew spurred along that faltering line of march late that night, carrying a message, he felt a creeping chill which was not born of the night wind nor a warning of swamp fever.

Before daylight there was another halt. He had to let

Shawnee pick his own careful path around and through groups of dismounted men sleeping with their weapons still belted on, their mounts, heads drooping, standing sentinel.

Saturday's dawn, and the advance had plowed ahead to the forks of the road some three miles out of Cynthiana. One brigade moved directly toward the town; the second— with a detachment of scouts—headed down the right-hand road to cross the Licking River and move in upon the enemies' rear. From the hill they could sight a stone-fence barricade glistening with the metal of waiting musket barrels. Then, suddenly, the old miracle came. Men who had clung through the hours to their saddles by sheer will power alone, tightened their lines and were alertly alive.

The ear-stinging, throat-scratching Yell screeched high over the pound of the artillery, the vicious spat of Minié balls. A whip length of dusty gray-brown lashed forward, flanking the stone barrier. Blue-coated men wavered, broke, ran for the bridge, heading into the streets of the town. The gray lash curled around a handful of laggards and swept them into captivity.

Then the brigade thundered on, driving the enemy back before they could reform, until the Yankees holed up in the courthouse, the depot, a handful of houses. Before eight o'clock it was all over, and the confidence of the weary raiders was back. They had showed 'em!

Drew had the usual mixture of sharp scenes to remember as his small portion of the engagement while he spurred Shawnee on past the blaze which was spreading through the center of the town, licking out for more buildings no one seemed to have the organization nor the will to save. He was riding with the advance of Giltner's brigade, doublequicking it downriver to Keller's Bridge. In town the Yankees were prisoners, but here a long line, with heavy reserves in wedges of blue behind, strung out across open fields.

Once more the Yell arose in sharp ululating wails, and the ragged line swept from the road, tightening into a semblance of the saber blades Morgan's men disdained to use . . . clashed . . . Then, after what seemed like only a moment's jarring pause, it was on the move once more while before it crumpled motes of blue were carried down the slope to the riverbank, there to steady and stand fast.

Drew's throat was aching and dry, but he was still croaking hoarsely, hardly feeling the slam of his Colts' recoils. They were up to that blue line, firing at deadly point-blank range. And part of him wondered how any men could still keep their feet and face back to such an assault with ready muskets. By his side a man skipped as might a marcher trying to catch step, then folded up, sliding limply to the trampled grass.

Men were flinging up hands holding empty cartridge boxes along the attacking line—too many of them. Others reversed the empty carbines, to use them in clubbing duels back and forth. The Union troops fell back, firing still, making their way into the railroad cut. Now the river was a part defense for them. Bayonets caught the sunlight in angry flashing, and they bristled.

"You . . . Rennie . . ."

Drew lurched back under the clutch of a frantic hand belonging to an officer he knew.

"Get back to the horse lines! Bring up the holders' ammunition, on the double!"

Drew ran, panting, his boots slipping and scraping on the grass as he dodged around prone men who still moved, or others who lay only too still. A horse reared, snorted, and was pulled down to four feet again.

"Ammunition!" Drew got the word out as a squawk, grabbing at the boxes the waiting men were already tossing to him. Then, through the haze which had been riding his mind since the battle began, he caught a clear sight of the fifth man there . . . And there was no disguising the blond hair of the boy so eagerly watching the struggle below. Drew had found Boyd—at a time he could do nothing about it. With his arms full, the scout turned to race down the slope again, only to sight the white flag waving from the railroad cut.

More prisoners to be marched along, joining the other dispirited ranks. Drew heard one worried comment from an officer: they would soon have more prisoners than guards.

He went back, trying to locate Boyd, but to no purpose. And the rest of the day was more confusion, heat, never-ending weariness, and always the sense of there being so little time. Rumors raced along the lines, five thousand, ten thousand blue bellies on the march, drawing in from every garrison in the blue grass. And those who had been hunted along the Ohio roads a year before were haunted by that old memory of disaster.

Once more they made their way through the streets of Cynthiana, where the acrid smoke of burning caught at throats, adding to the torturous thirst which dried a man's mouth when he tore cartridge paper with his teeth. Drew and Croxton took sketchy orders from Captain Quirk, their eyes red-rimmed with fatigue above their powder-blackened lips and chins. Fan out, be eyes and ears for the column moving into the Paris pike.

Croxton's grin had no humor in it as they turned aside into a field to make better time away from the cluttered highway.

"Looks like the butter's spread a mite thin on the bread this time," he commented. "But the General's sure playin' it like he has all the aces in hand. Which way to sniff out a Yankee?"

"I'd say any point of the compass now——"

"Listen!" Sam's hand went up. "Those ain't any guns of ours."

The rumble was distant, but Drew believed Croxton was right. Through the dark, guns were moving up. The wasps were closing in on the disturbers of their nest, and every one of them carried a healthy stinger. He thought of what he had seen today: too many empty cartridge boxes, Enfield rifles still carried by men who would not, in spite of orders, discard them for the Yankee guns with ammunition to spare. Empty guns, worn-out men, weary horses . . . and Yankee guns moving confidently up through the night.

3

On the Run—

THEY'RE comin'! Looks like the whole country's sproutin' Yankees outta the ground."

They were, a dull dark mass at first and then an arc of one ominous color advancing in a fast, purposeful drive, already overrunning the pickets with only a lone shot here and there in defiance. They rode up confidently, dismounted, and charged—to be thrown back once. But there were too many of them, and they moved with the precision of men who knew what was to be done and that they could do it. Confederates were trapped before they could reach their horses; there was a wild whirling scramble of a fight flowing backward toward the river.

Men with empty guns turned those guns into clubs, fighting to hold the center. But the enemy had already cut them off from the Augusta road and the bridge, and the river was at their backs. Water boiled under a lead rain. Drew saw an opening between two Union troopers. Flattening himself as best he could on Shawnee's back, he gave the roan the spur. What good could be accomplished by the message he carried now—to bring up half the horse holders as reinforcements—was a question.

However, he was never to deliver that message, for the horse lines had been stampeded by the first wave of flying men. Here and there a holder or two still tried to control at least one wild horse of the four he was responsible for, but there were no reserves for the fighting line. And—Drew glanced back—no battle to lead them into if there were.

Men and horses were struggling, dying in the river. The bridge . . . he gaped at the horror of that bridge . . . horses down, kicking and dying, barring an escape route to their riders. And the blue coats everywhere. Like a stallion about to attack, Shawnee screamed suddenly and reared, his front hoofs beating the air. A spurting red stream fountained from his neck; an artery had been hit.

Drew set teeth in lip, and plugged that bubbling hole with his thumb. Shawnee was dying, but he was still on his feet, and he could be headed away from the carnage in that water. Drew, his face sick and white, turned the horse toward the railroad tracks.

"Drew!"

Croxton? No, but somehow Drew was not surprised to see Boyd trying to keep his feet, being dragged along by two plunging horses, their eyes white-rimmed with terror. The only wonder was that the scout had heard that call through the din of screaming and shouting, the wild neighs of the horses, and the continual crackle of small arms' fire.

"Mount! Mount and ride!" He mouthed the order, not daring to pull up Shawnee, already past Boyd and his horses. The roan's hoofs spurned gravel from the track line now. And Boyd drew level with him and mounted one of the horses, continuing to lead the other. There was a cattle guard ahead to afford some protection from the storm churning along the river.

"Where?" Boyd called.

Drew, his thumb still planted in the hole which was becoming Shawnee's death, nodded to the guard. They made it, and Drew kneed the roan closer to the extra horse Boyd led, slinging his saddlebags across to the other mount. Then he dismounted, releasing his hold on the roan's wound. For the second time Shawnee cried, but this time it was no warrior's protest against death; it was the nicker of a question. The answering shot from Drew's Colt was lost in the battle din. He was upon the other horse before Shawnee had stopped breathing.

"Come on!" Drew's voice was strident as he spurred, herding Boyd before him. Two of them, then three, four, as they came out on the bank of a millpond. Across that stretch of water there was safety, or at least the illusion of safety.

"Drew!" For the second time he was hailed. It was Sam Croxton, holding onto the saddle horn with both hands, a stream of red running from a patch of blood-soaked hair over one ear. He swayed, his eyes wide open as those of the frightened horses, but fastened now on Drew as if the other were the one stable thing in a mad world.

"Can you stick on?" Drew leaned across to catch the reins the other had dropped.

A small spark of understanding awoke in those wide eyes. "I'll stick," the words came thickly. "I ain't gonna rot in that damned prison again—never!"

"Boyd . . . on his other side! We'll try gettin' him across together."

"Yes, Drew." Boyd's voice sounded unsteady, but he did not hesitate to bring his own mount in on Croxton's right.

"You'd best let me take that theah jump first, soldier." The stranger sent his horse in ahead of Drew's. "It don't necessarily foller that because that's water a man can jus' natcherly git hisself across in one piece. I'll give it a try quicker'n you can spit and holler Howdy."

As if he were one with the raw-boned bay he bestrode, he jumped his mount into the waiting pond. Still threshing about in the welter of flying water, he glanced back and raised a hand in a come-ahead signal.

"Bottom's a mite missin', but the drop ain't so much. Better make it 'fore them fast-shootin' hombres back theah come a-takin' you."

Though they did not move in the same reckless fashion as their guide, somehow they got across the pond and emerged dripping on the other side. The determination which had made Croxton try the escape, seemed to fade as they rode on. He continued to hold to the horn, but he slumped further over in a bundle of misery. Their pond guide took Boyd's station to the right, surveying the half-conscious man critically.

"This hoorawin' around ain't gonna do that scalpin' job no good," he announced. "He can't ride far 'less he gits him a spell of rest an' maybe has a medicine man look at that knock—"

Croxton roused. "I stick an' I ride!" He even got a measure of firmness into his tone. "I don't go to no Yankee prison . . ." He tried to reach for the reins, but Drew kept them firmly to hand.

There was a shot behind them, three or four more fugi-

tives plunged down to the millpond, and the last one in line
fired back at some yet unseen pursuer.

"Then we git!" But across Croxton's bowed shoulders the
other shook his head warningly at Drew.

He was young and as whipcord thin and tough as most
of those over-weary men from the badgered and now broken
command, but he was not tense, riding rather with the easy
adjustment to the quickened pace of a man more at home in
the saddle than on foot. His weather-browned face was
seamed with a scar which ran from left temple to the corner
of his mouth, and his hair was a ragged, unkempt mop of
brown-red which tossed free as he rode, since he was hatless.

With Croxton boxed between them, Drew and the stranger
matched pace at what was a lope rather than a gallop as
Boyd ranged ahead. Another flurry of shots sounded from
behind, and they cut across a field, making for the doubtful
cover of a hedge. There was no way, Drew decided after a
quick survey, for them to get back into town and join the
general retreat. The Yankees must be well between them
and any of the force across the Licking.

When they had pushed through the hedge they were faced
by a lane running in the general northwest direction. It provided better footing, and it led away from the chaos at
Cynthiana. With Croxton on their hands it was the best they
could hope for, and without more than an exchange of
glances they turned into it, the wounded man's horse still
between them.

The cover of the hedge wall provided some satisfaction and
Drew dared to slow their pace. Under his tan Sam was
greenish-white, his eyes half closed, and he rode with his
hands clamped about the saddle horn as if his grip upon

that meant the difference between life and death. But Drew knew he could not hope to keep on much longer.

There might be Confederate sympathizers in the next farmhouse who would be willing to take in the wounded scout. On the other hand, the inhabitants could just as well be Union people. It was obvious that Sam could not keep going, and it was just as obvious to Drew that they—or at least he—could not just ride on and leave him untended by the side of the road.

"Boyd!" So summoned, the youngster reined in to wait for them. "You ride on! You, too!" Drew addressed the stranger.

Boyd shook his head, though he glanced at the winding road ahead. "I ain't leavin' you!" His lip was sticking out in that stubborn pout.

At that moment Drew could have lashed out at him and enjoyed it, or at least found a satisfaction in passing on some of his own exasperation and frustration.

"We got a far piece to travel," commented the stranger. "An' I guess I'll string along with you, 'less, of course, this heah is a closed game an' you ain't sellin' any chips 'cross the table. Me, I'm up from Texas way—Anson . . . Anse Kirby, if you want a brand for the tally book. An' most all a Yankee's good for anyway is to be shucked of his boots." He freed one foot momentarily from the stirrup and surveyed a piece of very new and shiny footware with open admiration. It was provided with a highly ornate silver spur, not military issue but Mexican work, Drew guessed.

"You from Gano's Company?" the scout asked.

Kirby nodded. "Nowadays, but it was Terry's Rangers 'fore I stopped me a saber with this heah tough old head of mine an' was removed for a while. That Yankee almost fixed me so m' own folks wouldn't know me from a fresh-skinned buffala—not that I got me any folks any more." He grinned and that expression was a baring of teeth like a wolf's un-inhibited snarl. "You one of Quirk's rough-string scout boys, ain't you? We sure raised hell an' put a chunk under it back theah. Them Yankees are gonna be as techy as teased rattlers. An' I don't see as how we can belly through the brush with this heah hombre. He's got him a middle full of guts to stick it this far. Long 'bout now he must have him a horse-size headache . . ."

Croxton swayed and only Drew's crowding their horses together kept the now unconscious scout from falling into the road dust. Kirby steadied the limp body from the other side.

"Keep pullin' him 'round this way, amigo, an' he'll be planted permanent, all neat an' pretty with a board up at his head."

"There's a house—back there." Boyd pointed to the right, where a narrow lane angled away from their road, a small house to be seen at its end.

Drew, Croxton's weight resting against his shoulder, studied the house. The distant crackle of carbine fire rippled across the fields and came as a rumble of warning. It was plain that Croxton could not ride on, not at the pace they would have to maintain in order to outdistance pursuit; nor could he be left to shift for himself. To visit the house might be putting them straight into some Yankee's pocket, but it was the only solution open now.

"Hey, those mules!" Boyd had already ventured several horse lengths down the lane. Now he jerked a forefinger at two animals, heads up, ears pointed suspiciously forward, that were approaching the fence at a rocking canter. "Those are Jim Dandy's! You remember Jim Dandy, Drew?"

"Jim Dandy—?" the other echoed. And then he did recall the little Englishman who had been a part of the Lexington horse country since long before the war. Jim Dandy had been one of the most skillful jockeys ever seen in the blue grass, until he took a bad spill back in '59 and thereafter set himself up as a consultant trainer-vet to the comfort of any stable with a hankering to win racing glory.

To a man like Jim Dandy politics or war might not be all-important. And the fact that he had known the households of both Oak Hill and Red Springs could count for a better reception now. At least they could try.

"No use you gettin' into anything," Drew told the Texan. "You and Boyd go on! I'll take Croxton in and see if they'll take care of him."

Kirby looked back down the road. "Don't see no hostile sign heah 'bouts," he drawled. "Guess we can spare us some time to bed him down proper on th' right range. Maybeso you'll find them in theah as leery of strangers as a rustler of the sheriff—"

The Texan's references might be obscure, but he helped Drew transfer Croxton from the precarious balance in the wounded man's own saddle to Drew's hold, and then rode at a walking pace beside the scout while Boyd trailed with the led horse.

There was a pounding of hoofs on the road behind. A half dozen riders went by the mouth of the land at a distance-eating gallop. In spite of the dust which layered them Drew saw they were not Union.

"Them boys keep that gait up," Kirby remarked, "an' they ain't gonna make it far 'fore their tongues hang out 'bout three feet an' forty inches. That ain't no way to waste good hoss flesh."

"Got a good hold on him?" he asked Drew a moment later. At the other's nod he rode forward into the yard at the end of the lane.

"Hullo, the house!" he called.

A man came out of the stable, walking with a kind of hop-skip step. His blond head was bare, silver fair in contrast to Boyd's corn yellow, and his features were thin and sharp. It was Jim Dandy, himself.

"What's all this now?" he asked in that high voice Drew had last heard discussing the virtues of rival horse liniments at Red Springs. And he did not look particularly welcoming.

"Mr. Dandy—" Drew walked his horse on, Croxton sagging in his hold, his weight a heavy pull on his bearer's tired arms—"do you remember me? Drew Rennie, of Red Springs." He added that quickly for what small guarantee of respectability the identification might give. Certainly in his present guise he did not look Alexander Mattock's grandson.

Dandy rested his weight on his good leg and swung his shorter one a little ahead. And his hand went to the loose front of his white shirt.

"Now that's a right unfriendly move, suh. I take it right unfriendly to show hardware 'fore you know the paint on our faces—"

The smaller man's hand fell away from his concealed weapon, but Kirby did not reholster the Colt which had appeared through some feat of lightning movement in his grip.

"You're not going to take *my* horses!" Even if there was no gun in Dandy's hand, his voice stated a fact they could not doubt he meant.

"Nobody's takin' hosses," the Texan answered. "This heah soldier's got him a mighty sore head, an' he needs some fixin'. We ain't too popular round heah right now, an' he can't ride. So—"

Boyd pushed up. "Mr. Dandy, you know me—Boyd Barrett. And this *is* Drew Rennie. We have Yankees after us. And you never said you were Union—"

Dandy shrugged. "No matter to me what you wear . . . blue . . . gray—you're all a bunch of horse thieves, like as not. You, Mr. Boyd, what you doing riding with these here Rebs? And what's the matter with that man? Got him a lick on the head, eh? Well—" he crossed with his lurching walk to stand by Drew, studying the now unconscious Croxton—"all right." His voice was angry, as if he were being pushed along a path he disliked. "Get him into the stable. I ain't yet took sides in this here bloody war, and I ain't going to now. But the man's hurt. Unload him and don't tell me what he's been doing back there to get him that knock. I don't want to know."

He led the way into the stable, and moments later Croxton was as easy as they could make him on an improvised bed of straw and clean horse blankets. Dandy turned to them with Croxton's gun belt swinging free in his hand, still weighted down with two revolvers.

"You want these?"

Drew glanced at his two companions. His own carbine

was gone; he had dropped it at the verge of the millpond
when he had taken charge of Croxton. Boyd was without
any weapons, and Kirby had only side arms. Drew started
to reach for the belt and then shook his head. If Sam was
able to ride soon, he would need those. And the rest of them
could take their chances at getting more arms. Boyd opened
his mouth as if to protest, but he did not say anything as
Drew refused the Colts.

"You keep 'em—for him."

The ex-jockey nodded. "Better be riding on, Mr. Rennie.
They'll come looking, and I don't fancy having any fight
here. With luck we'll get your friend on his feet all right
and tight, and he can slip south when the dust is down a bit.
But you'd better keep ahead of what can come down the
pike now."

Kirby moved, the spurs jangling musically on his boots.
"I've been thinkin' 'bout that theah road," he announced.
"Any other trail outta heah we can take?"

"Cross the pasture—" Dandy directed with a thumb—
"then a cornfield, and you'll hit the pike again. Cuts off
about a mile."

"That sounds right invitin'." The Texan led the way back
to the yard and their waiting mounts. "Obliged to you, suh.
Now," he spoke to Drew, "I'd say it's time to raise some
dust. Ain't far to sundown, an' we oughta git some countryside between us an' them rip-snortin' javalinas—"

"Javalinas?" Drew heard Boyd repeat inquiringly.

"Kid—" the Texan reined his bay— "there is some mean
things in this heah world. Theah is Comanches an' Apaches,
an' a longhorn cow with a calf hid out in a thicket, an' a
rattler what's feelin' lowdown in his mind. An' theah's

javalinas, the wild boars of the Rio country. Then theah's men what have had to ride fast on a day as hot as this, swallerin' dust an' thinkin' what they're gonna do when they catch up to them as they're chasin'; an' those men're 'bout as mean as the boars—"

Drew lifted his hand to Jim Dandy and followed the other two through the pasture gate. Now he grinned.

"You sound like one speakin' from experience—of bein' chased, that is."

Kirby chuckled. "I'm jus' a poor little Texas boy, suh. 'Course we do a bit of fast ridin'. Mostly though I've been on the other end, *doin'* the chasin'. An' I know how it feels to eat dust an' git a mite riled doin' it. I'd say we could maybe help ourselves a bit though."

"How?" Boyd asked eagerly.

"You"—Drew rounded on him—"can cut cross-country and get home!" There was nothing in Boyd's clothing or equipment to suggest that he had been a part of the now scattered raiders. "If the Yankees stop you," Drew continued, "you can spin them a tale about riding out to see the fight. And Major Forbes's name ought to help."

Boyd's scowl was a black cloud on his grimy young face. "I'm one of General Morgan's men."

"Only a fool," remarked Kirby, "stops to argue with a mule, a skunk, a cook, or a boy what's run away to join the army. You figgerin' to take this kid home personal?"

"You'll have to tie me to a horse to do it!" Boyd flared up.

"No thanks for your help." Drew frowned at Kirby, then turned to Boyd again. "No, I can't take you back now. But I'll see that you do go back!"

Boyd laughed, high, with a reckless note. "I'm comin' along."

"As I was sayin'," Kirby returned to his half suggestion of moments before, "we can see 'bout helpin' ourselves. Them Yankees are mighty particular 'bout their rigs; they carry 'nough to outfit a squad right on one trooper."

Drew had already caught on. "Stage an ambush?"

"Well, now, let's see." Kirby looked down at his own gear, then critically inspected Drew and Boyd in turn. "We could do with carbines. Them blue bellies had them some right pretty-lookin' hardware—leastways them back by the river did. An' I don't see no ration bags on them theah hosses you two are ridin'. Yes, we could do with grub, an' rifle-guns . . . maybe some blue coats . . . Say as how we was wearin' them we could ride up to some farm all polite an' nice an' maybe git asked in to rest a spell an' fill up on real fancy eats. I 'member back on the Ohio raid we came into this heah farm . . . wasn't nobody round the place at all. We sashayed into the kitchen an' theah, jus' sittin' easylike an' waitin' right on the table, was two or three pies! Ain't had me a taste since as good as them theah pies. But maybe with a blue coat on us we could do as well heah 'bouts."

There was merit in the Texan's suggestion. Drew, from past experience, knew that. His only hesitation was Boyd. The youngster was right. Short of subduing him physically and taking him back tied to his saddle through the spreading Union web, Drew had no chance of returning Boyd to Oak Hill. But to lead him into the chancy sort of deal Kirby had outlined was entirely too dangerous.

"You mean—we hold up some Yankees and just take their

uniforms an' carbines an' things?" It was already too late. Boyd had seized upon what must have seemed to him an idea right out of the dashing kind of war he had been imagining all these past weeks.

"It has been done, kid," the Texan affirmed. " 'Course we got to find us two or three poor little maverick blue bellies lost outta the herd like. Then we cut 'em away from the trail an' reason with 'em."

"That ought to be easy." Boyd's enthusiasm was at the boiling point. "The Yankees are all cowards—"

Kirby straightened in his saddle, the lazy good humor gone from his face.

"Kid, don't git so lippy 'bout what you ain't rightly learned yet. Yankees can fight—they can fight good. You saw 'em do that today. And don't you ever forgit it!"

Boyd was disconcerted, but he clung doggedly to his belief. "One of Morgan's men can take on five Yankees."

Drew laughed dryly. "You saw *that* happen just this mornin', Boyd. And what happened? We ran. They fight just as hard and as long, and most of them just as tough as we do. And don't ever think that the man facin' you across a gun is any less than you are; maybe he's a little better. Keep that in mind!"

"Yes, you read the aces an' queens in your hand 'fore you spreads your money out recklesslike," Kirby agreed. "So, if we find the right setup, we move, but—"

Drew swung up one hand in the horseman's signal of warning. "Something—or someone—*is* on the move . . . ahead there!" he warned.

4

The Eleventh Ohio Cavalry

THEY had worked their way around the edge of the cornfield, and now they could look out on a hard-surfaced road which must be the pike. Riding along that in good order were a company of men—thirty, Drew counted. And four of those had extra horses on leading reins. He also saw ten carbines . . . and the owners of those were alert.

"Stand where you are!" The slight man leading that skeleton troop posted ahead. His shell jacket had the three yellow bars of a captain on its standing collar, and Drew saluted. This was the first group of fugitives he had seen who were more than frightened men running their horses and themselves into exhaustion.

"Rennie, Private, Quirk's Scouts," Drew reported himself.

Kirby's salute was delivered with less snap but as promptly. "Kirby, Private, Gano's."

"Captain William Campbell," the officer identified himself crisply. "Any more of you?" He looked to Boyd and then at the cornfield beyond.

"Barrett's a volunteer," Drew explained. This was no time to clarify Boyd's exact status. "There're just the three of us."

"You headin' somewheah special, Cap'n?" the Texan asked. "Or jus' travelin' for your continued health?"

Campbell laughed. "You might call it that, Kirby. But if we stick together, I think all of us may stay healthy."

Kirby turned his horse into the pike. "Sounds like a good argument to me, suh. You have any idea wheah at we are, or wheah we could be headin'?"

"Northwest is the best I can say. If we strike far enough to the west, we may be able to flank the troops spread out to keep us away from the river. Best plan for now, anyway. And the more men we can pick up, the better."

"Scattered some, ain't we?" Kirby assented. "You give the orders, Cap'n, suh. We ain't licked complete yet."

There was a low growl arising from the company on the pike as the Texan's comment reached them. They might have run and gone on running most of that long day, but they were no longer running; they were moving in reasonable order and to some purpose, with a direction in view and a form of organization, no matter how patched together they were. Campbell spoke directly to Drew: "You know anything about this section of the country?"

"Some, but it's been almost three years since I was here. I know nothin' about any Union garrison—"

"Those we'll have to worry about as they come. But you ride advance for us now. Send in any stragglers you come across. The night is almost here, and that's in our favor."

So Drew and Kirby, with Boyd trailing, ranged ahead of the small troop. And pick up more stragglers they did— some twenty men in the last hour before twilight closed down.

"I'm hungry," Boyd said, approaching Drew. "There're farms around. Why can't we get something to eat?"

"Here." Drew fumbled in the saddlebags he had transferred from Shawnee to this new mount back by the river. He handed over a piece of hardtack, flinty-surfaced and about as appetizing as a stone. "That's the best you'll get for a while."

Boyd stared at it in dismay. "You can't eat a thing like this! It's a piece of rock." Indignantly he hurled it away.

"You get down and pick that up! Now!"

Boyd, flushed and hot-eyed, gazed at Drew for a long moment. The flush faded and he moved uneasily in his saddle, but not out of the range of Drew's attention. At length, unhappily, he dismounted and went to pick the gray-white chunk out of a weed tangle. Holding it gingerly, he came back to his horse.

"If you don't want it—give!" Drew held out his hand.

Boyd, realizing the other meant just what he said, fingered the hardtack and finally dropped it into that waiting palm.

"You eat hard and you sleep on the soft side of a board— if you're lucky enough to find a board. You ride till your seat is blistered and until you can sleep in the saddle. You drink mud green with scum if that's all you can find to drink, and you think it's mighty fine drinkin', too. This ain't—" Drew's thoughts flitted back to his meeting with Aunt Marianna on the Lexington road—"all saber wavin' and chargin' the enemy and playin' hero to the home folks; this is sweatin' and dirt on you and your clothes, goin' mighty hungry, and cold and wet—when it's the season for goin' cold and wet. It's takin' a lot of the bad, with not much good.

And if you don't cut off home now, you'll ride our way, keepin' your mouth shut and doin' as you're told!"

Boyd swallowed visibly. "All right." But there was a firmness in that short answer which surprised Drew. The other sounded as if he meant it, as if he were swearing the oath of allegiance to the regiment. But *could* he take it? A few days on the run, and Boyd would probably quit. Maybe if they got into some town and the Yankees didn't smoke them out right away, Drew could send a telegram and Boyd would be collected. Drew tried to console himself with that thought all the time another part of him was certain that Boyd intended to prove he could stick through all the rigors Drew had just outlined for him.

But in any event the boy's introduction to war was going to be as unromantic as anyone could want, short of being thrown cold and untrained into a major battle. They must be prepared for a bad time until they made it out of the Union lines and south again.

The night closed down, dark and moonless, with a heaviness in the air which was oppressive. Campbell had to grant men and horses a breathing period. He put out pickets, leaving the rest of them to lie with their mounts saddled and to hand. Drew loosened the girth, stripped off saddle and blanket, and wiped down the sweaty back of his new mount. But he dared not leave the gelding free. So, against all good practice, he re-equipped the tired beast. No mount was going to be able to take that kind of treatment for long. They had a half dozen spare horses, and undoubtedly they could "trade" wornout mounts for fresh ones along the way. But such ceaseless use was cruel punishment, and no man wanted to inflict it. War was harder on horses than men. At least

the men could take their chances and had a fraction of free
will in the matter.

Drew awoke at a tug of his sleeve, flailed out his arm, and
struck home. Kirby laughed in the gray dawn.

"Now that theah, kid, is no way to go 'round wakin' up
a soldier. He may take you for a blue belly as has come
crawlin' into his dreams. It's all right, amigo—jus' time to
git on the prowl again."

Feeling as if he had been beaten, Drew slowly got to his
feet. Men were moving, falling into line. And one was ar-
guing with Captain Campbell.

"It could work, Cap'n," the trooper urged. "Ain't a lot of
the boys wearin' Yankee truck they took outta the warehouses? Them what ain't can act like prisoners. Jus' say
we're the Eleventh Ohio—they's stationed near Bardstown
and it would seem right, them ridin' down to take them
some prisoners. The old man, he's got a rich farm and
sets a powerful good table. Might even give us a right
smart load of provisions into the bargain. It's worth a try,
suh . . ."

"Rennie!" So summoned, Drew reported to their new
commander.

"Know anything about a Thomas McKeever livin' in this
section?"

Drew's memory produced a picture of a round-faced, cheerful man who liked to play chess and admired Lucilla's pickled
watermelon rind to the point of begging a crock of it every
time he visited Red Springs.

"Yes, suh. He's Union—got two sons with Colonel Wol-
ford. Owns a big farm and raises prime mules—"

"You know him personally?"

"Yes, suh. He's a friend of my grandfather; they used to visit back and forth a lot."

"Then he'd know you." Campbell's fingernails rasped through the stubble on his chin.

"So Rennie heah could be one of our prisoners, suh. That theah might convince Mistuh McKeever we's what we say—" the trooper pressed his point.

"Could be. It's gospel truth we ain't goin' to get far with our bellies flat on our backbones. And it might work. Now, all of you men, listen . . ." Campbell explained, gave orders, and put them through a small drill. A dozen men without any Union uniform loot to distinguish them were told to play the role of prisoners; the others exchanged and drew out of saddlebags pieces of blue clothing to make their appearance as the Eleventh Ohio.

"They ain't gonna expect too much." The trooper who had first urged the plan was optimistic. "We can pass as close to militia——"

"You hope!" Kirby was in the prisoner's section, and it was plain he did not relish a role which meant that he had to strip himself of weapons. "You—" he fixed his attention on the man to whom he must hand his Colts when the time came— "keep right 'longside, soldier. If I want to get those six-guns, I want 'em fast an' I want 'em sure—not 'bout ten yards away wheah I can't git my hands on 'em!"

Their gnawing hunger drove them all into agreeing to the masquerade. Drew could not recall his last really full meal. Just thinking about food made a warm, sickish taste rise in his mouth. He brought out the hardtack which Boyd had so indignantly rejected the night before, and holding the chunk balanced on his saddle horn, rapped it smartly with the butt of a revolver. It broke raggedly across, and then he was able to crack it again between his fingers.

"Here—" He held out a two-inch piece to Boyd, and this time there was no refusal. The younger boy's cheek showed a swollen puff as he sucked away at the fragment.

Drew offered a bite to the Texan.

"Right neighborly, amigo," Kirby observed. " 'Bout this time, me, I'm ready to exercise m' teeth on a stewed moccasin, Comanche at that, were anybody to ask me to sit down an' reach for the pot."

They rode on at a comfortable pace and for some reason met no other travelers on the pike. Drew found his new mount had no easy shuffle like Shawnee's. The gelding was a black with three white feet and a proudly held head—might even be Denmark stock—but for some reason he didn't relish moving in company. And, left without close enough supervision from his rider, he tended either to trot ahead or loiter until he was out of line. Drew was continually either reining him in or urging him on.

"Kinda a raw one," Kirby commented critically. "He ain't no rockin'-chair hoss, that's for sure. If I was you, I'd look round for somethin' better to slap m' tree on—"

Drew pulled rein for the tenth time, his exasperation growing. "I might do just that." Shawnee had been worth fifty of this temperamental blooded hunter.

"You take Tejano heah. He's a rough-coated ol' snorter—nothin' to make an hombre's eyes bug out—but he takes you way over yonder, an' then he brings you back . . . nothin' more you can ask."

Drew agreed. "Lost my horse back at the river," he said briefly. "This was a pickup—"

"Tough luck!" Kirby was sincerely sympathetic. "Funny about you Kaintuck boys . . . mostly you want a high-steppin' pacer with a chief's feathers sproutin' outta his head. They has to have oats an' corn an' be treated like they was glass. I'd'ruther have me a range hoss. You can ride one of 'em from Hell to breakfast—an' maybe a mile or two beyond—an' he never knows the difference. Work him hard all day, an' maybe the next mornin' when you're set to fork leather again, he shows you a bellyfull of bedsprings an' you're unloaded for fair. A hoss like that has him wind an' power to burn—"

"You raised horses before the war?"

Kirby swallowed what must have been the last soggy crumb of hardtack. "Well, we had a mind to try that. M'pa, he started him a spread down Pecos way. He had him a good stud—quarter hoss—one of Steel Dust's git. Won two or three races, that stud did. Called him Kiowa. Pa made a deal with a Mex mustanger; he got some prime stuff he caught in the Panhandle. One mare, I 'member—she was a natcherel pacer. Yeah, you might say as how we was gittin' a start at a first-rate string. Me an' m' brothers, we was breakin' some right pretty colts . . ."

His voice trailed into silence. Drew reined in the black again and asked another question:

"What happened . . . the war?"

"What happened? Well, you might say as how Comanches happened. Me, I was trailin' 'long with this Mex mustanger to learn some of his tricks. When I came back, theah jus' warn't nothin'—nothin' a man wants to remember after. Someday I'm gonna hunt me Comanches. Gonna learn me some tricks in this heah war I can use in that business!"

There was no change in his expression. If anything, his drawl was a little softer and lazier, but the deadly promise in it reached Drew as clearly as if the other had burst out with the Rebel Yell.

"This is it!" Captain Campbell rode back along their line. It was a larger company; they had gathered in more fugitives this morning and had no stragglers. All they lacked was adequate arms to present a rather formidable source of trouble behind the Union lines. "We're goin' into the McKeever place. You men—remember, you're prisoners!"

Very reluctantly those in that unhappy role unbuckled gun belts, passing their side arms over to their "captors." There was a graveled drive branching out of the pike to their right with a grove of trees arching over it, so they rode into a restful green twilight out of the punishing sun.

Fields rippled lushly beyond that border of trees. There was a cleanness, a contentment, a satisfaction about this place which was no part of them or any men who passed so, armed, restless, tearing apart just such peace as enfolded them here. They rode out of urgency when the gravel of that well-raked drive shifted under the hoofs of their mounts.

"I'm sayin' one thing loud an' clear," Kirby announced to those in his immediate vicinity as they neared a big brick house. "I may be playin' prisoner to you boys, but I ain't settlin' for no prisoner's rations. We all eat full plates in heah, let that be understood from the start."

Campbell laughed. "Noted, Kirby. We'll see that you desperate Rebs get all that's comin' to you."

"Now that, Cap'n, is jus' what I'm afraid of. We git all that's *comin'*—that sounds a right smart better!"

"Company ahead, Cap'n!" The trooper who had suggested

this action, indicated a man walking down the drive to meet their cavalcade.

"That's Mr. McKeever." Drew identified their host for Campbell.

But the captain was already moving ahead to meet the older man. He touched fingers to kepi—a neat blue kepi—in a smart salute.

"Chivers, Captain, Eleventh Ohio, sir. We'd like to make our noon halt here if you'll grant permission."

Thomas McKeever beamed. "No reason not, suh. Take your men over in the orchard, Captain. We can add a little something to your rations. Glad, always glad to entertain our boys." His attention wandered to the score of "prisoners" in the center of the troop.

"Prisoners, Captain?"

"Some of Morgan's horse thieves." Campbell glanced back at the shabby exhibit. "You've heard the news, of course, sir? We smashed 'em proper over at Cynthiana—"

"You did? Now that's good hearin', Captain. It deserves a regular celebration; it surely does. Morgan smashed! Was he taken too? Next time I trust they'll put him in something stronger than that jail you Ohio boys had him in last time; he's a slippery one."

"Haven't heard about that, sir. But his men are pretty well scattered. These aren't going to trouble any one for a while."

McKeever nodded. "I've a stout barn you're welcome to use for a temporary lockup, Captain. Though I must say they don't display much spirit, do they? Look pretty well beat."

Drew rubbed his hand across his face, hoping the grime there—a mixture of road dust, sweat, and powder blacking

—was an effective disguise. No use recalling the old days for Mr. McKeever. Allowing his shoulders to slump dispiritedly as he was herded by his file guard, he rode sullenly on to the orchard.

They stripped their saddles and allowed the horses freedom for the first time in hours, an act which was against prudence but which McKeever would expect of Union troops. Drew lay full length under the curving limbs of an apple tree, his head pillowed on saddlebags.

"Now I wonder"—Kirby dropped down, to sit with his back against the tree trunk—"why they always say a fella is dog-tired. A dog, he ain't got him much to do 'cept chase around on his own business. Soldier-tired—now that's another matter. How 'bout it, kid? You ready to ride right outta heah an' chase General Grant clean back to Lake Erie?"

Boyd had stretched out only a hand's length from Drew. There were dark smudges under his closed eyes, hardly to be told from the smears of dirt on his round cheeks, but there. He rolled his head on a hammock of grass and scowled at Kirby.

"General Grant can—" he added a remark which surprised Drew into opening his eyes. Kirby shook his head reprovingly.

"Now that ain't no way for a growin' boy to talk. An' it sits on your tongue as easy as a fly on a mule's ear, too. What kinda company you bin keepin', kid? Rennie, this heah colt ain't got no reason to cram grammar into a remark that way."

Drew stretched, folded his arms under his head, and answered, in a voice he tried to make as blighting as possible:

"Thinks it makes him sound like a man, probably. He's findin' out the army ain't quite what he expected."

"You shut up—!" Boyd might have added something to that, but Drew had moved. He leaned over the youngster, his hand hard and heavy on Boyd's shoulder. And it was plain that, much as he wanted to, the other did not quite dare to move or shake off that grip.

"I've had about enough," Drew said quietly. "The next town we hit you're goin' to stay there, until someone comes from back home to collect you. Nobody knows you're with us, and you can go back to Oak Hill without any trouble from Union troops."

Boyd's eyes blazed. His mouth wasn't shaping a small boy's pout this time; it was an ugly line tight against his teeth.

"I ain't goin' home! I said you can't make me, 'less you tie me on a horse and keep me tied all the way. And I don't think you can do that, Drew Rennie. I'd like to see you try it; I sure would!"

"He's got you on a stand-off, I'd say," Kirby remarked. "My, ain't he the tough one though, horns sticking up an' haired all over! Gentlemen—" he had glanced over their shoulder and was watching whatever was there—"company comin'. Mind your manners!"

Drew looked around. His hand clamped tighter on Boyd, keeping him pinned on his back. If he only had time ... but there was no way of disguising the younger boy. And Thomas McKeever, strolling with Captain Campbell, had already sighted them, stopped short, and now was moving swiftly in their direction.

"Boyd Barrett!"

Drew had to release his hold and Boyd sat up, brushing

bits of grass from his shirt sleeves even as he returned Mr. McKeever's stare with composure.

"Yes, suh?" Boyd was on his feet now, making his manners with the speed of one harboring a guilty conscience.

"What are you doing with this gang of cutthroats and banditti?" Mr. McKeever had an excellent voice to deliver such an inquiry; it could rattle the unaware into confusion, and sometimes even into quick confession, as he undoubtedly knew.

"I'm with General Morgan, Mr. McKeever." Boyd did not appear too ruffled.

"I refuse to believe that even that unprincipled ruffian is robbing cradles to fill up his ranks, depleted as they may be—"

Boyd reddened. "General Morgan ain't no . . . no unprincipled ruffian!"

"Yeah," Kirby drawled. As the other two, he had risen to his feet on the approach of the older man. "Them's pretty harsh words, suh. Cutthroat now—I ain't never slit me a throat in all my born days. What about you, Rennie? You done any fancy work with a bowie lately?"

Mr. McKeever favored the Texan with a passing frown; then his attention settled on Drew. "Rennie," he repeated, and then said the name again with the emphasis of one making a court identification. "Drew Rennie!"

"Yes, suh." As Boyd had done, Drew answered to the indictment of being where he was and who he was.

"I am most unhappy to see Alexander Mattock's grandson and Meredith Barrett's son in such company. Surely"—he turned to Captain Campbell— "these boys are not your regular prisoners—"

Campbell shook his head gravely. "Unfortunately, sir, they are indeed troopers with Morgan. And, as such, they are subject to the rules of war governing prisoners—"

"That does not prevent my seeing what I can do for both of you," their host said quickly. "At least, Boyd, you are young enough to be released by the authorities. Be sure I shall do all I can to bring that about."

As Boyd opened his mouth to protest, Drew spoke quickly: "Thank you, suh. I know Cousin Merry will appreciate that."

With a last assurance of his intention to help them, Mr. McKeever left. Boyd grinned.

"He did help me," he observed. "He knows now I'm with Morgan, and nobody can say that's not so!"

Kirby laughed. "Reckon that's true, kid. You locked yourself right into the corral along with the rest of us bad men. Look's like you've been outfought this time, Rennie."

Drew threw himself back under the tree. So Boyd had won this round—they were still in Kentucky and not too far from Oak Hill.

5

Bardstown Surrenders

N ow that's what I call true hospitality, gentlemen, true hospitality." Kirby caressed his middle section gently with both hands, smiling dreamily into the lacing of apple boughs over his head. "I ain't had me a feed like that since we took that sutler's wagon back outside Mount Sterlin'. 'Mos' forgot theah was such vittles lyin' 'bout to be sampled. An' you got us most of the cream, too, 'cause you're poor little misguided boys a-runnin' 'way to be with us desperate characters. Git me a bowie knife, an' I'll show you how to cut throats—all free, too."

Drew laughed, but Boyd did not appear amused. They had been favored with a short but pungent lecture from Mr. McKeever, served along with food, which to Drew made it worth the return of listening decorously to a listing of their sins.

"I ain't goin' home," Boyd repeated stubbornly.

"Well," Kirby pointed out, "if he rides up to the Yankee prison camp, he ain't gonna find you neither. So what's the difference? I think we oughta be movin' on, seein' as how we ain't really on speakin' terms with the law heah 'bouts."

It would appear that Captain Campbell agreed with that.

63

The order came to saddle up and move out. But they went with provision sacks slung from their saddles, a portion of McKeever's bounty stowed away against tomorrow. And once they were past the house, the word came down the line for Drew to quit his prisoner's role and join their commander.

Campbell held a fragment of map as he let his mount's pace fall to a slow walk. "There are about a hundred Union infantry stationed at Bardstown, according to Mr. McKeever. Know anything about the town?"

"I was there once. My cousin went to St. Joseph's for a term."

"Remember enough to find your way around?"

"I don't know, suh. But if there's a Union garrison—?" He ended the sentence with an implied question.

"What are we going to do there?" The captain grinned. "We're going to collect some arms, I hope. Supposing you were a Yankee commander, Rennie, and a bold, bad raider like General Morgan was to ride clean up to your door with a regiment or two tailing him and say: 'Your guns, suh, or your life!' What would you do, especially if your troops were mostly militia and green men who hadn't ever been in a real fight?"

Drew understood. "Probably, suh, I'd tell General Morgan that he could have his guns, providin' he kept his side of the bargain."

"As far as the Yankees in Bardstown may know, General Morgan could be headed their way right now with a regiment. I don't think they've had time yet to learn just how badly we were scattered back there by the Licking River. You willing to take the flag in when we get there, Rennie? Pick a couple of outriders to go with you!"

It was risky, but no more risky than bluffs he had seen work before. And they did need the weapons. Cutting westward now only kept them well inside Union territory. Somehow they would have to skulk or fight their way down through the southern part of Kentucky and then probably all the way across Tennessee—a tall order, but one which was just possible of accomplishment.

"I'll do it, suh." Riding into Bardstown was no worse than riding over the rest of this countryside where any moment they might be swept up by the enemy.

It was lucky they had brought rations with them from McKeever's, for they took no more chances of trying for such supplies again. Once more they altered their advance, riding the pikes at night, hiding out by day.

Hills then, and among them Bardstown. Drew borrowed a carbine, stringing a dubiously white strip of shirt tail from its barrel, and flanked by Kirby and Driscoll, a trooper Campbell had appointed, rode slowly up the broad street opening from the pike. Great trees arched overhead, almost as they had across the drive of the McKeever place, and the houses were fine, equal to the best about Lexington.

A carriage pulled to the side, its two feminine occupants leaning forward a little under the tilt of dainty parasols, eyes wide. While their coachman stared open-mouthed at the three dirty, tattered cavalrymen riding with an assumption of ease, though armed, down the middle of the avenue.

"You, suh." It was the coachman who hailed Drew. "You soldier men?"

Drew reined in the black, who this time obeyed without protest. The weary miles had taught the gelding submission if not perfect manners. Transferring his reins to the hand which also steadied the butt of his carbine against his thigh so that his "flag" was well in evidence, Drew swept off his dust-grayed hat and bowed to the ladies in the carriage.

"General Morgan's compliments, ladies," he said, loud enough for his words to carry beyond the vehicle to the townspeople gathering on the walk. "Flag of truce comin' in, ma'am." He spoke directly to the elder of the two in the carriage. "Would you be so kind as to direct me to where I may find the Union commander?"

"You're from John Hunt Morgan, young man?" She shut her parasol with a snap, held it as if she was considering its use as a weapon.

"Yes, ma'am. General Morgan, Confederate Army—"

She sniffed. "You'll find their captain at the inn, probably. Yankees and whiskey apparently have an affinity for one another. So John Morgan's coming to pay us a visit?"

"Maybe, ma'am. And where may I find the inn?"

"Straight ahead," the girl answered. "You really are Morgan's men?"

Kirby did not have a hat to doff, but his bow in the saddle was as graceful as Drew's.

"That's right, ma'am. My, did we know what we'd find in Bardstown now, we'd bin ridin' in right sooner!"

"Suh! . . . Louisa!" The elder lady's intimidating glare was divided, but Drew thought that Louisa got more than a half share of it.

"No offense meant, ma'am. It's jus' that ridin' 'bout the way we do an' all, we don't git us a chance to say Howdy to ladies." The Texan's expression was properly contrite; his voice all diffidence.

"The inn, young men, is on down the street. Drive on,

Horace!" she ordered the coachman. But as the carriage started, she pointed her parasol at Drew as a teacher might point an admonishing ruler at a pupil. "I hope you'll find what you're looking for, young man. In the way of Yankees . . ."

"We generally do, ma'am," Kirby commented. "For us Yankees jus' turn up bright an' sassy all over the place."

Drew laughed. "Bright and sassy, then on the run!" For the success of his present mission and all those listening ears he ended that boast in as fervent a tone as he could summon.

"See that you keep them that way!" She enforced that order with a snap of parasol being reopened as the carriage moved from the shade back into the patch of open sunlight.

"That sure was a pretty girl," observed Driscoll as Drew and the Texan wheeled back into line with him. "Wish we could settle down heah for say two or three days. Git some of the dust outta our throats and have a chance to say Howdy to some friendly folks—"

"You'd be more likely sayin' Howdy to a Yankee prison guard if you did that," Drew replied. "Let's find this inn and the garrison commander."

"That's the proper way of layin' it out—the inn an' *then* business. Yankees an' whiskey go together; that's what she said, ain't it? I maybe don't weah no blue coat regular, but whiskey sounds sorta refreshin', don't it, now?"

"Just so you only think that, Anse, and don't try any tastin'," Drew warned. "We make our big talk to this captain, and then we move out—fast. You boys know the drill?"

"Sure," Driscoll repeated. "We're the big raiders come to gobble up all the blue bellies, 'less they walk out all nice an' peaceful, leavin' their popguns behind 'em for better men to use. I'd say that theah was the inn, Rennie—"

They saw their first Yankees, a blot of blue by the horse trough at the edge of the center square. And Drew, surveying the enemy with a critical and experienced eye, was sure that he was indeed meeting either green troops or militia. They were as wide-eyed in their return stare as the civilians on the streets around.

Kirby chuckled. "Strut it up, roosters," he urged from the corner of his mouth. "Cutthroats, banditti, hoss thieves—jus' downright bad hombres, that's us. They expect us to be on the peck, all horns an' rattles. Don't disappoint 'em none! Their tails is half curled up already, an' they're ready to run if a horny toad yells Boo!"

To the outward eye the three riding leisurely down the middle of the Bardstown street had no interest in the soldiers by the trough. Drew in the middle, the white rag dropping from the barrel of his carbine, brought the black a step or two in advance. Just so had Castleman ridden into Lexington earlier, and that had been at night with a far more wary and dangerous enemy to face. The scout's confidence rose as he watched, without making any show of his surveillance, the uneasy men ahead.

One of them broke away from the group, and ran into the inn.

"Wonder who's roddin' this outfit," Kirby remarked. "That fella's gone to rout him out. Do your talkin' like a short-trigger man, Drew."

They pulled rein in front of the inn and sat their horses facing the door through which the soldier had disappeared.

His fellows edged around the trough and stood in a straggling line to front the Confederates.

"You!" Drew caught the eye of the nearest. "Tell your commanding officer General Morgan's flag is here!"

The Yankee was young, almost as young as Boyd, but he had less assurance than Boyd. Now the boy stammered a little as he answered:

"Yes . . . yes, sir," Then he added in a rush, "General who, sir?"

"General John Hunt Morgan, Confederate Cavalry, Army of the Tennessee, detached duty!" Drew made that as impressive as he could, whether it was worded correctly according to military protocol or not. It was, he thought with satisfaction, a nicely rounded, important-sounding speech, although a bit short.

"Yes, sir!" The boy started for the door, but he was too late.

The man who erupted from that portal was short and stout, his face a dramatic scarlet above the dark blue of his unbuttoned coat. He stopped short a step or two into the open and stood staring at the three on horseback, that scarlet growing more dusky by the second.

"Who . . . are . . . you?" His demand was expelled in heavy puffs of breath.

"Flag from General Morgan," Drew repeated. Then to make it quite plain, he added kindly, "General John Hunt Morgan, Confederate Cavalry, Army of the Tennessee, detached duty."

"But, but Morgan was defeated . . . at Cynthiana. He was broken—"

Slowly Drew shook his head. "The General has been re- ported defeated before, suh. No, he's right here outside Bardstown. And I wouldn't rightly say he was broken either, not with a couple of regiments behind him—"

"Couple of regiments!" The man was buttoning his coat, his red jowls sagging a little, almost as if Drew had used the carbine across his unprotected head. "Couple of regiments . . . Morgan . . ." he repeated dazedly. "Well," sullenly he spoke to Drew, "what does he want?"

"You're a captain," Drew spoke crisply. "You'll return with us to discuss surrender terms with an officer of equal rank!"

"Surrender!" For a moment some of the sag went out of the other.

"Two regiments—an' you have maybe eighty or ninety men." Kirby gazed with critical disparagement at such Union forces as were visible.

"One hundred and twenty-five," the officer repeated me- chanically and then glared at the Texan.

"One hundred and twenty-five then." Kirby was willing to be generous. "All ready to hold this heah town. I don't see no artillery neither." He rose in his stirrups to view the im- mediate scene. "Goin' to fight from house to house maybe—?"

"General Morgan," Drew remarked to the company at large, "is not a patient man. But it's your decision, suh. If you want to make a fight of it." He shrugged.

"No! Well, I'll talk . . . listen to your terms anyway. Get my horse!" he roared at the nearest soldier.

They escorted the captain with due solemnity out of Bards- town to meet Campbell, a well-armed guard in evidence strung out on the pike. The Union officer picked up enough assurance to demand to see the General himself, but Campbell's show of surprised hauteur at the request was an expert's weapon in rebuttal; and the other not only subsided but agreed without undue protest to Campbell's statement of terms.

The Union detachment in town were to stack their arms in the square, leaving in addition their rations. They were to withdraw, unarmed, to a field outside and there await the patroling officer who would visit them in due course. Having agreed, the Union captain departed.

Campbell was already signaling the rest of the company out of cover.

"This is where we move fast. You all know what to do."

But much had to be left to chance. Drew and Kirby surrendered their borrowed carbines to the rightful owners and prepared to join the first wave of that quick dash.

"*Yahhhh-aww-wha—*" There were no words in that, just the war cry which might have torn from an Indian warrior's throat, but which came instead from between Kirby's lips: the famous Yell with all its yip of victory as only an uninhibited Texan could deliver it. Then they were rushing, yelping in an answering chorus, four and five abreast, down the street under the shade of the trees, answered by screams and cries as the walks emptied before them.

Blue ranks broke up ahead, leaving rifles stacked, provisions in knapsacks. And the ragged crew struck at the spoil like a wave, lapping up arms, cartridge boxes, knapsacks. For only moments there was a milling pandemonium in the heart of Bardstown. Then once again that Yell was raised, echoed, and the pound of hoofs made an artillery barrage of sound. Armed, provisioned, and very much the masters of the scene, Morgan's men were heading out of town on the other side, leaving bewilderment behind.

They pushed the pace, knowing that the telegraph wires or the couriers would be spreading the news. Perhaps the reputation of their commander might slow the inevitable pursuit, but it would not deter it entirely. They must put as much distance between themselves and the out-foxed Union garrison as they could. And Campbell continued to point them westward instead of south, since any enemy force would be marching in the other direction to cut them off.

Even if men could stand that dogged pace, driven by determination and fear of capture, horses could not. And through the next two days the inference was very clear: fall behind at your own risk; there will be no waiting for laggards to catch up. Nor any mounts furnished; you must provide your own.

Drew discovered the black gelding an increasing problem, but at least the horse provided transportation, and he tried to save the animal as best he could. Though when it was impossible to unsaddle, when one had to ride—and did—some twenty hours out of twenty-four, there was not much the most experienced horseman could do to relieve his mount.

Drew pulled up beside Kirby as he returned from a flank scout. The Texan had dropped to the rear of the small troop, holding his horse to not much more than a walk. Now and then he glanced to the receding length of the road as if in search of someone.

"Where's Boyd?" Drew had ridden along the full length of the company and nowhere had he seen that blond head.

"Jus' what I'm wonderin'." Kirby came to a complete

halt. "I came back a little while ago, and nobody's seen him."

Drew pulled in beside the other. His horse's head hung low as the gelding blew in gusty snorts. He tried to remember when he had seen Boyd last and when he did, that memory was not too encouraging.

"With Hilders . . . and Cambridge . . ." he said softly.

"Yeah." Kirby's thought seemed to match his. "Hilder's mare is jus' about beat, an' Boyd rides light; that bay he got is holdin' up like a corn-fed stud."

"They were talkin' to him when I went out on point." Drew followed his own line of thought. "And he won't listen to me—"

"It don't foller that because you advise a hombre for his own good, he's goin' to take kindly to your interest in him," the Texan observed. "You tell him Hilders an' Cambridge are wearin' skunk stripes, an' he's apt to claim 'em both as compadres. Suppose he don't come in when we bed down; he coulda jus' cut his picket rope an' drifted, as far as we can prove."

"Not if his bay turns up with one of them on top," Drew replied.

"Them two are of the curly wolf breed." Kirby shifted his newly acquired Enfield. "No tellin' as how they would join up with us again did they make such a switch; might figure as how they could make it better time driftin' on their own."

The Texan had put his own fear into words. Drew pointed the gelding back down the road and booted the animal into a trot. A moment later he heard more drumming hoofs behind him; Kirby was following.

"This ain't your trouble," Drew reminded him.

"No, maybe it ain't. But then, me, I'm jus' a rough string

rider from way back, an' this may end in a smoke-up. Odds seem a mite one-sided now—Hilders is easy on the trigger. He won't take kindly to anyone tryin' to hang up his hide for dryin'—"

Drew studied the hoof-churned dust of the road. He could only hold a very slim hope of some trace along its margin. The gelding stumbled and tried to cut pace. Drew hardened his will, holding the animal to the trot. He knew that under saddle and blanket, sores were forming, that soon he would have no choice but a "trade" such as Hilders might be forcing now, though not at the expense of one of his own fellows.

Kirby was reading sign on the other side of the road. His sudden hand signal brought Drew to join him. Hoofprints marked the softer verge.

"Turned off not too long ago," Drew commented.

Kirby nodded toward the brush. They were facing a small woodland into which a thin trace of path led. Good cover for trouble. Looping reins over his arm, Drew walked forward, Colt in hand, using scout tricks to cover the noise of his advance into the green shimmer of the trees.

The trail led ahead without any attempt at concealment. The other two troopers must have tricked Boyd into taking that way; maybe they had even put a revolver on him once they were off the road. It was only too easy for a man to straggle from the company and not be missed until hours and miles later.

"Now, sonny, there ain't no use makin' a big fuss . . ."

Drew dropped the reins and slipped on.

"You can see for yourself, boy, that m' hoss ain't gonna be able to git much farther. You can nurse him along an' take it easy. Them blue bellies ain't gonna be hard on a nice little boy like you—no, suh, they ain't—even if they find you. We jus' trade fair an' square. No trouble . . ."

" 'Course," another, harsher voice cut in, "if you want to make it rough, well, that's what you'll git! We're takin' that hoss, no matter what!"

"You ain't!" There was a short snap of sound, the cocking of a hand gun.

"Pull that on me, will you!"

"I'll shoot! I'm warnin' you . . . touch m' horse, and I'll shoot!" Boyd's voice scaled higher.

Drew ran, his arm up to shield his face from the whip of branches. He came out at a small stream. Boyd was backed against a tree while the two others advanced on him from different directions.

"That's enough!" Drew's Colt was pointed at Hilders. The man's head jerked around. "Get goin'," the scout ordered.

Cambridge blinked stupidly, but Hilders took a step back to catch up the reins of a horse that stood dull-eyed, its head bent, pink foam roping from its muzzle as it breathed in heavy gasps.

"I said—get!" Drew advanced, and Hilders gave ground again, towing the trembling horse.

"Now, we don't want no trouble," Cambridge said hurriedly. "It woulda bin a fair trade . . . Sonny, heah, ain't got place in the company anyhow——"

"Get!" Drew's weapon raised a fraction of an inch. Cambridge's protest thickened into a mumble and he went. When both men had disappeared, Drew turned to Boyd.

"Put that away—" he flicked a finger at the other's Colt— "and mount up. We'll have to push to get back to the troop."

He watched the other lead the bay away from the stream

side. Kirby was right, the horse was in better condition than most of the others in the company, and sooner or later someone might again try to rank Boyd out of it. There were a good many in that hunted column who would see that in the same light as Hilders and Cambridge did and would say so, with the weight of public opinion to back them. Campbell had set their course for Calhoun—and in that town Boyd and the raiders must definitely part company.

6

Horse Trade

"WHAT's this heah Calhoun like?" Kirby watched Drew loosen the saddle blanket, lifting it from the gelding as gently as he could.

"Not much—" Drew was beginning, then he sucked in his breath and stood staring at the nasty sight he had just uncovered. He slung the blanket to the ground as Boyd came up, leading the bay. It was the younger boy who spoke first.

"You ain't goin' to try to ride him now, Drew!" That protest came spontaneously. Drew thought that Shawnee's end had put the last bit of steel over his feelings, but he had to agree with Boyd now: no one with any humanity could make the gelding carry so much as a blanket over that back, let alone saddle and rider.

"Here!" Roughly, his face flushed, Boyd jerked on the reins of his own mount, bringing the bay sidling toward Drew. "You can take Bruce . . ."

He stooped, reaching for Drew's saddlebags. "You have to ride scout. I'll walk this one a while. Maybe he can carry me later. I ride light."

Drew shook his head. "Not that light," he commented dryly. "No, I guess this is where I do some tradin'—"

"House-smoke yonder . . ." Kirby pointed. They could see the thin trail of smoke rising steadily this windless morning. "Best make it fast—the cap'n is already thinkin' about pointin' up an' headin' out."

Drew loosened his side arms in their holsters. He always hated this business, but it was part of a day's work in the cavalry now. He just hoped that he wouldn't have to do his impressing at gun point. He entrusted saddle and blanket to Boyd, but made the other wait outside the farmyard twenty minutes later as he shepherded the gelding into the enclosure where chickens squawked and ran witlessly and a dog hurled himself to the end of a chain, giving tongue like a hound on a hot scent.

Drew skirted that defender, moving toward the barn. But he was still well away from the half-open door when a woman hurried out, a basket in her hands, her face picturing surprise and apprehension. She stopped short to stare at Drew.

"Who are you—what do you want?" Her two questions ran together in a single breathless sentence. Drew looked beyond her. No one else issued from the barn or came in answer to the dog's warning. He took off his hat.

"I need a horse, ma'am." He said it bluntly, impatiently. After all, how could you make a demand like that more courteous or soft? The very fact that he had been driven to this made him angry.

For a moment she looked at him uncomprehendingly, and then her eyes shifted to the gelding. She came forward a step or two, and there was a blaze of anger in the gaze she directed once more to the man.

"That horse's galled raw!" She accused.

"Don't you think I know it?" he returned abruptly. "That's why I have to have another mount."

A quick step back and she was between him and the door of the barn, holding the basket as a shield between them. It was full of eggs.

"You won't get one here!" she snapped.

"Ma'am"—Drew had his temper under control now—"I don't want to take your horse if you have one. But I'm under orders to keep up with the company. And I'm goin' to do what I have to . . ."

He dropped the gelding's reins, walked forward, hoping she wouldn't make him push around her. But apparently she read the determination in his face and stood aside, her expression bleak now.

"There's only King in there," she said. "And I wish you the joy of him, you thief!"

King proved to be a stallion, stabled in a box stall. Drew hesitated. The stud might be mean, harder to handle even than the gelding. But it was either taking him or being put afoot. If he could back this one even as far as Calhoun tomorrow—or the next day—he might be able to make a better exchange in town. It would depend on just how hard the stallion was to control.

Making soothing noises, he worked fast to bit and bridle the big chestnut. His experience with the Red Springs stud led him aright now. He came out of the barn leading the horse while the dog, its first incessant clamor stilled, growled menacingly from the end of its chain. The woman had disappeared, maybe into the fields beyond in search of help. Drew departed at a swift trot to where he had left Boyd.

"That's all horse!" Boyd eyed Drew's trade excitedly.

"Too much so, maybe. We'll see." He saddled quickly, glad that so far the chestnut had proved amiable. But how the stud might behave in troop company he had yet to learn. He mounted and waited for any signs of resentment, remembering the woman's warning. King snorted, pawed the dust a bit, but trotted on when Drew urged him.

Kirby whistled from where he rode with the rear guard as they rejoined the company. But Captain Campbell frowned. And King put on a display of fireworks which almost shook Drew out of the saddle, rearing and pawing the air.

"Makes like a horny one on the prod," commented the Texan. "That's stud's a lotta hoss to handle, amigo."

"Too much," the captain echoed Drew's earlier misgivings. "Keep him away from the rest until you're sure he won't start anything!"

But that order fitted in with Drew's usual scouting duties. And when he did bed down for one of the fugitives' limited halts he was careful to stake King away from the improvised picket lines.

Drew was eating a mixture of hardtack and cold bacon, the last of their captured provision from Bardstown, when Driscoll sauntered over to the small mess Kirby, Boyd, and Drew had established without any formal agreement.

"The boys are plannin' 'em a high old time," Driscoll announced.

Kirby's left eyebrow slanted up in quizzical inquiry. Drew chewed energetically and swallowed. It was Boyd who asked, "What do you mean?"

"Calhoun—that's what I mean, sonny." Driscoll squatted

on his heels. "They 'low as how they're gonna do a little impressin' in Calhoun."

"The town's not very big," Drew observed. "A couple of stores, a church, maybe a smithy . . ."

Driscoll snickered. "Oh, the boys ain't particular 'long 'bout now. They won't be too choosy. Only thought I'd tell you fellas, seein' as how you been ridin' scout and ain't maybe heard the plans. If you want to load up, better git into town early. Some of them fast workers from B Company are gittin' set . . ."

"The cap'n know about this?" asked Kirby.

Driscoll shrugged. "He ain't deaf. But the cap'n also knows as how you can't be too big a gold-lace officer when you're behind the enemy lines with men on the run. We're gonna take Calhoun and take her good!" He grinned at the two veterans. "Jus' like we took Mount Sterlin'."

Kirby was sober. "There was a take theah which warn't no good. Somebody cleaned out the bank, or else I wasn't hearin' too well afterward. I can see some impressin'—stuff an hombre can put in his belly as paddin', an' maybe what he can put on his back. That's fair an' square. The Yankees do it too. But takin' a gold watch or money outta a man's pants—now that's somethin' different again."

Driscoll stood up. "Ain't nobody said anything about gold watches or money or banks," he replied stiffly. "There's stores in Calhoun, and there's men in this heah outfit what needs new shirts or new breeches. And since when have you seen any paymaster ridin' down the pike with his bags full of bills, not that you can use that paper stuff for anythin' like shoppin', anyway!"

"Thanks for the tip," Drew cut in. "We take it kindly."

Driscoll's ruffled feelings appeared soothed. "Jus' thought you boys oughta know. Me, I have in mind gittin' maybe two or three cans of them peaches like we got from the sutler's wagon. Them were prime eatin'. General store might jus' have some. Yankee crackers are right good, too. Say, that theah stud you got, Rennie, how's he workin' out?"

"So far no trouble," Drew remarked. "Only I'm lookin' for a trade—maybe in town."

"Trade? Why ever a trade?"

"We got a couple of river crossin's comin' up ahead," the scout explained. "And one of them is a good big stretch of deep water—you don't go wadin' across the Tennessee. I don't want to beg for trouble, headin' a stud into somethin' as dangerous as that."

Driscoll seemed struck by the wisdom of that precaution. "Now I heard tell," he chimed in eagerly, "as how a mule is a right sure-footed critter for a river crossin'. An' a good ridin' mule could suit a man fine——"

"A mule!" Boyd exploded, outraged. But Drew considered the suggestion calmly.

"I'll keep a lookout in town. May be swappin' for that mule yet, Driscoll. You'll have to pick up my share of peaches if that's the way it's goin' to be."

There were more plans laid for the taking of Calhoun as the hours passed and the harried company plodded or spurred —depending upon the nature of the countryside, the activity of Union garrisons, and their general state of energy at the time—southwest across the length of Kentucky. Days became not collections of hours they could remember one by one afterward, but a series of incidents embedded in a nightmare of hard riding, scanty fare, and constant movement.

Not only horses were giving out now; they dropped men along the way. And some—like Cambridge and Hilders—vanished completely, either cut off when they went to "trade" mounts, or deserting the troop in favor of their own plans for survival.

The remaining men burst into Calhoun as a cloud of locusts descending on a field of unprotected vegetation. Drew did not know how much Union sentiment might exist there, but he judged that their actions would not leave too many friends behind them. Jugs had appeared, to be passed eagerly from hand to hand, and the contents of store shelves were swept up and out before the outraged owners could protest.

It had showered that morning, leaving puddles of mud and water in the unpaved streets. And at one place there was a mud fight in progress—laughing, staggering men plastering the stuff over the new clothes they had looted. Drew rode around such a party, the stud's prancing and snorting getting him wide room, to tie up at the hitching rail before the largest store.

A man in his shirt sleeves stood a little to one side watching the excitement in the street. As Drew came up the man glanced at the scout, surveying his shabbiness, and his mouth took on the harsh line of a sneer.

"Want a new suit, soldier?" he demanded. "Just help yourself! You're late in gettin' to it . . ."

Drew leaned against the wall of the store front. He was so tired that the effort of walking on into that madhouse, where men yelled, grabbed, fought over selections, was too much to face. This was just another part of the never-ending nightmare which had entrapped them ever since they had fled from the bank of the Licking at Cynthiana. Listlessly he watched one trooper snatch a coat from another, drag it on triumphantly over a shirt which was a fringe of tatters. He plucked at the front of his own grimy shirt, and then felt around in the pocket he had so laboriously stitched beneath the belt of his breeches, to bring out one creased and worn bill. Spreading it out, he offered it to the man beside him. To loot an army warehouse was fair play as he saw it. Morgan's command had long depended upon Union commissaries for equipment, clothing, and food. And a horse trade was something forced upon him by expediency. But he still shrank from this kind of foraging.

"A shirt?" he asked wearily.

The man glanced from that crumpled bill to Drew's tired face and then back again. The sneer faded. He reached out, closed the scout's fingers tight over the money.

"That's just wastepaper here, son. Come on!" Catching hold of Drew's sleeve so tightly that the worn calico gave in a rip, he guided the other into the store, drawing him along behind a counter until he reached down into the shadows and came up with a pile of shirts, some flannel, some calico, and one Drew thought was linen.

"These look about your size. Take 'em! You might as well have them. Some of these fellows will just tear them up for the fun of it."

Drew fumbled with the pile, a flannel, the linen, and two calico. He could cram that many into his saddlebags. But the store owner thrust the whole bundle into his arms.

"Go ahead, take 'em all! They ain't goin' to leave 'em, anyway."

"Thanks!" Drew clutched the collection to his chest and edged back along the wall, avoiding a spirited fight now in progress in the center of the store. Mud-spattered men came bursting back, wanting to change their now ruined clothing for fresh. Drew stiff-armed one reeling, singing trooper out of his path and was gone before the drunken man could resent such handling. With the shirts still balled between forearm and chest, he led King away from the store.

"Ovah heah!"

That hail in a familiar voice brought Drew's head around. Kirby waved to him vigorously from a doorway, and the scout obediently rehitched King to another rack, joining the Texan in what proved to be the village barbershop.

Kirby was stripped to the waist, using a towel freely sopped in a large basin to make his toilet. His face was already scraped clean of beard, and his hair plastered down into better order than Drew had ever seen it, while violent scents of bay rum and fancy tonics fought it out in the small room.

"What you got there?" Boyd looked up from a second basin, a froth of soap hiding most of his face.

"Shirts—" Drew dropped his bundle on a chair. He was staring, appalled, into the stretch of mirror confronting him, unable to believe that the face reflected there was his own. Skinning his hat onto a shelf, he moved purposefully toward the row of basins, ripping off his old shirt as he went.

Where the barber had gone they never did know, but a half hour later they made some sweeping attempts to clean up the mess to which their efforts at personal cleanliness had reduced the shop, pleased once more with what they saw now in the mirror. They had divided the shirts, and while the fit was not perfect, they were satisfied with the windfall. Before he left the shop Kirby swept a half dozen cakes of soap into his haversack.

Boyd was already balancing a bigger sack, full to the top.

"Peaches, molasses, crackers, pickles," he enumerated his treasure trove to Drew. "We got us some real eats."

"Hey, you—Rennie!" As they emerged from the barber-shop Driscoll trotted up. "The cap'n wants to see you. He's on the other side of town—at the smithy."

Boyd and Kirby trailed along as Drew obeyed that summons. They found Campbell giving orders to the smith's volunteer aides, some engaged with the owner of the shop in shoeing the raiders' horses, others making up bundles of shoes to be slung from the saddles as they rode out.

"Rennie"—the captain waved him out of the rush and clamor of the smithy—"I want you to listen to this. You—Hart—come here!" One of the men bundling horseshoes dropped the set he was tying together and came.

"Hart, here, comes from Cadiz. Know where that is?"

Drew closed his eyes for a moment, the better to visualize the map he tried to carry in his head. But Cadiz—he couldn't place the town. "No, suh."

"It's south, close to the Tennessee line and not too far from the big river. There's just one thing which may be impor-tant about it; it has a bank and Hart thinks that there are Union Army funds there. We still have a long way to go, and Union currency could help. Only," Campbell spoke with slow emphasis, "I want this understood. We take army funds only. This may just be a rumor, but it is necessary to scout in that direction anyway."

"You want me to find out about the funds and the river crossin' near there?"

"It's up to you, Rennie. Hart's willin' to ride with you."

"I'll go." He thought the bank plan was a wild one, but they did have to have a safe route to the river.

"You'll move out as soon as possible. We'll be on our way as soon as we have these horses shod."

Drew doubted that. What he had seen in the streets suggested that it was not going to be easy to pry most of the company out of Calhoun in a hurry, but that was Campbell's problem. "I'll need couriers," he said aloud. It was an advance scout's privilege to have riders to send back with information.

Campbell hesitated as if he would protest and then agreed. "You have men picked?"

"Kirby and Barrett. Kirby's had scout experience; Barrett knows part of this country and rides light."

"All right, Kirby and Barrett. You ready to ride, Hart?"

The other trooper nodded, picked up a set of extra horseshoes, and went out of the smithy. Campbell had one last word for Drew.

"We'll angle south from here to hit the Cumberland River some ten miles north of Cadiz, Hart knows where. This time of year it ought to be easy crossin'. But the Tennessee—" he shook his head—"that is goin' to be the hard one. Learn all you can about conditions and where it's best to hit that . . ."

Drew found Hart already mounted, Kirby and Boyd waiting.

"Hart says we're ridin' out," the Texan said. "Goin' to cover the high lines?"

"Scout, yes. South of here. River crossin's comin' up."

"No time for shadin' in this man's war," Kirby observed.

"Shadin'?" Boyd repeated as a question.

"Sittin' nice an' easy under a tree while some other poor hombre prowls around the herd," Kirby translated. "It's a kinda restin' I ain't had much of lately. Nor like to . . ."

They put Calhoun behind them, and Hart led them cross-country. But at each new turn of the back country roads Drew added another line or two on the map he sketched in on paper which Boyd surprisingly produced from his bulging sack of loot.

The younger boy looked self-conscious as he handed it over. "Thought as how I might want to write a letter."

Drew studied him. "You do that!" He made it an order. There had been no chance to leave Boyd in Calhoun. But there was still Cadiz as a possibility. He did not believe this vague story about Union gold in the bank. And the company might never enter the town in force at all. So that Boyd, left behind, would not attract the unfavorable attention of the authorities.

It began to rain again, and the roads were mire traps. As they struggled on into evening Kirby found a barn which appeared to be out by itself with no house in attendance. The door was wedged open with a drift of undisturbed soil and Boyd, exploring into a ragged straggle of brush in search of a well, reported a house cellar hole. The place must be abandoned and so safe.

"We'll be in Cadiz tomorrow," Hart said.

"An' how do we ride in?" Kirby wanted to know. "Another bearer-of-the-flag stunt?"

"Is Cadiz a Union town?" Drew asked Hart.

The other laughed. "Not much, it ain't. This is tobacco country; you seen that for yourself today. An' there's guerrillas to give the Yankees trouble. They hole up in the Brelsford Caves, six or seven miles outta town. We can ride right in, and there ain't nobody gonna care."

"Nice to know these things ahead'a time," Kirby remarked. "So we ride in—lookin' for what?"

Hart glanced at Drew but remained silent. The scout shrugged. "Information about the rivers and any stray garrison news. You have kin here, Hart?"

"Some." But the other did not elaborate on that.

Drew was thinking about those guerrillas; their presence did not match Hart's story about the Yankee gold in the bank. Such irregulars would have been after that long ago. He didn't know why Hart had pitched Campbell such a tale, but he was dubious about the whole setup now. Better make this a quick trip in—and out—of town.

7

A Mule for a River

For a Confederate patrol, they looked respectable enough as they rode into Cadiz. Though they lacked the uniformity of a Yankee squad, their dark shirts, "impressed" breeches, and good boots gave an impression of a common dress, and Kirby had even acquired a hat.

They slung their captured rifles before entering town and progressed at a quiet amble which suggested good will. But there was no mistaking the fact that they attracted attention, immediately and to some purpose. A small boy, balancing on a fence, put his fingers to his mouth and released a piercing whistle.

King's response to that was vigorous. Rearing, until he stood almost upright on his hind feet, the stallion pawed the air. Drew barely kept his seat. He fought with all his knowledge of horsemanship to bring the stud back to earth and under control. And he could hear Kirby's laugh and Boyd calling out some inarticulate warning or advice.

"Better git that mule—or run down this one's mainspring some," the Texan said when Drew had King again with four feet on the ground, though weaving in a sideways dance.

"You men—what are you doing here?" A horseman looked over the heads of the crowd to the four troopers.

"Passin' through, suh. Leastwise we was, until greeted—" Kirby answered courteously.

Drew assessed the questioner's well-cut riding clothes, his good linen, and fine gloves. The rider was middle-aged, his authority more evident because of that fact. This was either one of the wealthy planters of the district or some important inhabitant of Cadiz. There was a wagon drawing up behind him, a span of well-cared-for mules in harness with a Negro driver.

The mules held Drew's attention. King's reaction to that sudden whistle was a warning. He had no wish to ride such an animal into a picket skirmish. The sleekness of the mules appealed to his desire to rid himself of the unmanageable stud.

Now he edged the sidling King closer to the wagon. The driver watched him with apprehension. Whether he guessed Drew's intention or whether he dreaded the near approach of the stallion was a question which did not bother the scout.

"You there," Drew hailed the driver." I'll take one of those mules!"

As always, he hated these enforced trades and spoke in a peremptory way, wanting to get the matter finished.

"You, suh—" the solid citizen turned his horse to face the scout—"what gives you the right to take that mule?"

With a visible sigh of relief, the Negro relaxed on the driver's seat, willing to let the other carry on the argument.

"Nothing, except I have to have a mount I can depend upon." Drew did not know why he was explaining, or even why he wanted the mule so acutely right now. Except that he was tired, tired of the days in the saddle, of being on the run, of these small Kentucky towns into which they rode to loot and ride off again. The Yankees in Bardstown had been fair game, and their bluff there had been an adventure. But Calhoun left a sour taste in his mouth, and he didn't like the vague order which had brought him to Cadiz. So his dislike boiled over, to settle into a sullen determination to rid himself of one irritation—this undependable horse.

"Do I assume, suh, that you are part of General Morgan's command?" Sharp blue eyes studied Drew across the well-curried backs of the mules.

"Yes, suh."

The man gave a nod, which might have been for some thought of his own.

"We have heard some rumors of your coming, suh," the other continued. "You, Nelson," he spoke to the Negro, "take this team up to the livery stable and tell Mr. Emory I want Hannibal saddled! Then you bring him back here and give him to this gentleman!"

"Yes, suh. Hannibal—wi' saddle—for this young gentle-m'n."

"Hannibal, suh," the man said to Drew, "is a mule, but a remarkable one, riding trained and strong. I think you will find him quite usable. Do I understand we are about to be favored by a visit from General Morgan?"

Drew dismounted. Now he made a business of squinting up at the sun as if to tell time. "Not for a while, suh." He remained cautious; though he guessed that his questioner's sympathies were at least not openly Union.

There was a stir in the gathering crowd. Hart was leaning

from his saddle, talking earnestly to two men flanking him on either side.

"May I offer you some refreshment, gentlemen. I am James Pryor, at your service—"

Automatically Drew responded to the manners of Red Springs. "Drew Rennie, suh. Anson Kirby, Boyd Barrett . . ." He looked around for Hart, only to see the other disappearing into an alley with his two companions from the crowd.

"Suh, that's a right heartenin' offer," Kirby said, smiling. "Trail dust sure does make a man's throat dryer'n an alkali flat!"

"Mark Hale over here has just the answer for that difficulty, gentlemen. If you will accompany me—"

They left the glare of the sunlit street, following their host into a small shop where a quantity of strange smells fought for supremacy. Kirby stared about him puzzled, but his look changed to an expression of pure bafflement and outrage as Pryor gave his order to the smaller man who came from a back room.

"Mark, these gentlemen need some of that good lemonade you make—if you have some cold and ready."

Drew heard Kirby's muffled snort of protest and wanted so badly to laugh that the struggle to choke off that sound was a pain in his chest. Mr. Pryor smiled at them blandly.

"M' boys, nothing better on a really hot day than some of Mark's lemonade. Nothing like it in this part of Kentucky. Ah, that looks like a draft fit for the gods, Mark, it certainly does!"

Hale had bobbed out of his inner room again, shepherding before him a Negro boy who walked with exaggerated caution, balancing a tray on which stood four tall glasses, beaded

with visible moisture. There was a sprig of green mint standing sentry in each.

"Drink up, gentlemen." Under Mr. Pryor's commanding
eye they each took a glass and a first sip.

But it was good—cool as it went slipping down the throat
bearing that blessed chill with it, tart on the tongue, and
fresh. Drew had sipped, but now he gulped, and he noted
over the rim of his own glass, that Kirby was following his
example. Mr. Pryor consumed his portion at a more genteel
rate of intake.

"This allays that trail dust of yours, Mr. Kirby?" He in-
quired with no more than usual solicitude, but there was a
faint trace of amusement in his small smile.

Kirby met the challenge promptly. "Ably, suh, ably!" He
raised his half-filled glass. "To your very good health, suh.
I don't know when I've had me a more satisfyin' drink!"

Pryor bowed. He was still smiling as he glanced at Drew.
"You have business in Cadiz, suh? Beyond that of swap-
ping that firebreather of yours for another mount, I mean?
Perhaps I can be of service in some other way . . ."

Drew cradled his glass in both hands. The condensing
moisture made it slippery, but the chill was pleasant to feel.

"Do you have any news about the Cumberland River, suh?"
he asked. Pryor might have usable information, and there
was no reason to disguise that part of their objective. Short
of turning about and fighting their way through about a
quarter of the aroused Yankee army, the fugitives did have to
cross the Cumberland and the Tennessee, and do both soon.

"The Cumberland, suh, is not apt to give you much
trouble." Pryor sipped at his glass with a relish. "If, of course,
you contemplate a try at the Tennessee—that will be a dif-

ferent matter. I trust your commander will be amply prepared for difficulties there. But General Morgan is not to be
easily caught napping, or so his reputation stands. I wish you
the best of luck."

"Is that your horse out there, young man?" the proprietor
of the drugstore addressed Drew. "That big stallion?"

Drew put his glass on the counter and spun around.
"What's he doin' now?"

"Nothing," Hale returned quickly. "Ransome!" Out of
nowhere Hale's servant appeared. "Get the saddlebags from
that horse."

Surprised at this highhanded demand for his property,
Drew waited for enlightenment. When Ransome returned
with the bags, Hale took them, moved quickly to a cabinet,
and unlocked it. By handfulls he took small boxes from the
shelves inside, added some paper packets, and then buckled
the straps tightly over the new bulge.

"I understand," he said in his dry, precise voice, "there is
a pressing need for quinine, morphine, and the like in the
South?"

Drew could only nod as Hale held out the bags.

"Give this to your surgeon, young man, with my compliments. There is little enough we can do, but this is something."

Drew stammered his thanks, knowing that those boxes
and packets crammed into his bags meant a fortune to a
blockade runner, but far more to men in the improvised hospitals behind the gray lines. Hale waved away Drew's thanks,
adding only a last warning: "Keep your bags dry if you contemplate a river crossing! I would like to make sure that
those drugs do reach the right hands intact."

"Rennie!" Hart hailed him from the door. "There's a boy here with a mule; he says it's for you."

Pryor put down his glass. "It's Hannibal. I think you will find him acceptable, suh. An even-tempered animal for the most part, and the surest-footed one I have ever ridden."

"Then you do *ride* him?" Boyd spoke for the first time.

"Naturally he has been ridden—by me. I would not offer him otherwise, suh!" Pryor's flash of indignation was quick. "Hannibal's dam was Dido, a fine trotting mare. He's an excellent mount."

The mule stood in the street, ears slightly forward, eyeing King warily. He was a big animal, groomed until his gray coat shone under the sun, wearing a well rubbed and oiled saddle and trappings. As Drew approached he lowered his head, sniffing inquiringly at the scout.

"Your new master, Hannibal," Pryor addressed the animal with the gravity of one making a formal introduction. "You are about to be mustered into the cavalry."

Hannibal appeared to consider this and then shook his big head up and down in a vigorous nod. Boyd laughed and Kirby offered vocal encouragement.

"Mount up an' see if you have to go smoothin' out any humps."

"If you're goin' to ride that critter, git on!" Hart called. His tone expressed urgency as if he had learned something in town which should send them out of Cadiz in a hurry.

Drew's previous experience with mules had not been as a rider. He had heard plenty about their sure-footedness, their ability to keep going as pack animals and wagon teams when horses gave out, their intelligence, as well as that stubbornness which lay on the darker side of the scales. He advanced on Hannibal now a little distrustfully, settling into the saddle on the animal's back with the care of one expecting some unpleasant reaction. But Hannibal merely swung his head about as if to make sure by sight, as well as pressure of weight on his back, that his rider was safely aloft.

Relaxing, Drew saluted Pryor. "My thanks to you, suh."

"Think nothing of it, young man. Luck to you—all of you."

"That we can use, suh," Kirby returned. "Adios . . ."

Hart's impatience was so patent that Drew had only hasty thanks for Hale before the trooper had them on their way out of town. When they were at a trot Kirby joined their guide.

"How come you workin' on your critter's rump with a double of rope? Git sight of some blue belly hangin' out to dry-gulch us?"

"We ain't too welcome hereabouts." Hart did look worried, and Drew was alert.

"Yankees?" he asked.

Hart shook his head. "Just some of the boys; they don't want no attention pulled this way, not right now."

The bank money—and the guerrillas. Yes, holding up the Cadiz bank if and when any gold reached there, would appeal to the local irregulars, who might be so irregular as to be on the cold side of the law, even in wartime with the enemy their victim. Drew fitted one piece to another and thought he could guess the full pattern.

Kirby looked from one to the other. Boyd was completely at a loss. A moment later the Texan spoke again.

"Me, I'm never one to argue with local talent, specially if they wear their Colts low and loose. Doin' that is apt to make a man wolf meat. Wheah to now—this heah river?"

Drew nodded. The Cumberland must be scouted. And, after that, the more formidable barrier of the Tennessee. He had not needed Pryor's warning about the latter. Ever since they had left Bardstown and knew they were headed for that barrier, Drew had been carrying worry at the back of his mind.

But Pryor was also right about the Cumberland. Hart agreed to ride back to the company with the information to direct them to the best crossing. While Drew, Kirby, and Boyd went on to the last barrier between them and eventual escape southwest.

Here the Tennessee was a flood, a narrow lake more than a river. As they traveled its eastern bank Boyd halted now and again to study the waste of water dubiously.

"It's wide," he said in a subdued voice. Kirby spat accurately at a leaf drifting just below.

"Need us some fish fixin's heah," he agreed. "You swim?" he asked the other two.

There had been ponds at home where both of them in childhood had paddled about with most of the young male populations of Red Springs and Oak Hill. But whether they could trust that somewhat limited skill to get them over this flood was another matter.

"Some." Boyd appeared to have discovered caution.

"Me, I'm not sayin' yet," Kirby commented. "Splashin' 'round some in a little-bitty wadin' pool, an' gittin' out in this, don't balance none. Ain't every hoss takes kindly to water, neither. I'd say we'd better see what's the chances of knockin' together a raft or somethin'. 'Less we can find us a boat."

But boats were not to be found, unless they were willing to risk discovery by trying to cross near a well-settled district. And when Captain Campbell joined them that afternoon he insisted on the need of speed over a longer reconnaissance.

"The Yankees are closing in," he told the trio by the river. "If we try to cross at a town, they'll have a point to center on. Rafts, yes, we can try to build rafts—have to ferry over the men who can't swim, and our gear. This is the time we must push—fast."

The remote section of bank which Drew had chosen became a scene of activity as the company came in—a tight bunch—not long after Campbell. The stragglers came later, pushing beat-out horses, one or two riding double. They had no tools other than bowie knives, and their attempts at raft-building were not only awkward but in the most cases futile. When they did have a mat which would stick together after a fashion, they were determined to put it to the test at once.

None of them had much practice in getting horses over such a wide body of water, and there were a great many freely voiced suggestions concerning the best methods.

Kirby stood watching the first attempt, his face blank of expression, a sign Drew had come to recognize as the Texan's withdrawal from a situation or action of which he did not approve. There were five men squeezed together on the flimsy-looking raft and they had strung out their mounts in a line, the head of one horse linked by leading rope to the tail of the one before him.

"You don't think it's goin' to work?" Drew asked Kirby.

The Texan shrugged. "Maybe, only hosses don't think like men. An' a lotta hosses don't take kindly to gittin' wheah theah ain't no footin'. Me, I want to see a little more, 'fore I roll out—"

Kirby's misgivings were amply justified. For that first voyage was doomed to a tragic and speedy end. The second horse in line, losing footing as the river bed fell away beneath him, reared in fright, caught his forefeet over the rope linking him to his fellow, and so jerked his head underwater by his own frenzied struggles. Before the men on the wildly dipping raft were able to cut the now fright-maddened animals loose, three in that string had drowned themselves by their uncontrolled plunges, and the others were being dragged under.

Boyd dived from the upper bank before Drew could stop him. It was madness to go anywhere near the struggling horses. But somehow Boyd's blond head broke water at the side of the last gasping animal. He took a grip on the water-logged mane, his body bobbing up and down with the jerks of the horse's forequarters, until he had sawed through the lead cord and was able to start the mount back toward the shore, swimming beside him.

Drew was waiting with Kirby to give Boyd a hand up the bank.

"You could have been pulled under!"

Boyd was grinning. "But I wasn't. And the horse's all right, too." He patted the wet haunch of the shivering animal. "That was bad—they pulled each other down."

It was a disheartening beginning. But as the hours slipped by they had better success. One horse, two, three could be towed on separate ropes behind the raft. And in the morning there was a cockleshell of a boat oared in by one of the men who had found it downriver.

They had ferried and crossed well into the dusk of the evening. And at the first dawn they were at it again. Drew tried to remember how many times he had made that trip, swimming or rowing, always with some mount as his special charge. More than half the company had sworn they could not swim, and so the burden of the transfer fell upon their fellows.

"Rennie—" That was Campbell climbing up from the raft after another weary passage across. "There's trouble on the other side. You've been using that mule of yours to get some of the horses over, haven't you?"

Drew was so tired that words were too much trouble to shape. He nodded dully. Pryor had been right about Hannibal. The big mule had not only taken his own passage across the Tennessee as a matter-of-course proceeding, but had shouldered and urged along three horses as he went. And twice since then Drew had taken him back and forth to bring in skittish mounts causing trouble.

"That horse of mine's running wild; he broke out of the water twice." The captain caught at Drew's bare arm so hard his nails cut. "Think you could get him over with the mule's help?"

Drew wavered a little as he walked slowly to where he had picketed Hannibal after their last trip. He was tired, and although he had eaten earlier that morning, he was hungry again. It was warm and the sun was climbing, but the air felt chill against his naked body and he shivered. The one thing they were all getting out of this river business, Drew decided, were much-needed baths.

Kirby, his body white save for tanned face and throat, sun-darkened hands and wrists, crouched on the raft as Drew brought Hannibal down to that unwieldy craft.

"Tryin' for the cap'n's hoss?"

"What's wrong with it?" Drew helped the Texan push off.

"Reaches no bottom, an' then it plain warps its backbone tryin' to paw down the sky. Maybe that mule can git some sense into the loco critter. But I'm not buyin' no chips on his doin' it."

Drew located Campbell's horse, a rangy, good-looking gray which reminded him a little of the colt he had seen at Red Springs, snorting and trotting back and forth along the path they had worn on the banks during their efforts of the past twenty-four hours. One of the rear guard held its lead rope and kept as far from the skittish animal as he could.

"He's plumb mean," the guardian informed Drew. "When he jumps, get out from under—quick!"

Yet when Drew, mounted on Hannibal now, brought the horse down to the water's edge, the horse appeared to go willingly enough. The scout tossed the lead rope to Kirby, waiting until the raft pushed off with its load of men and fringe of horses, then took to the river beside Campbell's horse. When they reached the deeper section he saw the gray go into action.

Rearing, the horse appeared about to try to climb onto the raft. And the man holding its lead rope dropped it quickly. Drew, swimming, one hand on Hannibal's powerful shoulder, tried to guide the mule toward the horse that was still splashing up and down in a rocking-horse movement. But the mule veered suddenly, and Drew saw those threatening hoofs loom over his own head. He pushed away frantically, but too late to miss a numbing blow as one hoof grazed his shoulder.

Somehow, with his other hand outflung, he caught Hannibal's rope tail and held on with all the strength he had left, while the water washed in and out of a long raw gouge in the skin and muscles of his upper arm.

8

Happy Birthday, Soldier!

N o WATER here either." Boyd climbed up the bank of what
might once have been a promising stream. Carrying
three canteens, he ran the tip of his tongue over his lips unhappily. "It sure is hot!"

They had turned off the road, which was now filled with
men, horses, men, artillery, and men, all slogging purposefully forward. They composed an army roused out before
daylight, on the move toward another army holed in behind
a breastworks and waiting. And over all, the exhausting
blanket of mid-July heat which pressed to squeeze all the
vital juices out of both man and animal.

Drew touched his aching arm soothingly. It still hurt, although the rawness had healed during the weeks between
that turbulent crossing of the Tennessee and this morning in
Mississippi as they moved at the Union position on the ridge
above the abandoned ghost town of Harrisburg. The remnant
of Morgan fugitives, some eighty strong, had fallen in with
General Bedford Forrest's ranging scouts at Corinth, and
had ridden still farther southward to join his main army
just on the eve of what promised to be a big battle.

"Hot!" echoed Kirby. "A man could git hisself killed to-day an' never know no difference."

They were reluctant to re-enter the stream progressing along the road. The dust was ankle-deep there, choking thick when stirred by feet and hoof to a powdery cloud. In contrast, there were no clouds in the sky, and the sun promised to be a ball of brass very soon.

Yesterday had been as punishing. Men wilted in the road, overcome by heat and lack of water. If there ever had been any moisture in this country, it had long ago been boiled away. The very leaves were brittle and grayish-looking where they weren't inches deep in dust.

As of last night, the Morgan men were an addition to Crossland's Kentuckians under General Buford. The speech of the blue grass was familiar, but nothing yet had made them a part of this new army with which they marched.

Drew reached for one of the canteens. His worry over Boyd, dulled by the passing of time, stirred sluggishly. The other had kept up the grueling pace which had brought the fugitives across half of Kentucky, all of Tennessee, and into this new eddy of war, making no complaint after his first harsh introduction to action—which might be in part an adventure, but which was mostly something to tbe endured—with the dogged stubbornness of a seasoned veteran. And Boyd had manifestly toughened in that process. After Drew's mishap in the river, Boyd had accepted responsibility, helping to keep the scout in the saddle and riding, even when Drew had been bemused by a day or two of fever, unaware of either their enforced pace or their destination.

No, somewhere along the line of retreat Drew had stopped

worrying about Boyd. And now, with the youngster already appointed horse holder for the day's battle, he need not think of him engulfed in action. Though any fighting future was decided mainly by the capricious chance which struck one man down and allowed his neighbor to march on unscathed.

"You men—over there—close up!" A officer, hardly to be distinguished from the men he rode among, waved them back to the column. Then they were dismounting. As Drew handed Hannibal over to Boyd's care, he was glad again that the other was safely behind the battle line moving up in the thin woods.

During the night the enemy had thrown together the breastworks on the ridge, weaving together axed trees, timbers torn out of the abandoned houses of the village—anything the Union leader could commandeer for such use. And between that improvised fortification and the cover in which the Confederates now waited was a section of open ground, varying in width with the wanderings of a now dry river. Where the Kentuckians were stationed, there must have stretched about three hundred yards of that open, Drew estimated, and the woods bordering it on this side were so thin that any charge would take them into plain sight for five hundred yards of approach.

Fieldpieces brought into line on the woods side, hidden above by the breastworks, opened up in a dull *pom-pom* duel. Drew saw a shell strike earth not far away, bounce twice, still intact, and roll on toward the Confederate lines.

The *zip-zip* of the Miniés had not yet begun. And this waiting was the hardest part of all. Drew tried to pin all his powers of concentration on a study of the ground immediately before him, the slope up which they would have to win in order to have it out with the now hidden enemy. He made himself calculate just which path to take when the orders to charge came. Although his arm prevented his using a carbine or rifle, his two Colts were loaded, and one was in his hand. He glanced around.

Kirby? There was a Morgan trooper next—Drew tried to remember his name. Laswell . . . Townstead . . . no, Clinton! Tom Clinton. He'd done picket duty with Drew. And beyond Clinton—there was Kirby, his lips pulled tight in what might have been a grin, but which Drew thought was not. Then . . . Boyd! But Boyd was back with the horses; he had to be!

Drew edged forward a little, trying to see better. If it were Boyd, he had to wrench him out of that line and get the boy back. A hot emotion close to panic boiled up in Drew.

Somewhere, through the pound of the artillery, a bugle blared. And Drew's muscles obeyed that call, even as he still tried to see who was fourth in line from him.

Slowly at first, they were on the move. The sun was up, shining directly into their faces. But in spite of the glare, they could still see the Union works and the flash of guns along it. They were moving faster, coming to a trot. Officers shouted here and there, trying to slow that steady advance—why?

Then, drowning out the bugles, the mutter and roar of the artillery, came the Yell. Their shambling trot quickened. Men were running now, forming a great wave to lick up at the breastworks. Men in that line did not know—or care—that they were moving without the promised support on right and left; they did not hear the disturbed orders of the officers still striving to slow them, to wrench them back into a battle plan already too broken to mend. All they cared about now was the field clear for running, the weapons in their hands, the enemy waiting under the hot morning sun.

Drew never remembered afterward that splendid useless charge except as chaos. He could not have told just when they were caught in a murderous crossfire which poured canister at their undefended flanks. A man went down before him, stumbling. The scout caught his foot against the writhing body, pitched head forward, and struck on his bad arm. For a moment or two the stabbing pain of that made the world red and black. Then Drew was up on one knee again, just in time to realize foggily that the Yankees were ripping at their flanks, that their charge was pocketed by lead and steel, being wiped out. He steadied his gun hand on the crook of his injured arm, tried to find some target, then fired feverishly without one, the gun's recoil sending shivers of pain through his whole shoulder and side.

The first wave of men had great gaps torn in its length. But those remaining on their feet still ran up the slope, screaming their defiance. A handful reached the breastworks. Drew saw one man by some strange fortune scramble to the top of that timber wall, stand balanced for a moment in triumph to take aim at a target below as if he himself were invulnerable, and then plunge, as might a diver cleaving a pool, out of sight on the other side.

Men faltered, the fire was breaking them, crumpling up the lines. All the Union might was concentrated in a lead-and-canister hail on the remnants of the brigade, making of the slope a holocaust in which nothing human could continue to advance.

But new lines of gray-brown came steadily from the wood-

land, racing, yelling, steadfast in their determination to storm
that barricade and pluck out the Yankees with their hands.
They were wild men, with no thought of personal safety. A
color bearer went down. His standard was seized by his right
rank man before its red folds hit the churned, stained ground,
the soldier flinging aside his rifle to take tight grip on the
pole. The line came on at a run. Now broken squads of
Kentuckians re-formed; a battered lacework of what had
been companies, regiments, joined the newcomers.

Drew was on his feet. Where Kirby or any others of the
small Morgan contingent had vanished—whether Boyd *had*
been with them—he did not know. He jammed his now
empty Colt into its holster, drew its twin, still not wholly
aware that the breastworks were too far away for small arms'
fire to have any effect.

Now the whole world was no larger than that stretch of
open ground and the breastworks, the men in blue behind
them. Only the flanking fire still withered the gray lines,
curling them up as the sun had withered and curled the leaves
on the shrubs by the dried stream bed. This was walking
stiff-legged through a bath of fire—sun fire, lead-death fire—
with no end except the hope of reaching the ridge top and the
fight waiting there.

But they could not reach that wall—except singly, or in
twos and threes, then only to fall. And the waves of men no
longer broke from the woods to lap up and recede sullenly
down the slope. Out of nowhere, just as they fell back to the
first fringe of trees, came an officer on a tall gray horse. His
coat was gone, he rode in his shirt sleeves, and a bullet-torn
tatter waved from one wide shoulder. Above prominent
cheekbones, his eyes were hot and bright, his clipped beard

pointed sharply from a jaw which must be grimly set, his face was flushed, and his energy and will was like a cloud to engulf the disheartened men as he bore down upon them.

His galloping course threaded through the shattered groups of Kentuckians, men fast disintegrating into a mob as the realization of their failure on the slope began to strike home—no longer a portion of an army believing in itself. But, sighting him, they followed his route with a rising wave of cheers—cheers which even though they came from dry throats rose in force and violence to that inarticulate Yell which had raised them past all fear up the hill.

From his saddle, the officer leaned to grab at a standard, whirling the flag aloft and around his head so that its scarlet length, crossed with the starred blue bands, made a tossing splotch of color, to hold and draw men's eyes. And now he was shouting, too, somehow his words carrying through the uproar in the woods.

"Rally! Rally on colors!"

"Forrest!" A man beside Drew whooped, threw his hat into the air. "The old man's here! Forrest!"

They were pulled together about that rider and his waving standard. Lines tightened, death-made gaps closed. They steadied, again a fighting command and not a crowd of men facing defeat. And having welded that force, Forrest did not demand a second charge. He was furiously angry—not with them, Drew sensed—but with someone or something beyond the men crowding about him. It was not until afterward that rumor seeped out through the ranks; it had not been Forrest's kind of battle, not his plan. And he now had five hundred empty saddles to weight the scales after a battle which was not his.

Drew leaned against a bullet-clipped tree. Men were at work with some of the same will as had taken them to attack, building a barricade of their own, expecting a counterthrust from the enemy. He wiped his sweaty face with the back of his hand. His throat was one long dry ache; nowhere had he seen a familiar face.

Somewhere among this collection of broken units and scrambled companies of survivors he must find his own. He stood away from the tree, fighting thirst, weariness, and the shaking reaction from the past few hours, to move through the badly mauled force, afraid to allow himself to think what —or who—might still lie out on the ridge under the white heat of the sun.

"Rennie!"

Drew rounded a fieldpiece which had been manhandled off the firing line, one wheel shattered. He steadied himself against its caisson and turned his head with caution, fearing to be downed by the vertigo which seemed to strike in waves ever since he had retreated to the cover of the woods. He wanted to find the horse lines, to make sure that he had not seen Boyd on the field just before the bugle had lifted them all into that abortive charge.

It was Driscoll who hailed him. He had a red-stained rag tied about his forearm and carried his hand tucked into the half-open front of his shirt. Drew walked toward him slowly, feeling oddly detached. He noted that the trooper's weathered face had a greenish shade, that his mouth was working as if he were trying to shape soundless words.

"Where're the rest?" Drew asked.

Driscoll's good hand motioned to the left. "Four . . . five . . . some there. Standish—he got it with a shell—no head . . .

not any more—" He gave a sound like a giggle, and then his hand went hastily to his mouth as he retched dryly.

Drew caught the other's shoulder, shaking him.

"The others!" he demanded more loudly, trying to pierce the curtain of shock to Driscoll's thinking mind.

"Four . . . five . . . some—" Driscoll repeated. "Standish, he's dead. Did I tell you about Standish? A shell came along and—"

"Yes, you told me about Standish. Now show me where the others are!" Still keeping his shoulder grip, Drew edged Driscoll about until the trooper was pointed in the general direction to which he had gestured. Now Drew gave the man a push and followed.

"Rennie!" That was Captain Campbell. He was kneeling by a man on the ground, a canteen in his hand.

Drew lurched forward. He was so sure that that inert casualty was Boyd, and that Boyd was dead.

"Boyd—" he murmured stupidly, refusing to believe his eyes. The man lying there had a brush of grayish beard on his chin, a mat of hair which moved up and down as he breathed in heavy, panting gasps.

"Boyd?" This time the scout made a question of it.

One of the men in that little group moved. "He got it—out there."

Drew shifted his weight. He felt as if he were striving to move a body as heavy and as inert as that of an unconscious man. It took so long even to raise his hand. Before he could question the trooper further, another was before him.

Kirby, his powder-blackened face only inches away from that of the man he had seized by a handful of shirt front, demanded: "How do you know?"

The man pulled back but not out of Kirby's clutch. "He was right beside me. Went down on the slope before we fell back—"

So—Drew's thinking process was as slow as his weary body—he had been right back there on the field! Boyd had been in the first line, and he was still out there.

Again, Drew made one of those careful turns to keep his unsteadiness under control. If Boyd was out there, he must be brought back—now! Hands closed on Drew's shoulders, jerking him back so that he collided with another body, and was held pinned against his captor.

"You can't go theah now!" Kirby spoke so closely to his ear that the words were a roaring in his head. But they did not make sense. Drew tried to wrench loose of that hold, the pain in his half-healed arm answering. Then there was a period he could not account for at all, and suddenly the sun was fading and it was evening. Somebody pushed a canteen into his hand, then lifted both hand and canteen for him so that he could drink some liquid which was not clear water but thick and brackish, evil-tasting, but which moistened his dry mouth and swollen tongue.

Through the gathering dusk he could see distant splotches of red and yellow—were they fires? And shells screamed somewhere. Drew held his head between his hands and cowered under that beat of noise which combined with the pulsation of pain just over his eyes. Men were moving around him, and horses. He heard tags of speech, but none of them were intelligible.

Was the army pulling out? Drew tried to think coherently. He had something to do. It was important! Not here— where? The boom of the field artillery, the flickering of those fires, they confused him, making it difficult to sort out his memories.

Again, a canteen appeared before him, but now he pushed it petulantly aside. He didn't want a drink; he wanted to think—to recall what it was he had to do.

"Drew—!" There was a figure, outlined in part by one of those fires, squatting beside him. "Can you ride?"

Ride? Where? Why? He had a mule, didn't he? Back in the horse lines. Boyd—he had left the mule with Boyd. Boyd! *Now* he knew what had to be done!

He moved away from the outstretched hand of the man beside him, got to his feet, saw the blot of a mount the other was holding. And he caught at reins, dragged them from the other's hand before he could resist.

"Boyd!" He didn't know whether he called that name aloud, or whether it was one with the beat in his head. Boyd was out on that littered field, and Drew was going to bring him in.

Towing the half-seen animal by the reins, Drew started for the fires and the boom of the guns.

"All right!" The words came to him hollowly. "But not that way, you're loco! This way! The Yankees are burnin' up what's left of the town; that ain't the battlefield!"

Drew was ready to resist, but now his own eyes confirmed that. Fire was raging among the few remaining buildings of the ghost town, and shells were striking at targets pinned in that light, shells from Confederate batteries, taking sullen return payment for that disastrous July day.

A lantern bobbed by his side, swinging to the tread of the man carrying it. And, as they turned away from the inferno which was consuming Harrisburg, Drew saw other such lights in the night, threading along the slope. This was the heartbreaking search, among the dead, for the living, who might yet be brought back to the agony of the field hospitals. He was not the only one hunting through the human wreckage tonight.

"I've talked to Johnson," Kirby said. "It'll be like huntin' for a steer in the big brush, but we can only try."

They could only try . . . Drew thought he was hardened to sights, sounds. He had helped bring wounded away from other fields, but somehow this was different. Yet, oddly enough, the thought that Boyd could be—*must* be—lying somewhere on that slope stiffened Drew, quickened his muscles back into obedience, kept him going at a steady pace as he led Hannibal carefully through the tangle of the dead. Twice they found and freed the still living, saw them carried away by search parties. And they were working their way closer to the breastworks.

"Ho—there—Johnny!"

The call came out of the dark, out of the wall hiding the Yankee forces.

Drew straightened from a sickening closer look at three who had fallen together.

"Johnny!" The call was louder, rising over the din from the burning town. "One, one of yours—he's been callin' out some . . . to your left now."

Kirby held up the lantern. The circle of light spread, catching on a spurred boot. That tiny glint of metal moved, or was it the booted foot which had twitched?

Drew strode forward as Kirby swung the lantern in a wider arc. The man on the ground lay on his back, his hands moving feebly to tear at the already rent shirt across his chest. There was a congealed mass of blood on one leg just above the boot top. Drew knew that flushed and swollen face in spite of its distortion; they had found what they had been searching for.

Kirby pulled those frantic hands away from the strips of calico, the scratched flesh beneath, but there was no wound there. The leg injury Drew learned by quick examination was not too bad a one. And they could discover no other hurt; only the delirium, the flushed face, and the fast breathing suggested worse trouble.

"Sun, maybe." Kirby transferred his hold to the rolling head, vising it still between his hands while Drew dripped a scanty stream of the unpalatable water from the Texan's canteen onto Boyd's crusted, gaping lips.

"I'll mount Hannibal. You hold him!" Drew said. "He can't stay in the saddle by himself."

Somehow they managed. Boyd's head, still rolling back and forth, moved now against Drew's sound shoulder. Kirby steadied his trailing legs, then went ahead with the lantern. Before they moved off, Drew turned his head to the breast-works.

"Thanks, Yankee!" He called as loudly and clearly as his thirst-dried throat allowed. There was no answer from the hidden picket or sentry—if he were still there. Then Hannibal paced down the slope.

"The Calhoun place?" Kirby asked.

Hannibal stumbled, and Boyd cried out, the cry becoming a moan.

"Yes. Anse . . ." Drew added dully, "do you know . . . this was his birthday—today. I just remembered."

Sixteen today . . . Maybe somewhere he could find the surgeon to whom last night he had turned over the drugs in his saddlebags. The doctor's gratitude had been incredulous then. But that was before the battle, before a red tide of broken men had flowed into the dressing station at the Calhoun house. The leg wound was not too bad, but the sun had affected the boy who had lain in its full glare most of the day. He must have help.

The saddlebags of drugs, Boyd needing help—one should balance the other. Those facts seesawed back and forth in Drew's aching head, and he held his muttering burden close as Kirby found them a path away from the rending guns and the blaze of the fires.

9

One More River To Cross

THE weather is sure agin this heah war. A man's either frizzled clean outta his saddle by the heat—or else his hoss's belly's deep in the mud an' he gits him a gully-washer down the back of his neck! Me—I'm a West Texas boy, an' down theah we have lizard-fryin' days an' twisters that are regular hell winds, and northers that'll freeze you solid in one little puff-off. But then all us boys was raised on rattle-snakes, wildcats, an' cactus juice—we're kinda hardened to such. Only I ain't seen as how this half of the country is much better. Maybe we shouldn't have switched our range—"

Drew grinned at Kirby's stream of whispered comment and complaint as they wriggled their way forward through brush to look down on a Union blockhouse and stockade guarding a railroad trestle.

"Weather don't favor either side. The Yankees have it just as bad, don't they?"

The Texan made a snake's noiseless progress to come even with his companion's vantage point.

"Sure, but then they should . . . they ought to pay up somehow for huntin' their hosses on somebody else's range.

We'd be right peaceable was they to throw their hoofs outta heah. My, my, lookit them millin' round down theah. Jus' like a bunch of ants, ain't they? Had us one of Cap'n Morton's bull pups now, we could throw us a few shells as would make that nest boil right over into the gully!"

"We'll do something when the General gets here," Drew promised.

Kirby nodded. "Yes, an' this heah General Forrest, too. He sure can ramrod a top outfit. Jus' prances round the country so that the poor little blue bellies don't know when he's goin' to pop outta some bush, makin' war talk at 'em. You know, the kid's gonna be hoppin' to think he missed this heah show—"

"At least we know where he is and what he's doin'."

Kirby propped his chin on his forearm. "Jus' 'bout now he's sittin' down at the table back theah in Meridian with a sight of fancy grub lookin' back at him. How long you think he's gonna take to bein' corraled that way?"

"General Buford gave him strict orders personally—"

"Nice to have a general take an interest in you," Kirby commented. "You Kaintuck boys, you're scattered all through this heah army. Want to stay with Boyd 'cause he's ailin', so you jus' find you a general from your home state an' talk yourself into a transfer—"

"Notice you wanted me to talk you into one, too."

"Well, Missouri, Mississippi, an' Tennessee are a sight nearer Texas an' home than Virginia. Anyway, theah warn't much left of our old outfit, an' this heah Forrest is headin' up a sassy bunch. So I'm glad you did find you a general to sling some weight an' git us into his scouts jus' 'cause he knew your grandpappy. Kaintucks stick together . . ."

There was a second of silence through which they could both hear the faint sounds of life from the stockade.

"M' father was a Texan," Drew said suddenly.

"Now that's a right interestin' observation," Kirby remarked. "Heah I was all the time thinkin' you was one of these heah fast-ridin', fine-livin' gentlemen what was givin' some tone to the army. Not jus' 'nother range drifter from the big spaces. What part of Texas you from—Brazos?"

"Oh, I wasn't born there. You had a war down that way, remember?"

"You mean when Santa Anna came trottin' in with his tail high, thinkin' as how he could talk harsh to some of us Tejanos?"

"No, later than that—when some of us went down to talk harsh in Mexico."

"Sure. Only I don't recollect that theah powder-burnin' contest, m'self. M'pa went . . . got him these heah fancy hoss ticklers theah." Kirby moved his hand toward the spurs he had taken off and tucked into his shirt for safekeeping to muffle the jingle while they were on scout. "Took 'em away from a Mex officer, personal. Me, I was too young to draw fightin' wages in that theah dust-up."

"My father wasn't too young, and he drew his wages permanent. My grandfather went down to Texas and brought my mother back to Kentucky just in time for me to appear. My grandfather didn't like Texans."

"An' maybe not your father, special?"

Drew smiled, this time mirthlessly. "Just so. You see, m' father came up from Texas to get his schoolin' in Kentucky. He was studyin' to be a doctor at Lexington. And he was pretty young and kind of wild. He had one meetin'—"

"You mean one of them pistol duels?"

"Yes. So my grandfather warned him off seein' his daughter. I never heard the rights of it, but it seems m' father didn't take kindly to bein' ordered around."

Kirby chuckled. "That theah feelin' is borned right into a Texas boy. He probably took the gal an' ran off with her—"

"You're guessing right. At least that's the story as I've put it together. Mostly nobody would tell me anything. I was the blacksheep from the day I was born—"

"But your ma, she'd give you the right of it."

"She died when I was born. That's another thing my grandfather had against me. I was Hunt Rennie's son, and I killed my mother; that's the way he saw it."

Kirby rolled his head on his arm so that his hazel eyes were on Drew's thin, too controlled features.

"Sounds like your grandpappy had a burr under his tail an' bucked it out on you."

"You might see it that way. You know, Anse, I'd like to see Texas—"

"After we finish up this heah war, compadre, we can jus' mosey down theah an' look it over good. Happen you don't take to Texas, why, theah's New Mexico, the Arizona territory . . . clean out to California, wheah they dip up that theah gold dust so free. Ain't nothin' sayin' a man has to stay on one range all his born days—"

"Looks like the war ain't doin' too well." Drew was watching the activity in the stockade.

"Well, we lost us Atlanta, sure enough. An' every time we close up ranks, theah's empty saddles showin'. But General Forrest, he's still toughenin' it out. Me, I'll trail along with him any day in the week."

"Hey!" Kirby was drawing a bead on a shaking bush. But the man edging through was Hew Wilkins, General Buford's Sergeant of Scouts. He crawled up beside them to peer at the blockhouse.

"They're pullin' out!" The men in blue coats were lining up about a small wagon train.

Wilkins used binoculars for a closer look. "Your report was right; those are Negro troops!" "No wonder they're clearin' out—fast."

"Cheatin' us outta a fight," Kirby observed with mock seriousness.

"All the better. Kirby, you cut back and tell the General they're givin' us free passage. We can get the work done here, quick."

"Back to axes, eh, an' some nice dry firewood—an' see what we can do to mess up the railroads for the Yankees. Only, seems like we're messin' up a sight of railroads, all down in our own part of the country. I'd like to be doin' this up in one of them theah Yankee states like New York, say, or Indiana. Saw me some mighty fine railroads to cut up, that time General Morgan took us on a sashay through Indiana."

Kirby got to his feet and stretched. Drew unwound his own lanky length to join the other.

"Maybe the old man will be leadin' us up there, too—" Wilkins put away the binoculars. "Rennie, we'll move on down there and see if we can pick up any information."

Two months or a little more since Harrisburg. The brazen heat had given way to torrents in mid-August, and the rain had made quagmire traps of roads, forming rapids of every creek and river—bogging down horses, men, and guns. But it had not bogged down Bedford Forrest. And one section of his small force, under the command of General Buford leading the Kentuckians, had held the Union forces in check, while the other, under Forrest's personal leadership had swung past Smith and his blue coats in a lightning raid on Memphis.

Now in September the rain was still falling in the mountains, keeping the streams up to bank level. And Forrest was also on the move. After the Memphis raid there had been a second honing of his army into razor sharpness, a razor to be brought down with its cutting edge across those railroads which carried the lifeblood of supplies to the Union army around Atlanta.

Blockhouses fell to dogged attack or surrendered to bluff, the bluff of Forrest's name. The Kentucky General Buford was leading his division of the command up the railroad toward the Elk River Bridge and that was below the scouts now, being abandoned by the Union troopers.

Two factors had brought Drew into Buford's Scouts. If Dr. Cowan, Forrest's own chief surgeon, had not been the medical officer to whom Drew had by chance delivered those saddlebags of drugs, and if Abram Buford had not been a division commander, Drew might not have been able to push through his transfer. But Cowan had spoken to Forrest, and General Buford had known both the Barretts and the Mattocks all his life.

Boyd had recovered speedily from the leg wound, but his convalescence from heat exhaustion and the ensuing complications was still in progress, though he had reached the point that only General Buford's strict orders had kept him from this second raid into enemy territory. Now he was safe in a private home in Meridian, where he was being treated as a son of the house, and Drew had even managed to send a letter to Cousin Merry with that information. He only hoped that she had received it.

As for the change in commands, Drew was content. Perhaps the more so since the news had come less than two weeks earlier that John Morgan was dead. He had gone down fighting, shooting it out with Yankee troopers in a rain-wet garden in Tennessee on a Sunday morning. Men were dying, dead . . . and maybe a cause was dying, too. Drew's thought flinched away from that line now, trying to keep to the job before them. There was the abandoned stockade to destroy, the trestle and bridge to knock to pieces, and if they had time, the tracks to tear up, heat, and twist out of shape.

Wilkins stood behind a pile of wood cut for engine fuel. "They are on the run, all right. Headin' toward Pulaski."

"Think they'll make a stand there?"

"One guess is as good as another. If they do, we'll smoke them out. Keep 'em busy and chase 'em clean out of their hats and back to camp."

The destruction of the blockhouse and the trestle could be left to the army behind; the scouts moved on again.

"The boys are havin' themselves a time." Kirby returned to his post with the advance. "Tyin' bowknots in rails gits easier all the time. When this heah campaign is over, we'll know more 'bout takin' railroads apart then the fellas who make 'em know 'bout puttin' 'em together."

"Trouble!" Drew reined in Hannibal and waved to Wilkins. "There's a picket up there . . ."

Kirby's gaze followed the other's pointing finger. "Kinda

green at the business," he commented critically. "Sorta makin' a sittin' target of hisself. Like to tickle him up with a shot. We don't git much action outta this."

"I'd say we're plannin' to go in now."

A squad of Buford's advance filtered up through the trees, and an officer, his insignia of rank two-inch strips of yellow-ish ribbon sewed to the collar of a mud-brown coat, was conferring with Wilkins. Then the clear notes of the bugle charge rang out.

Forrest's men were as adept as Morgan's raiders in making a show of force seem twice the number of men actually in the field. They now whirled in and out of a wild pattern which should impress the Yankee picket with the fact that at least a full regiment was advancing.

Three miles from Pulaski the Yankees made a stand, slamming back with all they had, but Buford was pushing just as hard and determinedly. Gray-brown boiled out of cover and charged, yelling. That electric spark of reckless determination which had taken the Kentucky columns up the slope at Harrisburg flashed again from man to man. Drew tasted the old headiness which could sweep a man out of sanity, send him plunging ahead, aware only of the waiting enemy.

The Union lines broke under those shock waves; men ran for the town behind them. But there was no taking that town. By early afternoon they had them fenced in, held by a show of force. Only in the night, leaving their fires burning, the Confederates slipped away.

Rains hit again; guns and wagons bogged. But they kept on into rough-and-rocky country. They had taken enough horses from the Union corrals at the blockhouses to mount the men who had tramped patiently along the ruts in just that hope. Better still, sugar and coffee from the rich Yankee supply depot at the Brown farm was now filling Rebel stomachs.

Drew sat on his heels by a palm-sized fire, watching with weary content the tin pail boiling there. The aroma rising from it was one he had almost forgotten existed in this world of constant riding and poor forage.

"Hope it kicks in the middle an' packs double." Kirby rested a tin cup on one knee, ready and waiting. "Me, I like mine strong enough to rest a horseshoe on . . . gentlelike."

"Yankees are obligin', one way or another." Drew licked his fingers appreciatively. He had been exploring the sugar supply. "I've missed sweetenin'."

"Drink up, boys, and get ready to ride," Wilkins said, coming out of the dark. "We've marchin' orders."

Kirby reached for the pot and poured its contents, with careful measurement, into each waiting cup. "Wheah to now, Sarge? Seems like we've covered most of this heah range already."

"Huntsville. We have to locate a river crossin'."

Drew looked up. "Startin' back, Sarge?"

"Heard talk," Wilkins admitted. "Most of the blue bellies in these parts are turnin' lines to aim square at us. We can't take on all of Sherman's bully boys—"

"Got him riled, though, ain't we? All right." Kirby was energetically fanning the top of his steaming cup with his free hand. "Git this down to warm m' toes, Sarge, an' I'll stick them same toes in the stirrups an' jingle off. Come on, Drew, no man never joined up with the army to git hisself a comfortable life . . ."

Certainly that last statement of the Texan's was proven correct during the next six days. A feint toward the Yankee garrison at Huntsville occupied the enemy until the wagon train and artillery moved on to the Tennessee River. And along its northern banks, Buford's Scouts ranged. Already high for the season the waters were still rising. And all the transportation they could collect were three ferry boats at Florence and a few skiffs, not enough to serve all the Confederate force pushing for that escape route.

Athens, which Forrest had occupied on the upswing of the raid, was already back in Union hands, and the blue forces were closing in, in a countrywide sweep, backing the gray cavalry against the river.

By the third of October Buford had the boats in action, ferrying across men, equipment, and artillery in a steady stream of night-and-day oar labor. The stout General, mounted on a big mule, a large animal to carry a large man, gave the scouts new orders.

"Try downriver, boys. We're in a pinchers here, and they may be goin' to nip us—hard!" He rolled a big cheroot from a Yankee commissary store between his teeth, watching the wind whip the surface of the river into good-sized waves about the laboring boats. "Anything usable below Florence . . . we want to know about it, and quick!"

Wilkins led them out at a steady trot. "We'll take a look around Newport. Rough going, but I think I remember a place."

However, the possibilities of Wilkins' "place" did not seem too promising to Drew when they came out on a steep bluff some miles down the Tennessee.

"This is a heller of a river," Kirby expressed his opinion

forcibly. "Always spittin' back in an hombre's face. We've had plenty of trouble with it before."

They were on a bank above a slough which was not more than two hundred feet wide. And beyond that was an island thickly overgrown with cane, oak, and hickory. The upper end of that was sandy, matted with driftwood, some of it partially afloat again.

"Use that for a steppin' stone?" Drew asked.

"Best we're goin' to find. And if time's runnin' out, we'll be glad to have it. Rennie, report in. We'll do some more scoutin', just to make sure there'll be no surprises later."

For more than thirty-six hours Buford had been ferrying. Artillery, wagons, and a large portion of his division were safely across. When Drew returned to the uproar along the river he found that the second half of the retreating forces, commanded by Forrest, were in town. And it was to Forrest that Drew was ordered to deliver his report.

He would never forget the first glimpse he'd had of Bedford Forrest—the officer sitting his big gray charger in the midst of a battle, whirling his standard to attract a broken rabble of men, knitting out of them, by sheer force of personality, a refreshed, striking force. Now Drew found himself facing quite a different person—a big, quiet, soft-spoken man who eyed the scout with gray-blue eyes.

"You're Rennie, one of that Morgan company who joined at Harrisburg."

"Yes, suh."

"Morgan's men fought at Chickamauga . . . good men, good fighters. Said so then, never had any reason to change that. Now what's this about an island downriver?"

Drew explained tersely, for he had a good idea that General Forrest wanted no wasting of time. Then at request he drew a rough sketch of the island and its approaches. Forrest studied it.

"Something to keep in mind. But I want to know that it's clear. You boys picket it. If there's any Union movement about, report it at once!"

"Yes, suh."

If Yankee scouts had sighted the island, either they had not reported it or their superiors had not calculated what its value might be for hunted men—and to a leader who was used to improvising and carrying through more improbable projects than the one the island suggested.

At Shoal Creek a rear guard was holding off the Union advance which had started from Athens, the two pronged pinchers General Buford had foreseen. And now the island came into use.

Saddles and equipment were stripped from horses and piled into the boats brought down from Florence. Then the mounts were driven to the top of the bluff and over into the water some twenty feet below. Leaders of that leap were caught by their halters and towed behind the boats, the others swimming after.

Men and mounts burrowed back into the concealment of those thick canebrakes and were hidden along the southern shore of the overgrown strip of water-enclosed land. The Union pursuers came up on the bluff, but they did not see the ferrying from the south bank of the island, ferrying which kept up night and day for some forty-eight hours.

"Cold!" Kirby and Drew crouched together behind a screen of cane on the north side of the island, watching the bank above for any hostile move on the part of the enemy.

"General Forrest says no fires."

"Yeah. You know, I jus' don't like this heah spread of water. This is the second time I've had to git across it with Old Man Death-an'-Disaster raisin' dust from my rump with a double of his encouragin' rope. Seems like the Tennessee ain't partial to raidin' parties."

"Makes a good barrier when we're on the other side," Drew pointed out reasonably.

"So—"

Drew's Colt was already out, Kirby's carbine at ready. But the man who had cat-footed it through the cane was General Forrest himself.

"I thought"—the General eyed them both— "I would catch some of you young fools loafin' back heah as if nothin' was goin' on. If you don't want to roost heah all winter, you'd better come along. Last boats are leavin' now."

As they scrambled after their commander Drew realized that the General had made it his personal business to make sure none of the north side pickets were left behind in the last-minute withdrawal.

They piled into one of the waiting boats, catching up poles. Forrest took another. Then he balanced where he stood, glaring toward the bow of the boat. A lieutenant was there, his hands empty.

"You . . . Mistuh—" Forrest's voice took on the ring Drew had heard at Harrisburg. "Wheah's your oar, Mistuh?"

The man was startled. "As an officer, suh—"

Still gripping his pole with one hand, the General swung out a long arm, catching the lieutenant hard on one cheek with enough force to send him over the gunwale into the river. The lieutenant splashed, flailing out his arms, until he caught at the pole Drew extended to him. As they hauled him aboard again, the General snorted.

"Now you, Mistuh officer, take that oar theah and git to work! If I have to knock you over again, you can just stay in. We shall all pull out of this together!"

The lieutenant bent to the oar hastily as they moved out into the full current of the river.

10

"Dismount!
Prepare To Fight Gunboats!"

D REW!"
He turned his head on the saddle which served him as a temporary pillow and was aware of the smell of mule, strong, and the smell of a wood fire, less strong, and last of all, of corn bread baked in the husk, and, not so familiar, bacon frying—all the aromas of camp—with the addition of food which could be, and had been on occasion, very temporary. Squinting his smarting eyes against the sun's glare, Drew sat up. With four days of hard riding by night and scouting by day only a few hours behind him, he was still extremely weary.

Boyd squatted by his side, a folded sheet of paper in his hand.

". . . letter . . ."

Drew must have missed part during his awakening. Now he turned away from the sun and tried to pay better attention.

"From who?" he asked rustily.

"Mother. She got the one you sent from Meridian, Drew! And when Crosely went home for a horse she gave him these to bring back through the lines. Drew, your grandfather's dead . . ."

Odd, he did not feel anything at all at that news. When he was little he had been afraid of Alexander Mattock. Then he had faced out his fear and all the other emotions bred in him during those years of being Hunt Rennie's son in a house where Hunt Rennie was a symbol of black hatred; he had faced up to his grandfather on the night he left Red Springs to join the army in '62. And then Drew had discovered that he was free. He had seen his grandfather as he would always remember him now, an old man eaten up by his hatred, soured by acts Drew knew would never be explained. And from that moment, grandfather and grandson were strangers. Now, well, now he wished—for just a fleeting second or two—that he did know what lay behind all that rage and waste and blackness in the past. Alexander Mattock had been a respected man. As hardly more than a boy he had followed Andy Jackson down to New Orleans and helped break the last vestige of British power in the Gulf. He had bred fine horses, loved the land, and his word was better than most men's sworn oaths. He had had a liking for books, and had served his country in Congress, and could even have been governor had he not declined the nomination. He was a big man, in many ways a great and honorable man. Drew could admit that, now that he had made a life for himself beyond Alexander Mattock's shadow. A great man . . . who had hated his own grandson.

"This is yours . . ." Boyd pulled a second sheet from the folds of the first. Drew smoothed it out to read:

My dear boy:
  Your letter from Meridian reached me just two days ago, having been many weeks on the way, and I am taking advantage of Henry Crosely's presence home on leave to

reply. I want you to know that I do not, in any way, consider you to blame for Boyd's joining General Morgan's command. He had long been restless here, and it was only a matter of time and chance before he followed his brother.

I know that you must have done all that you could to dissuade him after your aunt's appeal to you, but I had already accepted failure on this point. Just as I know that it was your efforts which established him under good care in Meridian. Do not, Drew, reproach yourself for my son's headstrong conduct. I know Boyd's stubbornness. There is this strain in all the Barretts.

You may not have heard the news from Red Springs, though I know your aunt has endeavored to find a means of communicating it to you. Your grandfather suffered another and fatal seizure on the third of August and passed away in a matter of hours.

I do not believe that it will come as any surprise to you, my dear boy, that he continued in his attitude toward you to the last, making no provision for you in his will. However, both Major Forbes and Marianna believe this to be unfair, and they intend to see that matters are not left so.

If and when this cruel war is over—and the news we receive each day can not help but make us believe that the end is not far off—do, I beg of you, Drew, come home to us. Sheldon spoke once of some plan of yours to go west, to start a new life in new surroundings. But, Drew, do not let any bitterness born out of the past continue to poison the future for you.

Perhaps what I say may be of value since I have always held your welfare dear to me, and you have a place in my heart. Melanie Mattock Rennie was my dearest friend for all of her life, your father, my cousin. And you were Sheldon's playmate and comrade for his short time on this earth.

Come home to us, I ask you to do this, my dear boy. We shall welcome you.

I pray for you and for Boyd, that you may both be brought safely through all the dangers which surround a soldier, that you may come home to us on a happier day. Your concern for and care of Boyd is something which makes me most grateful and happy. He had lost a brother, one of his own blood, but I content myself with the belief that he has with him now another who will provide him with what guidance and protection he can give.

Remember—we want you both here with us once more, and let it be soon.

With affection and love,

Drew could not have told whether her "Meredith Barrett" at the bottom of the page was as firmly penned as ever. To him it was now wavering from one misty letter to the next. Slowly he made a business of folding the sheet into a neat square of paper which he could fit into the safe pocket under his belt. A crack was forming in the shell he had started to grow on the night he first rode out of Red Springs, and he now feared losing its protection. He wanted to be the Drew Rennie who had no ties anywhere, least of all in Kentucky. Yet not for the world would he have lost that letter, though he did not want to read it again.

"Rennie! Double-quick it; the General's askin' for you!"

Boyd started up eagerly from his perch on another saddle. He was, Drew decided, like a hound puppy, so determined to be taken hunting that he watched each and every one of them all the time. He had been allowed to ride on this return visit to West Tennessee with the condition that he would act as one of Drew's scout couriers, a position which kept him under his elder's control and attached to General Buford's Headquarters Company.

Kirby reached out a brown hand to catch Boyd by the sleeve and anchor him.

"Now, kid, jus' because the big chief sends for him, it ain't no sign he's goin' to take the warpath immediately, if not sooner. Ease off, an' keep your moccasins greased!"

Drew laughed. Nobody who rode with Forrest could complain of a lack of action. He had heard that some general in the East had said he would give a dollar or some such to see a dead cavalryman. Well, there had been sight of those at Harrisburg and some at the blockhouses. Forrest stated that Morgan's men could fight; he did not have to say that of his own.

Now they were heading into another sort of war altogether. Drew hadn't figured out just how Bedford Forrest intended to fight river gunboats with horse soldiers, but the scout didn't doubt that his general had a plan, one which would work, barring any extra bad luck.

They were setting a trap along the Tennessee right now, lying in the enemies' own back pasture to do it. South, down-river, was Johnsonville, where Sherman had his largest cache of supplies, from which he was feeding, clothing, equipping the army now slashing through the center of the South. They had been able to cripple his rail system partially on that raid two weeks earlier; now they were aiming to cut the river ribbon of the Yankee network.

Buford's division occupied Fort Heiman, well above the crucial section. The Confederates also held Paris Landing. Now they were set to put the squeeze on any river traffic.

Guns were brought into station—Buford's two Parrots, one section of Morton's incomparable battery with Bell's Tennesseeans down at the Landing. They had moved fast, covered their traces, and Drew himself could testify that the Yankees were as yet unsuspecting of their presence in the neighborhood.

He found General Buford now and reported.

"Rennie, see this bend . . ." The General's finger stabbed down on the sketch map the scouts had prepared days earlier. "I've been thinkin' that a vedette posted right here could give us perhaps a few minutes of warning ahead when anything started to swim into this fishnet of ours. General Forrest wants some transports, maybe even a gunboat or two. We're in a good position to deliver them to him, but before we begin the game, I want most of the aces right here—" He smacked the map against the flat of his other palm.

"A signal system, suh. Say one of those—" Drew pointed to the very large and very red handkerchief trailing from Buford's coat pocket. "Wave one of those out of the bushes: one wave for a transport, two for a gunboat."

The General jerked the big square from his pocket, inspected it critically, and then called over his shoulder.

"Jasper, you get me another one of these—out of the saddlebags!"

When the Negro boy came running with the piece of brilliant cloth, Buford motioned for him to give it to Drew.

"Mind you, boy," he added with some seriousness, "I want that back in good condition when you report in. Those don't grow handily on trees. I have only three left."

"Yes, suh," Drew accepted it with respect. "I'm to stay put until relieved, suh?"

"Yes. Better take someone to spell you. I don't want any misses."

Back at the scout fire Drew collected Boyd. This was an assignment the boy could share. And shortly they had hollowed out for themselves a small circular space in the thicket, with two carefully prepared windows, one on the river, the other for their signal flag.

It was almost evening, and Drew did not expect any night travel. Morning would be the best time. He divided the night into watches, however, and insisted they keep watch faithfully.

"Kinda cold," Boyd said, pulling his blanket about his shoulders.

"No fire here." Drew handed over his companion's share of rations, some cold corn bread and bacon carefully portioned out of their midday cooking.

" 'Member how Mam Gusta used to make us those dough geese? Coffee-berry eyes . . . I could do with some coffee berries now, but not to make eyes for geese!"

Dough geese with coffee-berry eyes! The big summer kitchen at Oak Hill and the small, energetic, and very dark skinned woman who ruled it with a cooking spoon of wood for her scepter and abject obedience from all who came into her sphere of influence and control. Dough geese with coffee-berry eyes; Drew hadn't thought of those for years and years.

"I could do with some of Mam Gusta's peach pie." He was betrayed by memory into that wistfulness.

"Peach pie all hot in a bowl with cream to top it," Boyd added reverently. "And turkey with the fixin's—or maybe

young pork! Seems to me you think an awful lot about eatin'
when you're in the army. I can remember the kitchen at
home almost better than I can my own room . . ."

"Anse, he was talkin' last night about some Mexican
eatin' he did down 'long the border. Made it sound mighty
interestin'. Drew, after this war is over and we've licked the
Yankees good and proper, why don't we go down that way
and see Texas? I'd like to get me one of those wild horses
like those Anse's father was catchin'."

"We still have a war on our hands here," Drew reminded
him. But the thought of Texas could not easily be dug out
of mind, not when a man had carried it with him for most
of his life. Texas, where he had almost been born, Hunt
Rennie's Texas. What was it like? A big wild land, an outlaws' land. Didn't they say a man had "gone to Texas" when
the sheriff closed books on a fugitive? Yes, Drew had to
admit he wanted to see Texas.

"Drew, you have any kinfolk in Texas?"

"Not that I know about." Not for the first time he wondered about that. There had been no use asking any questions
of his grandfather or of Uncle Murray. And Aunt Marianna
had always dismissed his inquiries with the plea that she
herself had only been a child at the time Hunt Rennie came
to Red Springs and knew very little about him. Odd that
Cousin Merry had been so reticent, too. But Drew had pieced
out that something big and ugly must have happened to
begin all the painful tangle which had led from his grandfather's cold hatred for Hunt Rennie, that hatred which had
been transferred to Hunt Rennie's son when the original
target was gone.

When Drew first joined the army and met Texans he had hoped that one of them might recognize his name and say:

"Rennie? You any kin to the Rennies of—" Of where? The Brazos, the Rio country, West Texas? He had no idea in which part of that sprawling republic-become-a-state the Rennies might have been born and bred. But how he had longed in those first lonely weeks of learning to be a soldier to find one of his own—not of the Mattock clan!

"Yes, I would like to see Texas!" Boyd pulled the blanket closer about his shoulders, curling up on his side of their bush-walled hole. "Wish these fool Yankees would know when they're licked and get back home so we could do somethin' like that." He closed his eyes with a child's determination to sleep, and by now a soldier's ability to do so when the opportunity offered.

Drew watched the river. The dusk was night now with the speed of the season. And the crisp of autumn hung over the water. This was the twenty-ninth of October; he counted out the dates. How long they could hold their trap they didn't know, but at least long enough to wrest from the enemy some of the supplies they needed far worse than Sherman's men did.

General Buford had let four transports past their masked batteries today because they had carried only soldiers. But sooner or later a loaded ship was going to come up. And when that did—Drew's hand assured him that the General's red handkerchief was still inside against his ribs where he had put it for safekeeping.

In the early morning Drew slipped down to the river's edge behind a screen of willow to dip the cold water over his

head and shoulders—an effective way to clear the head and
banish the last trace of sleep.

The sun was up and it must have been shortly before
eight when they sighted her, a Union transport riding low
in the water, towing two barges. A quick inspection through
the binoculars he had borrowed from Wilkins told Drew that
this was what the General wanted. He passed the signal to
Boyd.

"*Mazeppa*," he read the name aloud as the ship wallowed
by their post. She was passing the lower battery now, and
there was no sign of any gunboat escort. But when their
quarry was well in the stretch between the two lower batteries, they opened fire on her, accurately enough to send
every shell through the ship. The pilot headed her for the
opposite shore, slammed the prow into the bank, and a stream
of crew and men leaped over at a dead run to hunt shelter
in the woods beyond.

Men were already down on the Confederate-held side of
the river, trying to knock together a raft on which to reach
their prize. When that broke apart Drew and Boyd saw one
man seize upon a piece of the wreckage and kick his way
vigorously into the current heading for the stern of the
grounded steamer. He came back in the *Mazeppa's* yawl
with a line, and she was warped back into the hands of
the waiting raiders.

There was a wave of gray pouring into the ship, returning
with bales, boxes, bundles. Then Drew, who had snatched
peeps at the activity between searching the upper waters for
trouble, saw the gunboats coming—three of them. Again
Boyd signaled, but the naval craft made better speed than
the laden transport and they were already in position to lob

shells among the men unloading the supply ships, though the batteries on the shore finally drove them off.

In the end they fired the prize, but she was emptied of her rich cargo. Shoes, blankets, clothing—you didn't care whether breeches and coats were gray or blue when they replaced rags—food.

Kirby came to their sentry post, his arms full, a beatific smile on his face.

"What'll you have, amigos—pickles, pears, Yankee crackers, long sweetenin'—" He spread out a variety of such stores as they had almost forgotten existed. "You know, seein' some of the prices on this heah sutlers' stuff, I'm thinkin' somebody's sure gittin' rich on this war. It ain't nobody I know, though."

They kept their trap as it was through the rest of the day and the following night without any more luck. When the next fish swam into the net it approached from the other side and not past the scout post. The steamer *Anna* progressed from Johnsonville, ran the gantlet of the batteries, and in spite of hard shelling, was not hit in any vital spot, escaping beyond. But when the transport *Venus,* towing two barges and convoyed by the gunboat *Undine,* tried to duplicate that feat they were caught by the accurate fire of the masked guns. Trying to turn and steam back the way they had come, they were pinned down. And while they were held there, another steamer entered the upper end of the trap and was disabled. Guns moved by sweat, force, will and handpower, were wrestled around the banks to attend to the *Undine*. And after a brisk duel her officers and crew abandoned her.

"We got us a navy," Kirby announced when he brought

their order to leave the picket post. "The Yankees sure are kind, presentin' us with a couple of ships jus' outta the goodness of their hearts."

The *Undine* and the *Venus,* manned by volunteers, did steam with the caution of novice sailors upriver when on the first of November troops and artillery started to Johnsonville.

"Hi!" One of the new Horse Marines waved to the small party of scouts, weaving in and out to gain their position at the head of the column. "Want to leave them feed sacks for us to carry?"

Kirby put a protecting hand over his saddle burden of extra and choice rations.

"This heah grub ain't gonna be risked out on no water," he called back. "Nor blown up by no gunboat neither."

Those fears were realized, if not until two days later, when the scouts were too far ahead to witness the defeat of Forrest's river flotilla. The *Undine,* outfought by two Yankee gunboats, was beached and set afire. The same fate struck the *Venus* a day afterward. But by that time the raiders had reached the bank of the river opposite Johnsonville and were making ready to destroy the supply depot there.

Drew, Kirby, and Wilkins, with Boyd to ride courier, had already explored the bank and tried to estimate the extent of the wealth lying in the open, across the river.

"Too bad we jus' can't sorta cut a few head outta that theah herd," Kirby said wistfully. "Heah we are so poor our shadows got holes in 'em, an' lookit all that jus' lyin' theah waitin' for somebody to lay a hot iron on its hide—"

"More likely to lay a hot iron on your hide!" countered Drew. But he could not deny that the river landing with its thickly clustered transports, gunboats and barges, the acres of shoreline covered with every kind of army store, was a big temptation to try something reckless.

They had illustrious company during their prowling that afternoon. Forrest himself and Captain Morton, that very young and very talented artillery commander, were making a reconnaissance before placing the batteries in readiness. And during the night those guns were moved into position. At midafternoon the next day the reduction of Johnsonville began.

Smoke, then flame, tore holes in those piles of goods. Warehouses blazed. By nightfall for a mile upriver and down they faced a solid sheet of fire, and they smelled the tantalizing odor of burning bacon, coffee, sugar, and saw blue rivers of blazing liquid running free.

"I still say it's a mighty shame, all that goin' to waste," commented Kirby sadly.

"Well, anyway it ain't goin' into the bellies of Sherman's men," Drew replied.

The Confederate force was already starting withdrawal, battery by battery, as the wasteland of the fire lighted them on their way. And now the Yankee gunboats were burning with explosions of shells, fired by their own crews lest they fall into Rebel hands. It was a wild scene, giving the command plenty of light by which to fall back into the country they still dominated. The reduction of the depot was a complete success.

Scouts stayed with the rear guard this time, so it was that Drew saw again those two who had so carefully picked the gun stands only twenty-four hours before. General Forrest and his battery commander came down once more to survey the desolation those guns had left as a smoking, stinking scar.

Drew heard the slow, reflective words the General spoke:

"John, if you were given enough guns, and I had me enough men, we could whip old Sherm clean off the face of the earth!"

And then the scout caught Kirby's whisper of assent to that. "The old man ain't foolin'; he could jus' do it!"

"Maybe he could," Drew agreed. He wished fiercely that Morton did have his guns and Forrest all the men who had been wasted, who had melted away from his ranks—or were buried. A man had to have tools before he could build, but their tools were getting mighty few, mighty old, and . . . He tried to close his mind to that line of thought. They were on the move again, and Forrest had certainly proven here that though Atlanta might be gone, there was still an effective Confederate Army in the field, ready and able to twist the tail of any Yankee!

11

The Road to Nashville

Sleet drove at the earth with an oblique, knife-edged whip. The half-ice, half-rain struck under water-logged hat brims, found the neck opening where the body covering, improvised from a square of appropriated Yankee oilcloth, lay about the shoulders.

"I'm thinkin' we sure have struck a stream lengthwise." Kirby's Tejano crowded up beside Hannibal. "Can't otherwise be so many bog holes in any stretch of country. An' if we ever do come across those dang-blasted ordnance wagons, we won't know 'em from a side of 'dobe anyway."

They had reined in on the edge of a mud hole in which men sweated—in spite of the sleet which plastered thin clothing to their gaunt bodies—swore, and put dogged endurance to the test as they labored with drag ropes and behind wheels encrusted with pendulous pounds of mud, to propel a supply wagon out of the bog into which it had sunk when the frozen crust of the rutted road had broken apart. The Army of the Tennessee, now fighting storms, winter rains, snow and hail, was also fighting men as valiantly, engaged in General Hood's great gamble of an all-out attack on Nashville. They had a hope—and a slim chance—to sweep through the Union lines back up into Tennessee and Kentucky, and perhaps to wall off Sherman in the south and repair the loss of Atlanta.

Hannibal brayed, shifting his weary feet in the churned-up muck of the field edge. The ground, covered with a scum of ice at night, was a trap for animals as well as vehicles. Breaking through that glassy surface to the glutinous stuff beneath, they suffered cuts deep enough to draw blood above hoof level.

Drew called to the men laboring at the stalled wagon.

"Ordnance? Buford's division?"

He didn't really expect any sort of a promising answer. This was worse than trying to hunt a needle in a stack of hay, this tracing—through the fast darkening night—the lost ordnance wagons, caught somewhere in or behind the infantry train. But ahead, where Forrest's cavalry was thrusting into the Union lines at Spring Hill, men were going into battle with three rounds or less to feed their carbines and rifles. Somehow the horse soldiers had pushed into a hot, full-sized fight and the scouts had to locate those lost wagons and get them up to the front lines.

A living figure of mud spat out a mouthful of that viscous substance in order to answer.

"This heah ain't no ordnance—not from Buford's neither! Put your backs into it now, yo' wagon-dogs! Git to it an' push!"

Under that roar the excavation squad went into straining action. Oxen, their eyes bulbous in their skulls from effort, set brute energy against yokes along with the men. The mud eventually gave grip, and the wagon moved.

Drew rode on, the two half-seen shapes which were Boyd

and Kirby in his wake. A dripping branch flicked bits of ice
into his face. The dusk was a thickening murk, and with
the coming of the November dark, their already pitiful
chance of locating the wagons dwindled fast.

There was a distant crackle of carbine and rifle fire. The
struggle must still be in progress back there. At least the
stragglers about them were still moving up. No retreat from
Spring Hill, unless the Yankees were making that. All Drew's
party could do was to continue on down the road, asking
their question at each wagon, stalled in the mud or traveling
at a snail's pace.

"D'you see?" Boyd cried out. "Those men were barefoot!"
Involuntarily he swung one of his own booted feet out of the
stirrup as if to assure himself that he still had adequate
covering for his cold toes.

"It ain't the first time in this heah war," Kirby remarked.
"They'll ketch 'em a Yankee. The blue bellies, they're mighty
obligin' 'bout wearin' good shoes an' such, an' lettin' themselves be roped with all their plunder on. Some o' 'em, who
I had the pleasure of surveyin' through Sarge's glasses
this mornin', have overcoats—good warm ones. Now that's
what'd pleasure a poor cold Texas boy, makin' him forget his
troubles. You keep your eyes sighted for one of them theah
overcoats, Boyd. I'll be right beholden to you for it."

Hannibal brayed again and switched his rope tail. His
usual stolid temperament showed signs of wear.

"Airin' th' lungs that way sounds like a critter gittin' set
to make war medicine. A hardtail don't need no hardware
but his hoofs to make a man regret knowin' him familiar-
like—"

Drew had reached another wagon.

"Ordnance? Buford's?" He repeated the well-worn question without hope.

"Yeah, what about it?"

For a moment the scout thought he had not heard that right. But Kirby's crow of delight assured him that he had been answered in the affirmative.

"What about it?" Boyd echoed indignantly. "We've been huntin' you for hours. General Buford wants . . ."

The man who had answered Drew was vague in the dusk, to be seen only in the limited light of the lantern on the driver's seat. But they did not miss the pugnacious set of knuckles on hips, nor the truculence which overrode the weariness in his voice.

"Th' General can want him a lotta things in this heah world, sonny. What the Good Lord an' this heah mud lets him have is somethin' else again. We've been pushin' these heah dang-blasted-to-Richmond wagons along, mostly with our bare hands. Does he want 'em any faster, he can jus' send us back thirty or forty fresh teams, along with good weather—an' we'll be right up wheah he wants us in no time—"

"The boys are out of ammunition," Drew said quietly. "And they are tryin' to dig out the Yankees."

"You ain't tellin' me nothin', soldier, that I don't know or ain't already heard." The momentary flash of anger had drained out of the other's voice; there was just pure fatigue weighting the tongue now. "We're comin', jus' as fast as we can—"

"You pull on about a quarter mile and there's a turnout; that way you'll make better time," Drew suggested. "We'll show you where."

"All right. We're comin'."

In the end they all pitched to, lending the pulling strength of their mounts, and the power of their own shoulders when the occasion demanded. Somehow they got on through the dark and the cold and the mud. And close to dawn they reached their goal.

But that same dark night had lost the Confederate Army their chance of victory. The Union command had not been safely bottled up at Spring Hill. Through the night hours Schofield's army had marched along the turnpike, within gunshot of the gray troops, close enough for Hood's pickets to hear the talk of the retreating men. Now they must be pursued toward Franklin. The Army of the Tennessee was herding the Yankees right enough, but with a kind of desperation which men in the ranks could sense.

Buford's division held the Confederate right wing. Drew, acting as courier for the Kentucky general, saw Forrest—with his tough, undefeated, and undefeatable escort—riding ahead.

They had Wilson's Cavalry drawn up to meet them. But they had handled Wilson before, briskly and brutally. This was the old game they knew well. Drew saw the glitter of sabers along the Union ranks and smiled grimly. When were the Yankees going to learn that a saber was good for the toasting of bacon and such but not much use in the fight? Give him two Colts and a carbine every time! There was a fancy dodge he had seen some of the Texans use; they strung extra revolver cylinders to the saddle horn and snapped them in for reloading. It was risky but sure was fast.

"They've got Springfields." He heard Kirby's satisfied comment.

"I'm goin' to get me one of those," Boyd began, but Drew rounded on him swiftly.

"No, you ain't! They may look good, but they ain't much. You can't reload 'em in the saddle with your horse movin', and all they're good for in a mixup is a fancy sort of club."

The Confederate infantry were moving up toward the Union breastworks, part of which was a formidable stone wall. And now came the orders for their own section to press in. They pushed, hard and heavy, while swirls of blue cavalry fought, broke, re-formed to meet their advance, and broke again. They routed out pockets of blue infantry, sending some pelting back toward the Harpeth.

A wave of retreating Yankees crossed the shallow river. Forrest's men dismounted to fight and took the stream on foot, the icy water splashing high. It was wild and tough, the slam of man meeting man. Drew wrested a guidon from the hold of a blue-coated trooper as Hannibal smashed into the other's mount with bared teeth and pawing hoofs. Waving the trophy over his head and yelling, he pounded on at a knot of determined infantry, aware that he was leading others from Buford's still-mounted headquarter's company, and that they were going to ride right over the Yankee soldiers. Men threw away muskets and rifles, raised empty hands, scattered in frantic leaps from that charge.

Then they were rounding up their blue-coated prisoners and Drew, the pole of the captured guidon braced in the crook of his elbow as he reloaded his revolver, realized that the shadows were thickening, that the day was almost gone.

"Rennie!" Still holding the guidon, Drew obeyed the beckoning hand of one of the General's aides. He put Hannibal to a rocking gallop to come up with the officer.

"Withdrawin'—behind the river. Pass the word to gather in!"

Drew cantered back to wave in Kirby, Boyd, and the others who had made that charge with him. It was retreat again, but they did not know then that Franklin had cost them Hood's big gamble. Forty-five hundred men swept out of the gray forces—killed, wounded, missing, prisoners. Five irreplaceable generals were dead; six more, wounded or captured. The Army of the Tennessee was slashed, badly torn . . . but it was not yet destroyed.

That night the cavalry was on the march, driven by Forrest's tireless energy. They hit skirmishers at a garrisoned crossroads, using Morton's field batteries to cut them a free path. And through the bitter days of early December they continued to show their teeth to some purpose.

Blockhouses along the railroads and along the Cumberland were taken, with Murfreesboro their goal. Life was a constant alert, a plugging away of weary men, worn-out horses, bogged-down wagons, relieved now and then from the morass of exhaustion by sharp spurts of fighting, the satisfaction of rounding up a Yankee patrol or blockhouse squad, the taking of some supply train and finding in its wagons enough to give them all mouthfuls of food.

Murfreesboro was strongly garrisoned by the enemy, too strong to be stormed. But on the morning of the seventh a Yankee detachment came out of that fort and Forrest's men deployed to entice them farther afield. Buford's command was lying in wait—let the blue bellies get far enough from the town and they could cut in between, perhaps even over-run the remaining garrison and accomplish what Forrest himself had believed impossible, the taking of Murfreesboro.

They made part of that ... fought their way into the town. Drew pounded along in a compact squad led by Wilkins. He saw the sergeant sway in the saddle, dropping reins, his face a clay-gray which Drew recognized of old. Snatching at the now trailing rein, Drew jerked the other's mount out of the main push.

The sergeant's head turned slowly; his mouth looked al-most square as he fought to say something. Then he slumped, tumbling from the saddle into the embrace of an ornamental bush as his horse clattered along the sidewalk. Drew knew he was already dead.

Buford's men went into Murfreesboro right enough, well into its heart. But they could not hold the town. Only that thrust was deep and well timed; it saved the whole command. For, though they did not know it yet, on the pike the in-fantry had broken. For the first time Forrest had seen men under his orders run from the enemy in panic-stricken terror. Only the cavalry had saved them from a wholesale rout.

Drew trudged over the stubble of a field, leading Hannibal and Wilkins' mount. There had been no way of bringing the sergeant's body out of town, and Drew had reported the death to Lieutenant Traggart, who officered the scouts. He felt numb as he headed for the spark of fire which marked their temporary camp, numb not only with cold and hunger, but with all the days of cold, hunger, fighting, and marching which lay behind. It seemed to him that this war had gone on forever, and he found it very hard to remember when he had slept soundly enough not to arouse to a quick call, when he had dared to ride across a field or down a road without watching every bit of cover, every point on the landscape which could mask an enemy position or serve the same purpose for the command behind him.

As he came up to the fire he thought that even the flames looked cold—stunted somehow—not because there had not been enough wood to feed them, but because the fire itself was old and tired. Blinking at the flames, he stood still, unaware of the fact that he was swaying on feet planted a little apart. He could not move, not of his own volition.

Someone coughed in the shadow fringe beyond the light of those tired flames. It was a short hard cough, the kind which hurt Drew's ears as much as its tearing must have hurt the throat which harbored it. He turned his head a fraction to see the bundle of blankets housing the cougher. Then the reins of mule and horse were twisted from his stiff fingers, and Kirby's drawl broke through the coughing.

"You, Larange, take 'em back to the picket line, will you?"

The Texan's hands closed about Drew's upper arms just below the arch of his shoulders, steered him on, and then pressed him down into the limited range of the fire's heat. From somewhere a tin plate materialized, and was in Drew's hold. He regarded its contents with eyes which had trouble focusing.

A thick liquid curled stickily back and forth across the surface of the plate as he strove to hold it level with trembling hands. Into the middle of that lake Kirby dropped white squares of Yankee crackers, and the pungent smell of molasses reached Drew's nostrils, making his mouth water.

Snatching at the crackers, he crammed his mouth with a dripping square coated with molasses. As he began to chew he knew that nothing before that moment had ever tasted so good, been so much an answer to all the disasters of the day. The world shrank; it was now the size of a battered tin plate smeared with molasses and the crumbs of stale crackers.

Drew downed the mass avidly. Kirby was beside him again, a steaming tin cup ready.

"This ain't nothin' but hotted water. But maybe it can make you think you're drinkin' somethin' more interestin'."

With the tin cup in his hands, Drew discovered he could pay better attention to his surroundings. He glanced around the small circle of men who messed together. There was Larange, coming back from the horse lines, Webb, the Tennesseean from the mountains, Croff and Weatherby, Cherokees of the Indian Nations, and Kirby, of course. But— Drew was searching beyond the Texan for the other who should be there.

Absently he sipped the hot water, almost afraid to ask a question. Then, just because of his inner fears, he forced out the words: "Where's Boyd?"

When Kirby did not answer, Drew's head lifted. He put down his cup and caught the Texan's arm.

"He made it out of town; I know that. But where *is* he?"

"Ovah theah." Kirby nodded at the blanket-wrapped figure in the shadows. "Seems like he ain't feelin' too well . . ."

Drew wasted no time in getting to his feet. On his hands and knees, he scrambled across the space separating him from the roll of blankets. His questing hand smoothed across a ragged bullet tear in the top one, recognizing it to be Kirby's by that mark. The pale oval of Boyd's face turned toward him.

"What's the matter, boy?"

Drew could hear the other's harsh, fast breathing just as he had when they had found the injured boy at Harrisburg. Drew's fingers touched a burning-hot cheek.

"Got . . . me . . . sniffles." Boyd's mumble ended in another bout of those sharp coughs. " 'Member—sniffles? Hot soup an' bricks in bed, an' onion cloth for the throat . . ." He repeated all the Oak Hill remedies for a severe cold.

Bricks to warm the bed, hot soup of Mam Gusta's expert concocting, a thick onion poultice to ease the pain in throat and chest and draw out inflammation: every one of those were as far beyond reach now as Oak Hill itself! For a moment Drew was gripped with a panic born of utter frustration.

"Shelly? You there, Shelly?" Boyd's hoarse voice came from the dark. "I'm sure thirsty, Shelly!"

Drew turned his head. Kirby had been behind him, but now the Texan was back to the fire, ladling more hot water out of the pot. When he returned, Weatherby was with him. Drew slipped his arm under that restlessly turning head to support the boy while the Texan held the tin cup to Boyd's lips. They got a few mouthfuls into him before he turned his head away with a ghost of some of his old petulance.

"I'm hungry, Shelly. Tell Mam Gusta . . ."

Weatherby squatted down on the other side of Boyd's limp body and put his hand to the boy's forehead.

"Fever."

"Yes." Drew knew that much.

"There's a farmhouse two miles that way." Weatherby nodded to the south. "Maybe nobody there, but it will be cover—"

"You can find it?" Drew demanded.

The Cherokee scout answered quickly. "Yes. You tell the lieutenant, and we'll go there."

Kirby's hand rested on Drew's shoulder for a moment. "I'll track down Traggart. You and Weatherby here get the kid into that cover as quick as you can. This ain't no weather for an hombre with a cough to be out sackin' in the bush."

Kirby was back again before they had rigged a blanket stretcher between two horses.

"The lieutenant says to stay with th' kid till mornin'. He'll send the doc along as soon as he can find him. Trouble is, we may have to ride on tomorrow . . ."

But Drew put that worry out of his mind. No use thinking about tomorrow; the present moment was the most important. With Weatherby as their guide, they started off at a walk, heading into the night across ice-rimmed fields while the rising wind brought frost to bite in the air they pulled into their lungs.

There was no light showing in the black bulk of the house to which Weatherby steered them. It was small, hardly better than a cabin, but the door swung open as Kirby knocked on it; and they could smell the cold, stale odor of a deserted and none-too-clean dwelling. But it was shelter, and exploring in the dark, Kirby announced that there was firewood piled beside the hearth.

By the light of the blaze Weatherby brought alive they found an old bedstead backed against the wall, a tangle of filthy quilts cascading from it. One look at them assured Drew that Boyd would be far better left in his blankets on the floor itself.

The Cherokee scout prowled the room, looking into the rickety wall cupboards, venturing through another door into a second smaller room, really a lean-to, and then going up the ladder into a loft.

"They left in a hurry, whoever lived here," he reported. "They left this—" He held out a dried, shrunken piece of shriveled salt beef.

"We can boil it," Kirby suggested. "Make a kinda broth; it might help the kid. Any sign of a pot—?"

There was a pot, encrusted with corn-meal remains. Weatherby took it outside and returned, having scrubbed its interior as clean as possible, and filling it with a cup or so of water. "There's a well out there."

Boyd was asleep, or at least Drew hoped it was sleep. The boy's face was flushed, his breathing fast and uneven. But he hadn't coughed for some time, and Drew began to hope. If he could have a quiet day or two here, he might be all right. Or else the surgeon could send him along on one of the wagons for the sick and wounded—the wagons already on the move south. If the doctor would certify that Boyd was ill . . .

Weatherby was busily shredding the wood-hard beef into the pot of water. His busy fingers stopped; his dark eyes were now on the outer door. Drew stiffened. Kirby's fingers closed about the butt of a Colt.

"What—?" Drew asked in the faintest of whispers.

The Cherokee dropped the remainder of the uncut beef into the pot. Knife in hand, he moved with a panther's fluid grace to the begrimed window half-covered with a dusty rag.

12

Guerrillas

B OYD stirred. "Shelly?" His call sounded loud in the now silent room. Drew set his hand across the boy's mouth, dividing his attention between Boyd and Weatherby. They had no way of putting out the fire, whose light might be providing a beacon through the dark. The Indian moved back a little from the window.

"Riders . . . coming down the lane." His whisper was a thread.

Now Drew could hear, too, the ring of hoofs on the iron-hard surface of the ground. A horse nickered—one of those which had brought Boyd's stretcher, or perhaps one of the newcomers.

Kirby whipped about the door and was now lost in the shadows of the next room. Weatherby looked to Drew, then to the loft ladder against the far wall. In answer to that unspoken question, Drew nodded.

As the Cherokee swung up into the hiding place, Drew eased one of his Colts out of the holster, pushing it under the folds of the blankets around Boyd. Then he swung the pot, with its burden of beef and water, out over the fire—to hang on its chain to boil.

"Shelly?" Boyd asked again. His eyes were open, too bright, and he stared about him, plainly puzzled. Then he looked up at his nurse, and his forehead wrinkled with effort. "Drew?"

But Drew was listening to those oncoming hoofs. The strangers would see two horses. If they came in, they would find two men—it was as simple as that. And if they wore the wrong color uniforms, Weatherby above, and Kirby in the lean-to, would be ready and waiting for trouble. Drew laid fresh wood on the fire. Since he could not hide, he felt he'd better get as much light as possible in case of future trouble. The last they had heard the Yankees were concentrating at Murfreesboro and Nashville. But scouts would be out, dogging the flanks of the Confederate forces, just as he had done the opposite during the past few days.

There was silence now in the lane, a suspicious quiet. Drew deduced that the riders had dismounted and might be closing in about the cabin. A prickle of chill climbed his spine. He touched the lump under the blanket which was his own insurance.

The door burst open, sent banging inward by a booted foot. And at the same time a small pane in an opposite window shattered, the barrel of a rifle thrust in four inches, covering him. Drew remained where he was, his left arm thrown protectingly across Boyd.

"Now ain't this somethin'?" The man who had booted in the door was grinning down at the two on the hearth. He wore a blue coat right enough, but it was slick with old grease across the chest, stained on one shoulder, and his breeches were linsey-woolsey, his boots old and scuffed. And his bush of unkempt hair was covered with a battered hat topping a woolen scarf wound about ears and neck.

The chill on Drew's spine was a band of ice. This was no Union trooper. The scout could identify a far worse threat now—bushwhacker . . . guerrilla, one of the jackals who hung on the fringe of both armies, looting, killing, and changing sides when it suited their purposes. Such a man was a murderer who would kill another for a pair of boots, a whole shirt, or the mere whim of the moment.

"Come in, Simmy, we's got us a pair o' Rebs," the man bawled over his shoulder, and then turned to Drew. "Don't you go gittin' no ideas, sonny. Jas' thar, he's got a bead right on yuh, an' Jas' he's mighty good with that rifle gun. Now, you jus' pull out that Colt o' yourn an' toss it here. Make it fast, too, boy. I'm a mighty unpatient man—"

Drew pulled free the Colt still in its holster, tossing it across the floor so that it spun against the fellow's boot. The big hairy hand scooped it up easily and tucked the weapon barrel down in his belt.

A second man, smaller, with a thin face which had an odd lopsided look, squeezed through the door and sidled along the wall of the room, his rifle pointed straight at Drew's head. He spat a blotch of tobacco juice on the hearth, spattering the edge of the top blanket which covered Boyd.

"What's th' matter wi' him?" he demanded.

"He's sick," Drew returned. "You Union?"

The big man grinned. "Shore, sonny, shore. We is Union . . . scouts . . . Union scouts." He repeated that as if pleased by the sound. "An' you is Rebs, which makes you our prisoners. So he's sick, eh? What's the matter?"

"I don't know." Drew's fingers were only inches away from the Colt under the blanket. But he could dare no such move with that rifle covering him from the window.

"Jas', any sign out thar?" the big man called.

"Petey ain't seen any, jus' two horses." The words came from behind the still ready rifle.

"Wal, tell him to look round some more. An' you kin come in, Jas'. These here Rebs ain't gonna be no trouble—is you, sonny?"

Drew shook his head. Luck appeared to be on his side. Once Jas' was in here, they could hope to turn tables on the three of them, with Weatherby and Kirby taking them by surprise.

Jas' appeared in the doorway a moment or so later. He was younger than his two companions, younger and more tidy. His coat was also blue, and he wore a forage cap pulled down over hair very fair in the firelight. There was a fluff of young beard on his chin, and he carried himself with the stance of a drilled man. Deserter, thought Drew.

The newcomer surveyed Drew and Boyd expressionlessly, his eyes oddly shallow, and tramped past them to hold his hands to the blaze on the hearth, keeping his rifle between his knees. Then he reached up with his weapon, hooked the barrel in the chain supporting the pot, and pulled that to him, sniffing at the now bubbling contents.

"You, Reb"—the big man towered over Drew—"git this friend o' yourn an' drag him over thar. Us wants to git warm."

"Drew?" Boyd looked up questioningly, his feverish gaze passing on to the guerrilla. "Where's Shelly?"

The big man's grin faded. His big boot came out, caught Drew's leg in a vicious prod.

"Who's this here Shelly? Whar at is he?"

"Shelly was his brother," Drew said, nodding at Boyd. "He's dead."

"Dead, eh? How come sonny boy here's askin' for him then?" He leaned over them, and his fingers grabbed and twisted at the front of Drew's threadbare shell jacket. "I ask yuh, Reb, whar at is this heah Shelly?" He seemed only to flick his wrist, but the strength behind that move whirled Drew away from Boyd, brought him part way to his feet, and slammed him against the wall—where the big man held him pinned with small expenditure of effort.

"Shelly's dead." Somehow Drew kept his voice even. Kirby ... Weatherby ... They were there. "Boyd's out of his head with fever."

Jas' let the pot swing back over the fire, moving toward Boyd to lean over and stare at the boy's flushed face.

"Might be so," Jas' remarked. "Two horses, two men. Neither one much to bother about."

"Better be so!" The big man held Drew tight to the wall and cuffed him with his other hand. Dazedly, his head ringing, Drew slipped to the floor as the other released him. "Now"—that boot prodded Drew again—"git your friend over thar, Reb."

Drew stumbled back and went on his knees beside Boyd. His fingers groped under the edge of the blanket, closing on the Colt. Jas' was inspecting the pot again, and Simmy had moved forward to share the warmth of the hearth. With the revolver still in his hand, though concealed by the blanket,

Drew pulled Boyd away from the fire as best he could, aware the big man was watching closely.

Jas' reached up to the crude mantel shelf, brought down a wooden spoon, and wiped it on a handkerchief he pulled from an inner pocket.

"This ain't fancy grub," he observed to the room at large, "but it's better than nothin'. You want Simmy to bring in Petey, Hatch?"

"Th' cap'n's comin'." Simmy's remark was made in a tone of objection.

Hatch swung his head around to eye the smaller man.

"You bring Petey in!" he ordered. "Now!" he added.

For a second or two it appeared that Simmy might rebel, but Hatch stared him down. Jas' scooped out a spoonful of the pot's contents and blew over it.

"You fixin' on havin' a showdown with the captain, Hatch?" he asked.

The big man laughed. "I has me a showdown with anyone what gits too big for his breeches, Jas'. You, Reb—" he indicated Drew, with a thumb poking through a ragged glove —"supposin' you jus' show us what you got in them pockets o' yourn."

Jas' laughed. "Don't figure to find anything worth takin' on a Reb do you, Hatch? Most of 'em are poorer'n dirt."

"Now that's whar you figger wrong, Jas'." Hatch shook his head as might one deploring the stupidity of the young. "Lotsa them little Reb boys has got somethin' salted 'way, a nice watch maybe, or a ring or such. Them what comes from th' big houses kinda hold on to things from home. What you got, Reb?"

"A gun—in your back!"

Jas' spun in a half crouch, his rifle coming up. There was the explosion of a shot, making a deafening clap of thunder in the room. The younger bushwhacker cried out. His rifle lay on the floor, and he was holding a bloody hand. Kirby stood in the doorway, a Colt in each hand. And now Drew produced his own hidden weapon, centering it on Hatch.

The door burst open for the second time as Simmy was propelled through it, his hands shoulder high, palm out, and empty. Weatherby came behind him, a gun belt slung over one shoulder, two extra revolvers thrust into his own belt.

"They got Petey," Simmy gabbled. "Got him wi' a knife!" His forward rush brought him against the wall, and he made no move to turn around to face them. He could only plaster his body tight to that surface as if he longed to be able to ooze out into safety through one of its many cracks.

"Shuck th' hardware!" Kirby ordered.

Hatch's grin was gone. The fingers of his big hands were twitching, and the twist of his mouth was murderous.

"Lissen—" the Texan's tone was frosty—"I've a finger what cramps on m' trigger when I git riled, an' I'm gittin' riled now. You loose off that theah fightin' iron, an' do it quick!"

Hatch's hand went to his gun. He jerked it from the holster and slung it across the floor.

"Now th' one you got holdin' up your belly . . . an' your knife!"

The Colt that Hatch had taken from Drew and a bowie with a long blade joined the armament already on the boards. Drew made a fast harvest of all the weapons.

"Well, we sure got us some bounty hunter's bag," Kirby

observed as he and Weatherby finished using the captives'
own belts to pinion them.

"There may be more comin'; they talked about some captain." Drew brought Boyd back to the warmth of the fire.

Weatherby nodded. "I'll scout." He disappeared out the
door.

Jas' was rocking back and forth, holding on one knee the
injured hand Kirby had roughly bandaged; his other arm
was fastened behind him. There were tears of pain on his
cheeks, but after his first outcry he had not uttered a sound.
Hatch, on the other hand, had been so foul-mouthed that
Kirby had torn off a length of the bed covering and gagged
him.

Simmy sat now with his back against the wall, watching
their every move. Of the three, he seemed the likeliest to talk.
Kirby appeared to share in Drew's thoughts on that subject,
for now he bore down on the small man.

"You expectin' some friends?" Compared to his tone of
moments earlier, the Texan's voice was now mildly friendly.
"We'd like to know, seein' as how we're thinkin' some hospitable thoughts 'bout entertainin' them proper."

Simmy stared up at him, bewildered. Kirby shook his head,
his expression one of a man dealing with a stubbornly stupid
child.

"Lissen, hombre, me—I'm from West Texas, an' that
theah's Comanche country, leastwise it was Comanche
country 'fore we Tejanos moved in. Now Comanches,
they're an unfriendly people, 'bout the unfriendliest Injuns,
'cept 'Paches, a man can meet up with. An' they have them
some neat little ways of makin' a man talk, or rather yell,
his lungs out. It ain't too hard to learn them tricks, not for a

bright boy like me, it ain't. You able to understand that?"

Kirby did not scowl, he did not even touch the little man. But as one drawling word was joined to the next, Simmy held his body tighter against the wall, as if to escape by pushing.

"I ain't done nothin'!" he cried.

"That's what I said, little man. You ain't done nothin'. But you're goin' to do somethin'—talk!"

Simmy's pale tongue swept across working lips. "What . . . you want-wantta . . . know?" he stuttered.

"You expectin' to meet some friends heah?"

"Th' rest o' the boys an' th' cap'n; they may be ketchin' up."

"How many 'boys' ?"

Simmy's tongue tripped again. He swallowed. Drew thought he was trying to produce a crumb of defiance. Kirby reached out, selecting Hatch's bowie knife from the cache of captured weapons. He weighed it across the palm of his hand as if trying its balance and then, with deceptive ease, flipped it. The point thudded into the wall scant inches away from Simmy's right ear, and the little man's head bobbed down so that his nose hit one of his hunched-up knees.

"How many 'boys' ?" Kirby repeated.

"Depends . . ."

"On what?"

"On how good th' raidin' is. After a fight thar's always some pickin's."

Drew was suddenly sick. What Simmy hinted at was the vulture work among the dead and the wounded too enfeebled to protect themselves from being plundered. He saw Kirby's lips set into a thin line.

"Kinda throw a wide rope, don't you, little man? How many 'boys'?"

"Maybe five . . . six . . ."

"An' this heah cap'n?"

"He tells us wheah thar's good pickin's." For a moment the man produced a spark of spite. "He's a Reb, like you——"

"Have you used this place before?" Drew broke in. If this were either a regular or temporary rendezvous for this jackal pack, the quicker they were away, the better.

"No, the cap'n said to meet here tonight."

"I don't suppose he said *when?*" Kirby's question was answered by a shake of Simmy's unkempt head.

Boyd suddenly moved in his cocoon of blankets, struggling to sit up, and Drew went to him.

He was coughing again with a strangling fight for breath which was frightening to watch. Drew steadied him until the attack was over and he lay in the other's arms, gasping. The liquid in the pot on the fire was cooked by now. Perhaps if Boyd had some of that in him . . . But dared they stay here?

Kirby squatted back on his heels as Drew settled Boyd on his blankets and went to unhook the pot. Then the Texan supported the younger boy as Drew ladled spoonfuls of the improvised broth into his mouth.

"Th' doc'll come," Kirby murmured. "Croff promised to guide him heah. But this gang business—"

"I don't see how we can move him now . . ." Drew was feeding the broth between Boyd's lips, trying to ease the cough, his wits too dulled to tackle any problem beyond that.

"Which means we gotta keep company from movin' in.

If we could raise us a few of the boys now . . ." Kirby was speculative.

"If you went back to camp, gave the alarm. Traggart doesn't want a gang like this runnin' loose around here. They say they're Union; maybe they do have some connection with the Yankees."

"With a Reb cap'n throwin' in with 'em? Most of these polecats play both sides of the border when it'll git them anythin' they want. An' they could try an' pay their way with the Yankees by tellin' 'bout our movements heah."

"Could you make it to camp, fast?"

Kirby grunted. "Sure, easy as driftin' downriver on one of them theah steamers. But leavin' you heah with that mess of skunks is somethin' else."

"Weatherby's out there. Anything or anyone gettin' by him would have to come in on wings."

"An' wings don't come natural to this breed of critter! All right, I don't see how theah's much else we can do. We can't go pullin' the kid 'round any more. I'll give Weatherby the high sign an' make it back as quick as I can. Let's see if these heah ropes is staked out tight."

He made a careful inspection of their three captives' bonds, and Drew laid the assorted armament to hand. But Kirby hesitated by the door.

"You keep your eyes peeled, amigo. Weatherby—he can pull that in-and-out game through the loft like he did before. But one man can't be all over the range at once."

"I know." Drew studied the remnants of battered furniture about the room. He thought he could pull the bed frame across the outer door, and shove the table and bench in front of the door to the lean-to. And there was a section of wall right under the broken window which could not be seen by anyone outside. "I've some precautions in mind."

"I'm ridin' then. See you." Kirby was gone with a wave of hand.

Boyd was quiet again. The broth must have soothed him. Drew shifted the other's body to the floor on the spot of safety under the window. As he returned to gather up the arms he noted that Jas' was watching him.

Some of the first shock of his wound had worn off so that the guerrilla was not only aware of his present difficulties but was eyeing Drew in a manner which suggested he had not accepted the change in their roles as final. Drew hesitated. He could tie back that wounded hand, too, but he was sure the other could not use it to any advantage, and Drew could not bring himself to cause the extra pain such a move would mean. Not that he had any illusions concerning the bush-whacker's care for him, had their situation been reversed.

Simmy, once Kirby had gone, moved against the wall, holding up his head with a sigh of relief. He, too, watched Drew move the furniture. And when the scout did not pay any attention to him he spoke. "Wotcha gonna do wi' us, Reb?"

Hatch's eyes, over the gag, were glaring evil; Jas' was watching the two Confederates with an intent measuring stare; but Simmy wilted a little when Drew looked at him directly.

"You're prisoners of war. As Union scouts . . ."

Simmy wriggled uncomfortably, and Drew continued the grilling.

"You *are* Union scouts?"

"Shore! Shore! We's Union, ain't we, Jas'?" he appealed eagerly to his fellow.

Jas' neither answered nor allowed his gaze to wander from Drew.

"Then you'll get the usual treatment of a prisoner." Drew was short, trying to listen for any movement beyond the squalid room. Weatherby was out there, and Drew put a great deal of trust in the Cherokee's ability. But what if the "captain" and the remaining members of this outlaw gang arrived before Kirby returned with help? Seeing that Boyd appeared to be asleep, Drew once again inspected his weapons, checking the loading of revolvers and rifle.

Jas's rifle was one of the new Spencers. The Yankees loaded those on Sunday and fired all week, or so the boys said. It was a fine piece, new and well cared for. He examined it carefully and then looked up to meet Jas's flat stare, knowing that the guerrilla's hate was the more bitter for seeing his prized weapon in the enemy's hands.

The Spencer, Simmy's Enfield, old and not very well kept, five Colts beside his own, Hatch's bowie knife and another, almost as deadly looking, which had been found on Jas', equipped Drew with a regular arsenal. But it was not until he settled down that Drew knew he faced a far more deadly enemy—sleep. The fatigue he had been able to battle as long as he was on the move, hit him now with the force of a clubbed rifle. He knew he dared not even lean back against the wall or relax any of his vigilance, not so much over the prisoners and Boyd, as over himself.

Somehow he held on, trying to move. The pile of wood by the hearth was diminishing steadily. He would soon have to let the fire die out. To venture out of the house in quest of more fuel was too risky. And always he was aware of Jas's tight regard. Simmy had fallen asleep, his thin, weasel face hidden as his head lolled forward on his chest. Hatch's eyes were also closed.

Drew straightened with a start, conscious of having lost seconds—or moments—somewhere in a fog. He jerked aside, perhaps warned by his scout's sixth sense more than any real knowledge of danger. There was a searing flash beside his head, the bite of fire on his cheek. If he had not moved, he would have received that blazing brand straight between the eyes. Now he rolled, snapping out a shot.

A man shouted hoarsely and Drew strove to avoid a kick, struggling to win to his feet, unable to tell just what was happening.

13

Disaster

Simmy's animallike howling filled the room. Jas', his hand bleeding afresh, sopping through the bandage his captors had twisted about the wound, sprawled forward, clawing with those reddened fingers for the Spencer. While Hatch, eyes and upper portions of his hair-matted cheeks bulging over the gag, kicked out, striving to come at Drew with the frenzy of a man making a last desperate play.

The brand Jas' had hurled was smoldering on Boyd's blankets. Drew sent it flying with the toe of his boot and made a quick movement to stamp out a small spurt of flame. Then he kicked it again, spinning the Spencer back against the wall.

Simmy's cry died to a whimper. A wide stain spread over his nondescript coat just above the belt, and Drew knew that his first shot had found that target. But he was in charge of the situation once again. Both Hatch and Jas' had subsided, the one eyeing the threat of Drew's weapon, the other again nursing his hand, his face drawn into a grin of agony.

The smell of burning cloth was a sour stench. Drew moved to beat out a new blaze in the bedcovers. He coughed in acrid smoke and felt the smart of the burn along his neck and jaw where the brand had hit him. Simmy rolled on the floor, bent double.

"Drew!" Boyd was struggling free of his blankets, up on one elbow, staring about him as one who had wakened into a nightmare rather than having come out of such a dream. "It's all right . . ."

But was it? Hatch had subsided. Jas' was quiet; there was nothing to fear from Simmy. Only that same sense which was part of any scout's equipment nagged at Drew, warning him that the crisis was not over.

He went down on one knee beside Simmy, endeavoring to roll him over to examine his wound. The guerrilla's mouth was slackly open, his small, predator's eyes were oddly bewildered, as if he could not comprehend what had happened to him or why. As Drew fumbled with his clothing to lay bare the wound, Simmy twisted, his legs pulling up a little. Then his head rolled, and Drew sat back on his heels. There was no longer any need for aid.

Boyd still rested on his elbow, listening. He could hear Hatch's thick breathing and Jas's, a crack of charred wood breaking on the hearth, a slashing against the broken window . . . the storm had begun again. Only those were not the sounds they were listening for.

Drew visited in turn each of the flimsy barricades he had erected after Kirby left. He had no way of telling time. How long had it been since the Texan left? It could not be too far from morning now, yet the sky outside the windows was still as black as night.

"Drew!" Boyd pulled his other hand free, pointing to the ceiling over their heads.

The loft! And the route Weatherby had made use of when he had gone up that ladder, dropped out of a window above, and returned with his prisoner through the front door. But if the Cherokee had come back to the cabin, surely the disturbance in the room below would have brought him down. Unless he was otherwise occupied . . . How? And by whom?

Drew went to the foot of the ladder, not looking up to show his suspicion, but only to listen. He was certain he heard a scraping sound. Was it someone making his way through a small window? No one who had been weeks in Weatherby's company could believe that the Indian would betray his movements in that manner.

Drew left the ladder, collected the Spencer, and joined Boyd. The rest of the weapons lay at hand, and Drew sorted them out swiftly, piling them between Boyd and his own post. From here, as he had earlier planned, they had both doors, two windows, and the ladder to the loft under surveillance. The other window was over the level of their heads. As long as they kept below its sill, anyone shooting through it could not touch them.

Boyd hitched his shoulders higher against the wall. He was still flushed, his eyes too bright, but he was certainly more himself than he had been any time since they had brought him here. Now he reached for one of the Colts, resting it on his body at chest level.

"Who are they?" he whispered, glancing at the prisoners.

"Guerrillas," Drew replied.

"More company comin'?"

"Might be. Anse went for the boys."

But Boyd's chin lifted an inch or two, a slight gesture to indicate the ceiling again. He brought his other hand up, and using both, cocked the Colt, that click carrying with almost a shot's sharp twang through the room.

Jas' was again staring at Drew, his lips a silent snarl. But the scout believed that as long as he was alert, weapons in hand, he had nothing more to fear from his prisoners. They had made their reckless gamble and had lost.

The opening at the top of the ladder was a square of dark, hardly touched by the flickering light of the dying fire.

"You theah . . ." The barking hail came from without, strident, startling. "We have you surrounded."

It was the voice of an educated man with the regional softening of vowels. Simmy's cap'n? What then had happened to Weatherby? Boyd braced the barrel of his Colt on a bent knee, its sights centered on the front door. But Drew still watched the loft opening.

"Last chance . . . come out with your hands up!" The voice was very close now. And the unknown apparently knew at least part of the situation in the cabin. Which meant either very clever scouting, or that they had taken Weatherby. But Drew, knowing the habits of the guerrillas, dared not follow that last thought far. He tried to locate the man outside; he was in front all right, but surely not directly in line with the door.

"Cap'n!" Jas' called, his gaze daring Drew to shoot. "There's only two of 'em, and one's sick."

There was a flicker of movement in the trap opening. Drew fired, to be answered by a yelp of pain and surprise. Perhaps he had not entirely removed one of the attackers from the effective list, but the fellow would be more cautious from now on.

There was only a short second between his shot and an

answering fusillade from outside. The panes in the other windows shattered and Hatch, gurgling incoherently behind his gag, kicked to roll himself behind the flimsy protection of the bedstead.

"You almost got one of your own men then!" Drew called. Feverishly he tried to think of a way to play for time. Weatherby might be dead, but Kirby could have reached the headquarters camp and already be well on his way back with reinforcements.

Hatch's gurgling was louder. And now Jas' had transferred his attention to the broken windows and what might be beyond them. There was a creaking above. Drew tried to deduce from those sounds whether one man or two moved overhead. The fire was dying fast. Should he try to urge it into new life with the last of the wood, or would the dark be more to his benefit?

Shots again, but not crashing through the windows now; these were outside. A man screamed shrilly. Then a horse cried in pain. Drew heard the pounding of hoofs, and in the loft a quick shuffling. More shots . . .

Boyd laughed hysterically, and then coughed, until he bent over the Colt he still grasped, gasping. Drew steadied him against his shoulder, trying to picture for himself what was happening outside. It sounded very much as if Kirby's relief force had arrived and that the "cap'n" and his gang were in retreat.

"Drew! Everythin' all right?" There was no mistaking Kirby's voice.

He had brought not only four other scouts from the camp, but also Lieutenant Traggart and the doctor. And as the major portion of that relief force crowded into the room Drew leaned back against the wall, very glad to let other authority take over.

"Guerrilla scum," was the lieutenant's verdict on their prisoners. "They say they're Union . . . or ours, whichever works best at the time. There's another one dead out there, and he's wearing one of *our* cavalry jackets!"

"Officer's?" Drew wondered if they had picked off the "cap'n."

"No, you thinkin' he was this renegade officer Kirby was talkin' about? I don't think this is the one. He's a pretty nasty-lookin' specimen, though. Four of 'em at least got away. We'll take these two into camp and see what they can tell us. The General will be interested. I'd say this one's a Yankee deserter." He studied Jas'.

The young man in the blue jacket spat, and one of the scouts hooked his fingers in the other's collar, jerking him roughly to his feet.

"Mount and start back with them!" Traggart ordered. "How's the boy, suh?"

Boyd had wilted back into his blankets when the stimulation of the fight was gone. He was still conscious, but his coughing shook his whole body.

"Lung fever, unless he gets the right care." The surgeon was going about his business with dispatch. "I hate to move him, but there's no sense in remaining here as a target for more of this trash." He glanced at Jas' and Hatch impersonally. "Lucky we brought the wagon. Tell Henderson to bring it up. We'll take him to the Letterworth house for now—"

Reeling a little when he tried to walk, Drew found himself sharing the accommodation of the wagon with Boyd, a canvas slung across them to keep off the gusts of rain. He fell asleep as they bumped along, unable to fight off exhaustion any longer.

Twenty-four hours later he was back on duty with the advance. Boyd was housed in such comfort as any could hope to find, and the cavalry was on the move. Buford's men were to picket along the Cumberland River. There was a new feel to the army. Drew sensed it as he rode with the small headquarters detachment. Empty saddles, too many of them, and the growing belief—evidenced in mutters passed from man to man—that they were engaged in a nearly hopeless bid.

Franklin, which for Drew had been a wild gallop across some fields, a strip of cloth seized from the enemy to set beneath a guidon of their own, had been a major disaster for the Army of the Tennessee. Forrest's energy and drive kept the cavalry a sharp-edged weapon, still to be used with telling effect. But they all sensed the clouds gathering over their heads, not those laden with the eternal chill rain, but ones which carried with them a coming night.

It was so cold that men had to use both hands to cock their revolvers. And Drew saw Croff swing from the saddle, draw his belt knife to cut the hoof from a dead horse. The Cherokee glanced up as he looped his grisly trophy to his saddle horn.

"Need the shoe," he explained briefly. "Runner has one worn pretty thin." He patted the drooping neck of his mount.

Hannibal walked around the dead horse carefully. The mule was only a skeleton copy of the sturdy, well-cared-for animal Drew had ridden out of Cadiz. But he would keep going until he dropped, and his rider knew it.

"Any trace of Weatherby?" Drew asked. The disappearance of the other Cherokee scout at the cabin battle had con-

tinued as a mystery for their own small company. None of
those who had known him could credit the Indian being
taken unawares by the guerrilla force. He had vanished somewhere in the dark of the night, and none of their searching
a day later, interrupted by orders to move, had turned up a
clue.

"Not yet," Croff answered. "He may have made too wide a
circle and run into a Yankee picket. Someday, perhaps, we
shall know. Look there!"

From their screen of cover they watched a blue cavalry patrol trot along a lane.

"Headin' for th' home corral, an' lookin' twice over each
shoulder while they do it," commented Kirby. "Was we to
let out a yell now, they'd drag it so fast they'd dig their
hoofs in clear down to the stirrup leathers."

Drew shook his head. "Those are General Wilson's men
... can't be sure with them that they wouldn't come poundin'
up, sabers out, tryin' to take a prisoner or two. Anyway, we
don't stir them up, that's orders."

Kirby sighed. "Too bad. Cold as it is, a little fightin' would
warm an hombre up some. You know, for sure, the only way
we're gonna git outta this heah war is to fight our way out."

Croff reined his patient mount around. "The big fight is
comin'—"

"Nashville?" Drew asked, aware of a somber shadow closing in on them all.

The Cherokee shrugged. "Nashville? Maybe. The signs
are not good."

"It's when the signs ain't good," Kirby observed, "that
fellas lean on their hardware twice as hard. Heard tell of
gunfighters knotchin' their irons for each man they take in

a shootout. Me, I'm kinda workin' the same idea for battles. An' I have me a pretty good tally—Shiloh, Lebanon, Chicka-mauga, Cynthiana twice, Harrisburg, an' a mixed herd o' little ones. Gittin' pretty long, that line o' knotches." His voice trailed away as he watched the disappearing Yankee cavalrymen, but somehow Drew thought he was seeing either more or less than blue-coated men riding under a sullen December sky.

Yes, a long tally of battles, and all those small fights in between which sometimes a man could remember better than the big ones, remember too often and too well.

"The wagons pulled out of the Letterworth place this mornin'," Drew said. "They were gone when I stopped by at noon—"

"Goin' south? Any news of the kid?"

"They took him along." There was a faint ray of comfort in the thought that Boyd had been judged well enough to be moved with the rest of the sick and wounded up from the temporary hospitals and shelters in the neighborhood. The seriously ill certainly could not be moved. But he wished he could have seen the boy; there was no telling when and where they would meet again.

"Well," Kirby pointed out, "if the doc took him, it means they thought he was able to make it. He's young an' tough. Bet he'll be back in line soon."

"They'll travel slow," Croff added. "Drivin' hogs and cattle and all those wagons, they ain't goin' to push."

Forrest, along with his prisoners, wagons, sick and wounded, the barefoot, and dismounted men, was driving four-footed supplies south on his way to the Tennessee River, and he was not likely to risk or relinquish any of the spoil.

Buford's Kentuckians lay in wait along the Cumberland, hoping perhaps to echo, if only faintly, their earlier successes against the gunboats and supply transports. And at Nashville a battle was shaping. . . .

Drew had ridden in to report when the first of the new retreat orders came. General Buford, who had invited Drew up to the fire, sat listening as the scout held his stiff hands to the blaze and listed the sum total of the day's comings and goings as far as Yankee patrols were concerned.

"No sign of that missin' scout?" the General asked when Drew's account was finished. "Pour yourself a cup of that, boy! It ain't coffee. In fact, I don't inquire too deeply into what Lish does bring me to drink nowadays. But it's kind of comfortin' to have something warm under your belt in this weather. Blame-coldest, wettest winter I ever did see! No sign of Weatherby?" he repeated as Drew sipped from the tin cup his superior had pushed into his hands, not only grateful for the warmth spreading through his insides, but also for the heat of the container he cupped between his palms.

"No, suh, no sign at all."

"Hmm. That's strange." The General edged his solid bulk forward on his stool, which creaked as his weight shifted. He poured himself a cup of the same brew he had urged upon the scout. "Those were guerrillas right enough. Scum from both sides, just out like buzzards to pick up what they could. Only they were too far into our lines . . . and bolder than most. Doesn't fit somehow."

"Might be cover for Union scouts after all, suh?"

Buford shrugged. "Not very likely. If Weatherby does report in, send him to me! Oh, by the way, Rennie, you're promoted to sergeant to take Wilkins' place." The General sat gazing into the cup he held, but it was plain his thoughts were far from the current substitute for coffee.

"Thank you, suh."

Buford glanced up. "Thank—? Oh, the sergeant business. Lieutenant Traggart put you in for the first openin' some time ago. You had your trainin' with Morgan, and you learned well. John Morgan . . . hard to think of him dead now. And Pat Cleburne . . . and all the rest. We have to close ranks and do double duty for all of them." Again he was speaking his thoughts, Drew was sure. "Well, Sergeant Rennie, we will, we will!"

The courier who stumbled into the room, lurched against the rude wooden table, almost rebounding from it to fall. He was nearly out on his feet, feet where broken boots were mired within inches of their tops. Drew put down his cup and jumped up to steady the man.

"General Forrest's compliments, suh. Will you bring up the division to join General Chalmers? The battle's on at Nashville, and it may be necessary to form a rear guard for a retreat—" He got the message out mechanically in a croak.

So they went to start the first move in a vast job of salvage. Buford's men marched fast to come between a broken army and the full force of enemy pursuit. For Franklin, having bled the Army of the Tennessee of its strength, was only the beginning of chaos. Nashville crushed the remains, and the remnants fled, a crippled despairing flight of the defeated. The big gamble was totally lost.

It was Forrest who commanded that hastily formed rear guard. Its stiff spine was his cavalry, with the addition of two brigades of infantry—Alabama and Georgia troops. Snapping

at them was Union cavalry in full force. Not snapping at their
heels, for it was fang to fang; the Confederates only gave
ground fighting. Day darkened on the field and they were
in hand-to-hand assault. A man marked musket or carbine
flash to sight on the enemy.

And as time became a nightmare of almost continuous
battle, the rain lashed at the struggling men with a whip of
icy water. Fighters crouched behind rail fences while the
Union cavalry charged across black fields, hoofs drumming
on the ground, and the sputtering fire of carbines making an
uneven kind of lightning along the improvised wood barricades. Black tree trunks gleamed greasily in the wet; and here
and there, out of defiance, the war whoop of the Yell cut
eerily through the melee.

After evacuating Columbia, they closed ranks and stiffened
again, knowing that they must be the wall between the disorganized rabble of the army and the thrust of the Yankee
forces coming confidently to finish them off. Cavalry, volunteers from the infantry, fragments of commands all, but still
with enough cohesion behind a commander they trusted to
fall back in fighting order . . . and fighting—even to coun-
tercharge when the need and the occasion offered.

Drew, Kirby, Croff, and Webb circled around a wagon,
bringing the driver to a halt, his mule team standing with
drooping heads, blowing and puffing so that their ribs showed
as bony bars through their wet hides.

"Git!" The driver raised his whip as a weapon of offense
until he saw where Croff's carbine was aimed. A little pale,
he sank back on the seat. A bush of whiskers hid most of his
dirty face, and there was something about him which reminded Drew of the guerrilla Simmy.

"Watta yuh want?" he whined.

"Orders," Drew told him shortly. "Pull over there and dump your load!"

"Whose orders?" The driver bristled, still fingering his whip.

"General Forrest's. Now get to it!" Drew put snap in that. "All right, boys," he called to the patiently waiting line of infantrymen, "here's another one ready to carry you as soon as you empty it."

The ragged half company fanned forward, bearing down upon the wagon as if it were a Yankee stronghold. They swarmed over and in it, pitching the contents out on the ground in spite of the futile protests of the driver.

"Lordy! Lordy!" One of the willing unloaders paused, his arms about a box. He was staring into its interior, bemused. "Lookit what's heah! I ain't seen such a lovely, lovely sight since I had me a chance on the river at that blue-belly supply ship!"

He placed the box with exaggerated care on the ground and dived into it, coming up with a can in each hand. "Boys, we has us a treasure; we sure enough has!" He was immediately the core of a group eager to share in his find. The driver half raised his whip. Kirby brought his horse closer to the wagon, caught at the lash, pulling the stock out of the other's hands with a quick jerk.

"Reckon the boys must have lighted on your own private cache, eh, fella? Don't hump your tail none 'bout it. They ain't in no mood to listen to any palaver on the subject. Better ride it out peaceablelike."

"Much obliged, Sarge." The original finder of the treasure

trove broke from the circle and handed Drew some crackers. "The boys want you should have a taste, too."

Drew laughed and began sharing the windfall with the scouts.

"Better break it up, soldiers. The General wants us on the move."

They were already busy throwing the last articles out of the wagon, settling in. Barefoot, cold, hungry, until the last few minutes, they were Forrest's indomitable rear guard, riding between brisk spats with the enemy.

Kirby tested the edge of a cracker between his teeth as they trotted on in search for another wagon to turn over to the infantry.

"This heah army is bound to git mounted, one way or the other," he commented. "Hope we have some more luck like that in the next wagon, too."

14

Hell in Tennessee

"A T LEAST we have that river between us now," Drew said. Behind them was Columbia, where Forrest had bought them precious hours of traveling time with his truce to discuss a prisoner exchange. Along the banks of the now turbulent Duck River not a bridge or boat remained to aid their pursuers. Buford's Scouts had had a hand in that precaution.

"Yeah, an' Forrest's waitin' for the Yankees to try an' smoke him out. It's 'bout like puttin' your hand in a rattler's den to git him by the tail, I'd say. But I'd feel a mite safer was theah an ocean between us. Funny, a man is all randy with his tail up when he's doin' the chasin', but you git mighty dry-mouthed an' spooky when the cards is slidin' the other way 'crost the table. Seems like we has been chased back an' forth over these heah rivers so much, they ought to know us by now. An' be a little more obligin' an' do some partin', like in that old Bible story—let us through on dry land. Man, how I could do with some *dry* land!" Kirby spoke with unusual fervor.

Croft laughed. "No use hopin' for that. Anyways, we have business ahead."

Just as they had rounded up wagons to transport the infantry between skirmishes, so now they were on the hunt for oxen to move the guns. The bogs—miscalled "roads" on their maps—demanded more animal power than the worn-out horses and mules of the army could supply. Oxen had to be impressed from the surrounding farms for use in moving the wagons and fieldpieces relay fashion, with those teams sometimes struggling belly deep. Having pulled one section to a point ahead, they were driven back to bring up the rear of the train.

"Not enough ice on the ground; it's rainin' it now!" Kirby's shoulders were hunched, his head forward between them as if, tortoisewise, he wanted to withdraw into a nonexistent protecting shell.

"Just be glad," Drew answered, "you ain't walkin'. I saw an ox fall back there a ways. Before it was hardly dead the men were at it, rippin' off the hide to cover their feet—bleedin' feet!"

"Oh, I'm not complainin'," the Texan said. "M'boots still cover me, anyway. Me, I'm thankful for what I got—can even sing 'bout it."

His soft, clear baritone caroled out:

"And now I'm headin' southward, my heart is full of woe,
I'm goin' back to Georgia to find my Uncle Joe,
You may talk about your Beauregard an' sing of General Lee,
But the gallant Hood of Texas played Hell in Tennessee."

Some sardonic Texan, anonymous in the defeated forces, had first chanted those words to the swinging march of his western command—"The Yellow Rose of Texas"—and they had been passed from company to company, squad to squad, by men who had always been a little distrustful of Hood, men who had looked back to the leadership of General Johnston as a good time when they actually seemed to be getting somewhere with this endless-seeming war.

There was a soft echo from somewhere—". . . played Hell in Tennessee–ee–ee."

"Sure did," Webb commented. "But this country comin' up now ain't gonna favor the blue bellies none."

He was right. Both sides of the turnpike over which the broken army dragged its way south were heavily wooded, and the road threaded through a bewildering maze of narrow valleys, gorges, and ravines—just the type of territory made for defensive ambushes to rock reckless Yankees out of their saddles. The turnpike was to be left for the use of the rear guard of fighting men, while the wagon trains and straggling mass of the disorganized Army of the Tennessee split up to follow the dirt roads toward Bainbridge and the Tennessee River.

"Know somethin'?" Webb demanded suddenly, hours later, as they were on their way back with their hard-found quota of oxen and protesting owners and drivers. "This heah's Christmas Eve—tomorrow's Christmas! Ain't had a chance to count up the days till now."

"Sounds like we is gonna have us a present—from the Yankees. Hear that, amigos?" Kirby rose in his stirrups, facing into the wind.

They could hear it right enough, the sharp spatter of rifle and musket fire, the deeper sound of field guns. It was a clamor they had listened to only too often lately, but now it was forceful enough to suggest that this was more than just a skirmish.

Having seen their oxen into the hands of the teamsters, they settled down to the best pace they could get from their mounts. But before they reached the scene of action they caught the worst of the news from the wounded men drifting back.

". . . saw him carried off myself," a thin man, with a bandaged arm thrust into the front of his jacket, told them. "Th' Yankees got 'cross Richland Creek and flanked us. General Buford got it then."

Drew leaned from his saddle to demand the most important answer. "How bad?" Abram Buford might not have had the dash of Morgan, the electric personality of Forrest, but no one could serve in his headquarters company without being well aware of the steadfast determination, the regard for his men, the bulldog courage which made him Forrest's dependable, rock-hard supporter in the most dangerous action.

"They said pretty bad. General Chalmers, he took command."

"Christmas present," Kirby repeated bleakly. "Looks like Christmas ain't gonna be so merry this year."

They had lost Buford and they were forced back again, disputing savagely—hand to hand, revolver against saber, carbine against carbine—to Pulaski. Seven miles, and the enemy made to pay dearly for every foot of that distance.

It was Christmas morning, and Drew chewed on a crust of corn pone, old and rock-hard. He wondered dully if his capacity to hold more than a few crumbs had completely vanished. And he allowed himself for one or two long moments to remember Christmas at Oak Hill—where he had managed to spend a more festive day than at Red Springs in the chilly neighborhood of his grandfather. Christmas at Oak Hill . . . Sheldon, Boyd, Cousin Merry, Cousin Jeff, too, before he died back in '59.

Drew opened his eyes and saw a fire, not the flames of brandy flickering above a plum pudding, or the quiet, welcoming fire on a hearth, but rather a violent burst of yellow-and-red destruction punctured by bursts of exploding ammunition. These were the stores Forrest had ordered destroyed because the men could transport them no further.

The word was out that they were going to make a firm stand near Anthony's Hill, again to the south. And they had been hard at work there to fashion a stopper which would either suck the venturesome enemy into a bad mauling, as Forrest hoped, or else just hold him to buy more time.

There the turnpike descended sharply with a defile between two ridges, ridges which now housed Morton's battery, ready to blast road and hollow below. Felled timber, rails, stones, anything which could shelter a man from lead and steel long enough for him to shoot his share back, had been woven together, and a mounted reserve waited behind to prevent flanking. A good stout trap—the kind Forrest had used to advantage before and which had enough teeth in it to crush the unwary.

"Dilly, Dilly, come and be killed," Drew repeated to himself that tag from some childhood rhyme or story as he waited at the mouth of the gorge to play his own part in the action to come. A small force of mounted men, scouts, and volunteers from various commands were bait. It was their job to make a short stiff resistance, then fly in headlong retreat, enticing the Union riders into the waiting ambush.

"Who's this heah Dilly?" Kirby wanted to know. "Some Yankee?"

Drew laughed. "Might be." He sagged a little in the saddle. Sleep during the past ten days had come in small snatches. Twice he had caught naps lying in stalled wagons waiting for fresh teams to arrive, and both times he had been awakened out of dreams he did not care to remember, to ride with gummy eyelids and a sense of being so tired that there was a fog between him and most of the world. It was two days now since Buford had been wounded. The news was that the big Kentucky general would recover. And it was a whole twenty-four hours since he watched the Christmas fires Forrest had lit in Pulaski, the fires which had devoured what they no longer had the animal power to save.

Here in the mouth of the gorge the silence was almost oppressive. He heard a smothered cough from one of the waiting men, a horse blow in a kind of wheeze. Then came the call of a bugle from down the road.

Theirs, not ours, Drew thought. Hannibal shook his head vigorously, as if bitten by a sadly out-of-season fly. The captain commanding their company of bait signaled an advance. And they followed the familiar pattern of weaving in and out of cover to enlarge the appearance of their force.

Firing rent the quiet of a few minutes earlier. Drew snapped a shot at the Yankee guidon bearer, certain he saw the man flinch. Then, with the rest, he sent Hannibal on the best run the mule could hold, back into the waiting mouth of the hollow. They pounded on, eager to present such a picture of wholesale rout that the Union men would believe a soft strike, perhaps an important bag of prisoners, lay ahead, needing only to be scooped in.

Perhaps it was the reputation for wiliness Forrest had earned which put the Yankee commander on his guard. There was no headlong chase down the ambush valley as they had hoped and planned to intercept. Instead, dismounted men came at a careful, suspicious pace, cored around a single fieldpiece, a small answer to their trap.

But when that blue stream funneled into the hollow, the jaws snapped away. Canister from Morton's guns laid a scythe along the Union advance, cutting men to ground level. The Yell shrilled along the slopes, and men jumped trees and rail barricades, pouring down in an assault wave not to be turned aside. The Yankee gun, its eight-horse team, men who stood now with their hands high, horses for riders who were no longer to need them. Three hundred of those horses from the lines behind the dismounted skirmishers—far more valuable than any inanimate treasure to men who had lost mounts —one hundred and fifty prisoners.

Kirby rode back from the eddy in the road, his mouth a wide grin splitting his skin-and-bone face. He had a length of heavy blue cloth across the saddle before him and was smoothing it lovingly with one chilblained hand.

"Got me one of them theah overcoats," he announced. "Sure fine, like to thank General Wilson for it personal. If I could git me in ropin' distance of him to do that."

The small success of the venture was not a complete victory. His dismounted cavalry overrun or thrust back, Wilson brought up infantry, and they settled down to a dogged attack on the entrenched Confederates on the ridges.

Union forces bored in steadily, slamming the weight of regiments against the flanks of the defenders. And slowly but inexorably, that turning movement pushed the Confederates in and back. Drew, riding courier, brought up to the ridge where Forrest sat on the big gray King Phillip, statue-still, immovable.

"General, suh, the enemy is in our rear—"

Forrest turned his head abruptly, the statue coming to life. And there was impatience in the answer which was certainly meant for all the doubters at large and not to one sergeant of scouts relaying a message.

"Well, ain't we in theirs?"

General Armstrong, his men out of ammunition, made his own plea to fall back. But the orders were to hold. Hood was at Sugar Creek with the army; he must have time to cross. It was late afternoon when Forrest at last ordered the withdrawal, and they made it in an orderly fashion.

Through the night the rear guard toiled on and a little after midnight they reached the Sugar in their turn. Drew splashed cold water on his face, not only to keep awake, but to rinse off the mud and grime of days of riding and fighting. He could not remember when he had had his clothes off, had bathed or worn a clean shirt. Now he smeared his jacket sleeve across his face in place of a towel and tramped wearily back to the fire where his own small squad had settled in for what rest they could get.

Croff was sniffing the air, hound fashion.

"Ain't gonna do you no good," Webb told him sourly. "Theah ain't nothin' in the pot, nor no pot neither—'less Kirby 'membered to stow it last time. Lordy, m' back an' m' middle are clean growed together, seems like."

"Feast your eyes, man! Jus' feast your eyes!" Kirby unrolled his prized coat. In its folds was a greasy package which did indeed give up a treasure—a good four-inch-thick slab of bacon squeezed in with a block of odd, brownish-yellow stuff.

They crowded around, dazzled by the sight of bacon, real bacon. Then Drew pointed at the accompanying block.

"What's that? New kind of hardtack?"

"Nope. That theah's vegetables." Kirby spoke with authority.

"Vegetables?"

"Yeah. These heah Yankee commissaries bin workin' out new tricks all th' time. They takes a lot of stuff like turnips, carrots, beets, all such truck, an' press it into cakes like this. 'Course you have to be careful. I heard tell as how one blue belly, he chawed the stuff dry an' then drank water; it bloated him up like a cow in green cane. Poor fella, he jus' natchelly suffered from bein' so greedy. But you drop it in water an' give it a boil . . ."

"Looks like hay," Drew commented without enthusiasm. He picked it up and sniffed dubiously.

"Man," Webb said, "if the Yankees can eat hay, then we can too. An' I'm hungry 'nough to chaw grass, were you to show me a tidy patch an' say go to it! How come you know all 'bout this hay-stuff, Anse?"

"We found some of it on the *Mazeppa*. The lieutenant told us how it worked—"

"The *Mazeppa*!" Webb breathed reverently, and there was a moment of silence as they all recalled the richness of that capture. "We shore could do with another boat like that one. Too bad this heah crick ain't big 'nough to float a nice bunch of supplies in, right now."

Kirby produced the pail dedicated to the preparation of coffee. But since coffee was so far in the past they could not even remember its smell or taste, no one protested his putting the vegetable block to the test by setting it boiling in the sacred container.

"Don't look like much." Webb fanned away smoke to peer into the pail. Kirby had also produced a skillet, made from half of a Yankee canteen, into which he was slicing the bacon.

"It's fillin'," he retorted sharply. "An' you didn't pay for it, did you? A man who slangs th' cook—an' the grub—now maybe he ain't gonna find his plate waitin' when it's time to eat—"

Webb drew back hurriedly. "I ain't sayin' nothin', nothin' at all!"

Drew grinned. "That's being wise, Will. Times when a man can talk himself right out of a good piece of luck. It's hot and fillin', and you got bacon to give it some taste . . ."

With hot food under their belts, a fire, and no sign of orders to move, they were content. Kirby and Croff followed the old Plains trick of raking aside the fire, leaving a patch of warmed earth on which all four could curl up together, two men sharing blankets. As the Texan squirmed into place beside him Drew felt the added warmth of the plundered coat Kirby pulled over them. This had not been too bad a day after all, or rather yesterday had not; it was now not too far before dawn. They had made their play at Anthony's Hill and had come out of it with horses, some food, and a few incidental comforts like this coat. Now after eating, they had a chance to sleep. It seemed that Forrest was going to pull it off neatly again. Drowsily Drew watched the rekindled fire. They would make it, after all.

He awoke to find a thick white cotton of fog enfolding

the bivouac. The preparations they had made again of rail and tree breastworks to greet the Union advance were no easier to see than the men crouched in their shadows. It would be a blind battle if Wilson's pursuit caught up before this cleared; one would only be able to tell the enemy by his position.

But there was no hanging back on the part of the Yankees that morning. Slowly, maybe blindly, but with determination, they were picking their way ahead, reaching the creek bank. If they could cut through Forrest's present lines, thrust straight ahead, they could smash the demoralized straggle of Hood's main command, and the Army of the Tennessee would cease to exist.

The blue coats were shadows in the fog, the first advance wading the creek now, their rifles held high. And as that line closed up and solidified into a wall of men, a burst of flame met them face-on. It was brutal, almost one-sided. The Yankees were on their feet, pacing into a country they could not clearly distinguish. While their opponents had "picked trees" and were firing from shelter with accuracy to tear huge gaps in that line.

Men stopped, fired, then broke, running back to the creek for the safety which might lie beyond that wash of icy water. And as they went, ranks of the defenders rose and raced after them, hooting and calling as if on some holiday hunt. Now the cavalry moved in in their turn, cutting savagely at the Union flanks, herding the dismounted Yankees back through the lines of their horse holders as the Morgan men had been driven at Cynthiana. Wild with fright, horses lunged, reared, tore free from men, and raced in and out, many to be caught by the gray coats. It was a rout and they pushed the Union troops back, snapping up prisoners, horses, equipment—whipping out like a thrown net to sweep back laden with spoil.

These attackers were the rear guard of a badly beaten army, but they did not act that way. They rode, fought, and out-maneuvered their enemies as if they were the fresh advance of a superior invading force. And the swift, hard blows they aimed bought not only time for those they defended, but also the respect, the irritated concern of the men they turned time and time again to fight against.

Having pushed Wilson's troopers well back, the Con-federates withdrew once more to the creek, waiting for what might be a second assault. They ate, if they were lucky enough to have rations, and rested their horses. Corn was long gone, so mounts were fed on withered leaves pulled from field shocks, from any possible forage a man could find.

Drew led the gaunt rack of bones that was Hannibal to the creek, letting the mule lip the water. But it was plain the animal was failing. Drew shifted his saddle from that bony back to one of the horses they had gathered in during the morning. But the Yankee gelding was little improvement. In the mud, constantly cut by ice, too wet most of the time, a horse's hoofs rotted on its feet. And the dead animals, many of them put out of their misery by their riders, marked with patches of black, brown, gray, the path of the army. A man had to harden himself to that suffering, just as he had to harden himself to all the other miseries of war.

War was boredom, and it was also quick, exciting action such as they had had that morning. It was fighting gunboats along the river; it was the heat and horror of that slope at Harrisburg, the cold and horror of Franklin. It was riding with men such as Anson Kirby, being a part of a fluid weapon forged and used well by a commander such as Bedford Forrest. It was a way of life . . .

The scout's hand paused in his currying of Hannibal as that idea struck him for the first time. Now he thought he could understand why Red Springs and all it stood for was so removed and meaningless, was lost in the dim past. To Drew Rennie now, the squad, his round of duties, the army —these were home, not a brick house set in the midst of green fields and smooth paddocks. The house was empty of what he had found elsewhere—acceptance of Drew Rennie as a person in his own right, friendship, an occcupation which answered the restlessness which had ridden him into rebellion. He stood staring at nothing as he thought about all that.

Kirby startled him out of his self-absorption. "Butt your saddle, amigo! We're hittin' the trail again."

As he swung up on the Yankee horse and took Hannibal's lead halter, Drew asked a question:

"Ever seem to you, Anse, like the army's home? Like it's always been, and you've always been a part of it?"

Kirby shot him a quick glance. "Guess we all kinda feel that sometimes. Gits so you can hardly remember how it was 'fore you joined up. Me, I sometimes wonder if I jus' dreamed Texas outta m' head. Only I keep remindin' myself that someday I can go back an' see if it's jus' the way I dreamed it. Kinda nice to think 'bout that."

They cut away from the main line of march, ranging out and ahead. Stragglers from the army must be moved forward, directed. And they came upon one of those, a tall man, limping on feet covered with strips of filthy rag. But he still had his musket, and on its bayonet was stuck a goodly portion of ham. He had been sitting on a tree trunk, but at the approach of the scouts he moved to meet them.

"Howdy, fellas," he spoke in a hoarse voice, and wiped a running nose on his sleeve. "What command you in?"

"Forrest's Cavalry . . . Scouts—"

"Forrest's!" He took another eager step forward. "Now theah's a command! Ain't bin for you boys, th' blue bellies woulda gulped us right up! Nairy a one of us'd got out of Tennessee."

"You ain't rightly out yet, amigo," Kirby pointed out. "Kinda lost, ain't you?"

The man shrugged and grinned wryly. "Feet ain't too good. But I'm makin' it, fast as I can."

"Can you fork a mule?" Drew asked. "This one is for ridin'. We'll take you to one of the wagons—"

"Now that's right kind of you boys, right kind." The man hobbled up to Hannibal as if he feared they might withdraw their offer. "Say, you hungry? Git us wheah we can light a spell, an' I'll divide my rations with you." He waved the musket with its impaled ham.

"Maybe we'll do jus' that," Kirby promised.

Drew dismounted to give the straggler a leg up on Hannibal before they headed on toward the Tennessee and the promise of a breathing space.

15

Independent Scout

"WHAT did the doc say?" Kirby, his blue overcoat a splotch of color against the general drabness of the winter scene, came up towing Hannibal and his own mount.

"Doesn't think he should try it." Drew made a lengthy business of pulling on the knitted gloves he had acquired only that morning as a swap for a captured Yankee Colt.

The infantry, back under the solid security of Joe Johnston's leadership, had marched on into North Carolina—to face Sherman's destructive sweep there. In the west, the only effective Confederate force still in the field east of the Mississippi was Forrest's Cavalry. And they had been granted twenty days' furlough to return home if they could get there, and gather clothing and fresh horses. The sun was far down the western horizon of the Confederacy, but to the men who rode with Forrest it had not yet set.

"Th' kid wants to go . . ."

That was the worst of it. When they listened to Boyd's eager talk, saw him make the effort to get on his feet again, they were almost convinced that the youngster could make the trip back through enemy-held territory to Oak Hill. Kirby, though he had no ties in Kentucky, was willing to

chance the journey to help Boyd home. But those miles between, where they must skulk and maybe even fight their
way—living out, eating very light—Boyd could not stand
that. The surgeon's verdict was that such an idea was utter
folly.

"I'll try to get a letter through with one of the boys," Drew
said. "Major Forbes ought to be able to furnish Cousin Merry
with safe conduct on that side; we could have the General
take care of it from this end. Then she could take him home
with her when he was able to travel."

"You write the letter fast. The Kaintucks are makin' tracks
today—"

Drew swung into the saddle, and they headed back to
camp.

"Now that we ain't headin' north, you thinkin' of joinin'
Croff an' Webb?"

Men on furlough had been given their orders to collect
supplies from home, but also to devil the Yankees when and
where they could. They were to fire into transports along the
rivers and rout and capture any Union patrols small enough
to be attacked when and where they came across them. The
Cherokee scout and others who could not return home asked
for their own type of furlough, determined to hunt the district below Franklin. Since such men could be of great
nuisance value well within the enemy lines, they were
granted permission and were even now preparing to move
out.

Drew, who had held off from committing himself to the
expedition until he had the final verdict on Boyd, knew that
Kirby was eager to go. And Drew felt that old restlessness,
which gripped him whenever he thought of spending days in

camp. He could do nothing for Boyd, but they might be able
to accomplish something in Tennessee.

"All right." He saw Kirby grin at his answer. The plan was
one after the Texan's heart, and Drew knew what it had
meant to him to hold back from it.

"You tell the kid?"

"Dr. Fairfax did." At least he had not had to deliver that
blow, a small relief which did not, however, lighten his sense
of responsibility.

"How'd he take it?"

"Quiet—on the surface."

The Boyd who once would have fought stubbornly to get
his own way, the Boyd who would have pulled himself out
of that big rocker and announced fiercely that he was riding
home whether the doctor said Yes or No—that Boyd was
gone. Perhaps this new acceptance of hard facts was a matter
of growing up. Drew clung to that. There was little he could
do, except not go home without him.

"The kid's gonna be all right?"

"Doc hopes so, if he takes it easy."

"Ever feel like this heah war's runnin' down?"

"I don't see how we can keep on much longer."

"Some of the boys are talkin' Texas. Git us down theah an'
we can go off—be a republic again. Wouldn't be the first
time the Tejanos stood up all by themselves. Supposin' this
fightin' heah stops . . . you ridin' for Texas?"

"I might."

Kirby slapped his hand on the horn of his Mexican saddle.
"Now that's what an hombre wants to hear. You change
pasture on a good colt, makes him even fatter! Come blue
bellies all ovah this heah territory, we jus' shift range. An'

nobody gonna take Texas! Even the horny toads would spit straight in a Yankee's eye—"

"How 'bout it, Sarge?" They were at the cluster of rail-walled huts where the scouts had established a temporary headquarters. Webb hailed them from the door of one of those dwellings where he was rolling up the rubber cloth laid over corn husks to form the floor. "You Kaintuck bound?"

"No. Ridin' with you boys. Doc thinks Boyd can't try it."

"Good enough, Sarge. We're pullin' out soon as Injun draws us some travelin' rations. Jus' enough to get us theah. We can eat off the Yankees later."

Since 1861 the clothing of the Confederate Army at large had never matched the colorful sketches hopefully issued by the Quartermaster General's department. Perhaps in Richmond or some state capitol the gold-lace exponents did appear in tasteful and well-tailored gray with the proper insignia of rank. Forrest's men, equipped from the first by the unwilling enemy, wore blue, a blue tempered tactfully and ingeniously by butternut shirts, dyed breeches—when there was time to do any dyeing—and slouch hats. But as Drew rode out with his squad he might have been leading a Union rather than a Rebel patrol, which, of course, was part of the necessary cover for venturing into the jaws of a very alert lion.

Parts of West Tennessee were still Confederate-held and through those they rode openly. But the countryside could offer them nothing in the way of forage. Two armies had stripped it bare during the past few months. Sometimes foraging parties on opposite sides had been known to combine forces under a private truce, or had fought brisk, bitter skirmishes to decide which would collect the spoils. If there remained a hog or chicken still running loose, it certainly possessed the power of invisibility.

They slipped across the river in one of the boats kept by local contacts acting in the scouts' service. Drew questioned the boy who owned their transportation.

"Sure they's bummers-out. Yankees say they's ourn, but they ain't!" he returned indignantly. "They ain't ridin' for nobody but their own selves. Cut off a Yankee an' shoot him for the boots on his feet—do the same if they want a hoss. Git ketched an' they tell as how they's scouts, workin' secret-like. Scouts o' ourn—if we ketch 'em; Yankees—do the blue bellies take 'em. But they ain't nothin' but lowdown trash as nobody wants, for sure!" He dug his pole into the water as if he were impaling a guerrilla on it. "They's mean, plenty mean, suh. Don't go foolin' 'round them!"

"Any special place they hang out?" Drew wanted to know.

The boy shook his head. "Oh, they holes up now an' then somewheahs. But they's a lotta empty houses 'bout nowadays. An' the bummers kin hide out good without no one knowin' they be theah—till they git ready to jump. Cut off a supply wagon or raid a farm or somethin' like that."

"Ridin' the south side of the law." Kirby settled his gun belt in a more comfortable circle about his thin middle. "Bet they know all the tricks of hoppin' back an' forth 'cross the border ahead of the sheriff, too. Time somebody collected bounty on those wolves' scalps."

Ridding the country of such vermin was indeed a worthy occupation. And their private quest for an answer to Weatherby's fate might be a part of that. But their first duty was to the army: The gathering of information, and any discomfort they could deal the Yankees, must be their primary project.

Croff brought them into a camping site he had chosen for just such use. It lay at the head of a small rocky ravine down the center of which ran an ice-sealed thread of stream. It was not quite a cave, but provided shelter for them and their mounts. It was a clear night, and the ground was reasonably hard.

They ate hard salt beef and cold army bread made with corn meal, grease, and water the night before.

"Leave here in the early mornin'." The Cherokee outlined his suggestions. "There's a road leadin' to the turnpike that's three or four miles from here. Last I heard, a bridge had washed out on the pike. Anybody ridin' from Pulaski to Columbia has to turn out and take this other way—"

"Good cover on it?" Drew asked.

"The best."

"I jus' got me one question," Kirby interrupted. "Say we was to gobble us up a bunch of strayin' Yankees along this road, what're we gonna do with 'em after? Four of us don't make no army, an' we ain't gonna be able to detach no prisoner guard. 'Course theah are them what's said from the first that the only good Yankees are them laid peacefullike in their graves. But I don't take natural to shootin' men what are holdin' up the sky with both hands."

"Orders are to spread confusion," Drew observed. "I'd say if we hit quick and often, take a prisoner's boots, maybe, and his horse, and his gun—"

"Also," Webb added, "his rations an' his overcoat, be he wearin' one."

"Then turn him loose, after parolin' him—"

"The Yankees don't honor a parole no more," Kirby objected.

"What if they don't? A lot of men comin' in sayin' they've been paroled will stir up trouble. Remember, from what we've heard, a lot of the Yankees ain't any happier about fightin' on and on than we are. So we take prisoners, get their gear, keep what we can use, destroy the rest, and turn the men loose. If we can move around enough, maybe we can draw some of Wilson's men out of that big army he's supposed to be gatherin' to hit us south. It's the old game Morgan played."

Croff grunted. "It may be old, but I've seen it work. All right, we parole prisoners and light out cross-country after a strike."

"I've been thinkin'—" Kirby was checking the loading of his Colts—"if we start heah, we can sorta work our way in, coyote right up close to Franklin. They'll be expectin' us to light out for the home range, not go jinglin' in to wheah they've forted up. Might raise a sight of smoke that way. Git Wilson's boys on the prod, for sure."

"Franklin—?" Croff repeated.

"Little below, maybe. From what that boy said, those bushwhackers move around pretty free," Drew reminded him, certain the Cherokee was back to the desire to search for Weatherby.

"We'll see what kind of luck we have along this road, Injun-scouted. You take first watch, Injun?"

"Yeah." Drew heard rather than saw the Cherokee leave their camp, bound for a lookout point. The other three bedded down, anxious to snatch as much rest as possible.

Long before dawn they were on the move again, threading

through the winter-seared woods. Croff brought them out unerringly behind a sagging rail fence well masked with the skeleton brush of the season. There was equally good cover on the other side of the road. Kirby climbed the fence, investigating a dark splotch on the surface of the lane.

"Fresh droppin's. Been a sight of trailin' 'long heah recent."

The rest was elementary. There was no need for orders. Croff and Webb holed up on one side of the lane well apart; Drew and Kirby did the same on the other. Waiting would be sheer boredom and in this weather the height of discomfort.

The gray of early morning sharpened the land about them. Boyd would have enjoyed this game of tweaking a wildcat's tail. Drew chewed his lower lip, tasting the salt of sweat, the grit of road dust. Just now was no time to think of Boyd; he must concentrate on the business before him.

He heard the sharp chittering of an aroused squirrel, repeated in two shrill bursts. But his own ear close to the ground told him they were to expect company. There was the regular thud of horses' hoofs, the sound of mounts ridden in company and at an even pace. The only remaining question was whether it was a Union patrol and small enough for the four of them to handle.

One, two . . . two more . . . five of them, topping a small rise. A cavalry patrol . . . and the odds were not too impossible.

Drew sighted sergeant's stripes on the leader's jacket. It would depend upon how alert that noncom was. Wilson was drawing in new levies, so these men could be new to the district, even green in the army.

The Yankee sergeant was past Kirby's post now, and after

him the first two of his squad. He paid no attention to the bushes.

Webb's carbine and Kirby's Colts cracked in what seemed like a single spat of sound. One of the troopers in the rear shouted, grabbing at a point high on his shoulder, the other one was thrown as his horse reared, its upraised forefeet striking another man from the saddle as he endeavored to turn his mount.

Drew fired, and saw the sergeant's carbine fall as he caught at the saddle horn, his arm hanging limp.

"Surrender!" As Drew shouted that order into the tangle below, he leaped to the right. A single shot clipped through the bushes where he had been, answered by a blast from Webb.

Then hands were up, men stared white-faced and sullen at the fence behind which might be a whole company of the enemy. Drew came into the open, the Spencer he had taken from Jas' covering the sergeant. For the expression on the noncom's face suggested that, wounded as he was, he would like nothing better than to carry on the struggle—with Drew as his principal target.

"Go ahead, get it over with!" He spat at Drew.

For a second Drew was bewildered, and then he suddenly guessed that the Union soldier expected to be shot out of hand.

His anger was hot. "We don't shoot prisoners!"

"No? The evidence is not in favor of that statement," the Yankee spoke dryly, his accent and choice of words that of an educated man.

"What brand you think we're wearin', fella?" Kirby had come out of concealment, his Colt steady on the captives.

"Guerrillas, I'd say," the sergeant returned hardily. Drew realized then that their mixture of clothing must have stamped them as the very outlaws they wanted to hunt down, as far as the Union troopers were concerned.

"Now that's wheah you're sure jumpin' your fences," Kirby's half grin vanished. "We're General Forrest's men, not guerrillas. Or ain't you never heard tell of Forrest's Cavalry? Seems like anyone wearin' blue an' forkin' a hoss ought to know who's been chasin' him to Hell an' gone over most of Tennessee. Lucky I ain't in a sod-pawin' mood, hombre, or I might jus' want to see how a blue-belly sarge looks without an ear on his thick skull, or maybe try a few Comanche tricks of hair trimmin'! Guerrillas—!"

The Union sergeant glanced from Kirby and Drew to his own men. One was sitting on the edge of the road, nursing his head between his hands. Another had his hand to his shoulder, and the sticky red of fresh blood showed between his fingers. The two others, very young, stood nervously, their hands high. If the Yankee noncom was thinking of trying something, his material was not promising. Drew broke the moment of silence with a warning.

"You're surrounded, subject to fire from both sides, Sergeant! I suggest surrender. You will be treated as prisoners of war and given parole. We *are* from General Forrest's command. We're scouts. Believe me, if we had wished to, we could have shot every one of you out of the saddle before you knew we were here. Guerrillas would have done just that."

The logic of that argument reached the Union sergeant. He still eyed Drew straightly, but there was a ruefulness rather than hostile defiance in his voice as he asked:

"What do you plan to do with us?"

"Nothing." Drew was crisp. "Give us your parole, leave your arms, your horses, your rations—if you are carrying any. Then you are free to go."

"We've been ordered not to take parole," the sergeant objected.

"General Forrest hasn't given any orders not to grant it," Drew countered. "As far as I am concerned, you can take it, we'll accept your word."

"All right." The other dismounted awkwardly, and with one hand unbuckled his saber, dropping his belt and gun.

Kirby went among the men gathering up their weapons. Then he and Drew tended the slight wounds of their enemies.

"You'll both do until you can get to town," Drew told them. "And you've a road and plenty of daylight to help you foot it . . ."

To Drew's surprise, the sergeant suddenly laughed. "This ain't going to sit well with the captain. He swore all you Rebs were run out of here a couple of weeks ago."

"You can assure him he's wrong." Drew saw a chance to confuse the enemy. "We're very much around. You'll be seein' a lot of us from now on, a lot more."

They watched the squad in blue, now afoot, plod on down the road. When they were out of sight around a bend, Webb and Croff came out of hiding to inspect the spoil. Unfortunately the Yankees had not possessed rations, but their opponents acquired five horses, five Springfields, four sabers, and three Colts, as well as welcome rounds of ammunition— a fine haul.

Croff methodically smashed the stocks of the Springfields against a rock and pitched the ruined weapons back of the fence. They had seen during the retreat just how useless those rifles were for mounted men. The sabers were broken the same way, but the rest of the plunder was shared.

Webb appropriated one of the captured mounts. They stripped the others of their gear, taking what they wanted in the way of blankets and saddle equipment, and were putting the horses on leading ropes when a volley of shots ripping through the early morning froze them. Croff whirled to face the road down which the Yankees had vanished.

"Came from that direction—"

They mounted, taking not the open road but a cross route the Cherokee indicated. Coming out on the crest of a slope, they were above another of those hollows through which the road ran. And in that way lay still blue figures. Drew's carbine swung up as men broke from ambush and headed toward those forms. No Confederate force would have wantonly butchered unarmed and wounded men, nor would the Yankees. Which left the scum they both hated—the bushwhackers!

Just as the crack of the murder guns had earlier torn the quiet, so did the Confederate answer come now. Three of those advancing on their victims dropped. One more cried out, staggering toward the concealing bush. Then more broke from cover beyond, going into flight up the other rise.

"Croff! Webb! After them!" The Cherokee scout was already booting his horse into a run.

Drew and Kirby reached the road together. Slipping from Hannibal, Drew knelt by the Union sergeant, turning the man over as gently as he could. But there was no hope. The Yankee's eyes opened; he stared up with a cold and terrible hate.

"Shot us . . . after all . . . murder—" he mouthed.

"No!" Drew cried his protest. "Not us—"

But that head rolled on his arm, and Drew was forced to swallow the fact that the other had died believing that treachery. Kirby arose from the examination of the rest of the bodies.

"Got 'em all. Musta bin as easy as shootin' weanlin's. They didn't have a chance! We got three—" He made a circle about one of the dead guerrillas—"but that don't balance none."

Drew lowered the dead sergeant to the surface of the road.

"It sure doesn't!" he said bleakly. "We'll go after them—if we have to ride clear to the Ohio!"

16

Missing in Action

I'VE COUNTED twenty at least," Webb said over his shoulder. The scouts were belly-flat in cover, looking down into a scene of some activity. It almost resembled the cavalry camp they had left behind them to the south. There were the same shelters ingeniously constructed of brush and logs and a picket line for horses and mules. This hole must harbor a high percentage of deserters from both armies.

"Only four of us," Kirby remarked. " 'Course I know we're the tall men of the army, but ain't this runnin' the odds a mite high?"

Croff chuckled. "He's got a point there, Sarge."

"Seein' as how what happened back there on the road could be pinned on us, we have to do something," Drew returned. This whole section of country would boil over when those bodies were discovered. "And we ain't the only ones. Any of our boys comin' through here on furlough are like to be jumped for it if the Yankees catch them."

"That's the truth if you ever spoke it, Sarge. I can see some hangin's comin' out of that ambush."

"Theah's still twenty hombres down theah, an' four of us. We can pick off a few from up heah, but they ain't gonna

wait around to git sniped. So, how we gonna spread ourselves—?"

Kirby's was the unanswerable question. They had trailed
the fugitives from the ambush back to this tangled wilderness
with infinite caution, bypassing two sentries so well posted
and concealed they had been forced to judge that the motley
collection of guerrillas were as experienced at this trade as
the scouts. There was no time to try to round up any other
bands of homing Confederates or prowling scouts, even if
they knew where they could be located. This was really a
Yankee problem partly as well.

Because of that murderous ambush, the local Union commander should be out for blood. But how could they get into
enemy hands the information about this rats' nest?

"We can't take 'em ourselves, and we've no time to round
up any of the boys who might be passin' through."

"So we jus' leave heah an' forgit it?" Webb demanded.

"There's another way—risky, but it might work. Take
the Yankees off our trail and put them to doing something
for us . . ."

"Sic 'em in heah, eh?" Kirby was watching Drew with
dancing eyes. "How?"

"Yeah, how? Ride up to their camp an' say, 'We know
wheah at theah's some bushwhackers, come'n see'?" Webb
asked scornfully. "After this mornin' they won't even listen
to a truce flag, I'm thinkin'."

Croff nodded. "That's right."

"Supposin' those sentries we passed back there were
knocked out and two of us took their places and the other
two then laid a trail leadin' here?"

"Showin' themselves for bait, plainlike?" Kirby asked.

"If we have to. The alarm will have gone out. I'm bettin' there're patrols thick on that road."

"Any blue bellies travelin' theah now are gonna be bunched an' ready to shoot at anything movin'.."

"So," Croff cut in over Webb's instant objection, "you get some Yankees a-hittin' it up after you, and you run for here. They're not all dumb enough to ride right into this kind of country."

"We'll have to work it so they'll keep comin'. When you see them headin' into the gorge after us, you move out of the sentry posts back across this ridge and start cuttin' this camp down to size—pick off those horses and put 'em afoot. That'll keep them here till the Yankees come."

"You know," Kirby said, "it's jus' crazy enough to work. Lordy—if it was summer, I'd say we all had our brains sun-cured, but I'm willin' to try it. Who does what?"

"Croff and Webb'll take out the sentries. We'll go hunt us up some Yankees." As Kirby said, it was a wild plan anchored here and there on chance alone. But the scouts were familiar with action as rash as this, which *had* worked. And they still had a few hours of daylight left in which to try it.

They let a supply train go by on the road undisturbed. It was, Drew noted, well guarded and the guard paid special attention to the woods and fields flanking them. The word had certainly gone out to expect dire trouble along that section of countryside.

"Have to be kinda hopin' for the right-sized herd," Kirby observed. "Need a nice patrol. Too bad we ain't able to rope in, to order, jus' what we need."

He went to a post farther south along the pike, and Drew

settled himself in his own patch of cover, with Hannibal close at hand. The passing of time was a fret, but one they were used to. Drew thought over the plan. Improvisation always had to play a large part in such a project, but he believed they had a chance of success.

A bird note, clear and carrying, broke the silence of the winter afternoon. Drew cradled the Spencer close to him. That was Kirby's signal that around the bend he had sighted what they wanted.

It was a patrol, led by a bearded officer with a captain's bars on his shoulders—quite an impressive turnout, consisting of some thirty men and two officers. Watching them ride toward him, Drew's mouth went dry, a shiver ascending his spine. To play fox to this pack of hounds was going to be more of a task than he had anticipated. But it had to be done.

He fired, carefully missing the captain by a small margin, as he saw the spark his bullet struck from a roadside stone. Then he pumped one shot after another over the heads of the startled men. As he mounted Hannibal he caught a glimpse of Kirby cutting across the slope. The Texan rode Indian fashion with most of his mount between him and the return fire from the road. Drew kicked Hannibal into a leap, taking him half way out of range and out of sight.

Then, with Kirby, he was pounding away. A branch was bullet-clipped over his head, and he heard the whistle of shots. Unless he was very lucky, this might be one piece of recklessness he would pay for dearly. But he also heard what he had hoped for—the shouts of the hunters, the thud of hoofs behind.

Now it was a game, much the same as the one they had

played to lead the Union troops into the cavalry trap at Anthony's Hill. They showed themselves, to fire and fall back,
riding a crisscross pattern which would confuse the Yankees
as to whether they were pursuing two men or more. Drew
watched for the landmarks to guide them back. Less than
half a mile would bring them to the gorge. Then they must
ride fast to put a bigger gap between them and the enemy
so they could go to cover before they struck the valley of the
guerrilla camp.

They must depend upon Croff and Webb having success-
fully taken over the sentry posts. But Drew faced those
heights with some apprehension. Kirby, on one of his cross
runs, pulled near.

"They're laggin'. Better give 'em somethin' to try an' bite
on!" He brought his bay to a complete stop and aimed. When
his carbine barked, a horse neighed and went down. Then
Kirby flinched, his weapon fell from his hand, and he caught
quickly at the horn of his saddle. From the foremost of the
blue riders there was a wild yell of exultation.

Drew whirled Hannibal and brought him at a run to the
Texan's side.

"How bad?"

"Jus' creased me." But Kirby's expression gave the lie to his
words. "Git goin' . . . don't be a dang-blasted fool!"

Drew scooped up the reins the other had let fall. Kirby
must not be allowed to lag. To be captured now was to lose
all hope of being taken as an ordinary prisoner of war. He
booted Hannibal into the rocking gallop the big mule was
capable of upon occasion, and pulled the bay along. Kirby
was clinging to the horn, his language heated as he alter-
nately ordered or tried to abuse Drew into leaving him.

The Texan's plight had applied any spur the pursuers might have needed. Confident they were now going to gather in at least two bushwhackers, the shouting behind took on a premature shrilling of triumph. There was a blast of shooting, and Drew marveled that neither man nor horse was hit again.

He was into the mouth of the gorge, still leading Kirby's horse, but a glance told him that the Texan would not be able to hold on much longer. He was gray-white under his tan, and his head bobbed from side to side with the rocking of the horse's running stride.

Their pursuers pulled pace a little, maybe fearing a trap. Drew gained a few precious seconds by the headlong pace he had set from the time Kirby had been wounded. But they dared not try to get up the steep sides of the cut now.

He dared not erupt into the bushwhacker campsite, or could he? If Croff and Webb were now making their way to the heights above, ready to fire into the camp as they had planned, wouldn't that keep the men there busy and cover his own break into the valley?

He heard firing again; this time the sound was ahead of him. Croff and Webb were starting action, which meant that the Yankees would be drawn on to see what was up. Kirby's horse was running beside Hannibal. The Texan's eyes were closed, his left shoulder and upper sleeve bloody.

Riding neck and neck, they burst out of the gorge as rifle bullets propelled from a barrel. The impetus of that charge carried them across an open strip. There were yells . . . shots . . . But Drew's attention was on keeping Kirby in the saddle.

Hannibal hit a brush wall and tore through it. Branches whipped back at them with force enough to throw riders.

Kirby was swept off, gone before Drew could catch him. Then Hannibal gave a wild bray of pain and terror. He reared and Drew lost grasp of the bay's reins. The riderless horse drove ahead while Drew tried to control the mule and turn him.

Tossing his head high, Hannibal brayed again. A man scuttled out of the brush, and Drew only half saw the figure snap a shot at him.

He was aware of the sickening impact of a blow in his middle, of the fact that suddenly he could pull no air into his straining lungs. The reins were out of his hands, but somehow he continued to cling to the saddle as the mule leaped ahead. Then under Hannibal's hoofs the ground gave way, both of them tumbling into the icy stream. And for Drew there was instant blackness, shutting out the need for breath, the terrible agony which shook him.

". . . dead. Get on after the others!"

The words made no sense. He was cold, wet, and there was a throbbing pain beating through him with every thrust of blood in his veins. But he could breathe again and if he lay very still, his nausea eased.

Then he heard it—not quite a bray, but a kind of moaning. The sound went on and on—shutting everything else out of his ears—to hurt not flesh, but spirit. He could stand it no longer.

With infinite labor, Drew turned his head. He felt the rasp of grit on the skin of his burned cheek, and that small pain became a part of the larger. He opened his eyes, setting his teeth against a wave of nausea, and tried to understand what had happened to him.

Water washed over his legs and boots, numbing him to the

waist. But his arms, shoulders, and head were above its surface as he lay on his side, half braced against a rock. And he could see across the stream to the source of that mournful sound.

Hannibal was struggling to get to his feet. There was a wound in his flank, a red river rilling from it to stain the water. And one of his forelegs was caught between two rocks. Throwing his head high, the mule bit at the branches of a willow. Several times he got hold and pulled, as if he could win to his feet with the aid of the tooth-shredded wood. Shudders ran across his body, and the sound he uttered was almost a human moan of pain and despair.

Drew moved his arm, dully glad that he could. His fingers seemed stiff—as if his muscles were taking their own time to obey his will—but they closed on one of the Colts which had not been shaken free from his holster when he fell. He pulled the weapon free, biting his lip hard against the twinges that movement cost him.

Steadying the weapon on his hip, he took careful aim at Hannibal's head and fired. The recoil of the heavy revolver brought a small, whistling cry of pain out of him. But across the stream, the mule's head fell from the willows, and he was mercifully still.

The sky was gray. Drew heard a snap of shots, but they seemed very far away. And the leaden cold of the water crept farther up his body, turning the throb into a cramp. He tried not to cry out; for him there would be no mercy shot.

The rising tide of cold brought lethargy with it. He felt as if all his strength had drained into the water tugging at him. Again, the dark closed in, and he was lost in it.

Warm . . . he was warm. And the painful spasms which

had torn at him were eased. He still had a dull ache through his middle, but there was warm pressure over it, comforting and good. He sighed, fearful that a sudden movement might cause the sharp pains to return.

Then he was moved, his head was raised, and something hard pressed against his lower lip so that he opened his mouth in reflex. Hot liquid lapped over his tongue. He swallowed and the warmth which had been on the outside was now within him as well, traveling down his throat into his stomach.

More warmth, this time on his forehead. Drew forced his eyes open. Memory stirred, too dim to be more than a teasing uneasiness. Action was necessary, important action. He focused his eyes on a brown face bearing a scruff of beard on cheeks and chin.

"Webb . . ." It was very slow, that process of matching face to name. But once he had done it, memory brightened.

"What happened—?"

They had ridden into the guerrilla camp site, he and Kirby, with the Yankees on their heels. Painfully he could recall that. Then, later he had been lying half in, half out of a creek, sicker than he had ever been in his life. And Hannibal . . . he had shot Hannibal!

Webb's hand came out of the half dark, holding the tin cup to his mouth again.

"Drink up!" the other ordered sharply.

Drew obeyed. But he was not so far under, now. Objects around him took on clarity. He was lying on the ground, not too far from a fire, and there were walls. Was he in a cabin?

There had been a cabin before, but he had not been the sick one then. The guerrillas!

"Bushwhackers?" He got that out more clearly. A shadow which had substance, moved behind Webb. Croff's strongly marked features were lined by the light.

"Dead . . . or the Yankees have them."

Webb was making him drink again. With the other supporting his head and shoulders, Drew was able to survey his body. A blanket was wrapped tightly about his legs, and over his chest and middle a wet wad of material steamed. When Webb laid him flat again, the two men, working together, wrung out another square of torn blanket, and substituted its damp heat for the one which had been cooling against him.

"What's the . . . matter—? Shot?"

Croff reached to bring into the firelight a belt strap. Dangling it, he held the buckle-end in Drew's line of vision. The plate was split, and embedded in it was an object as big as Drew's thumb and somewhat resembling it in shape.

"We took this off you," the Cherokee explained. "Stopped a bullet plumb center with that."

"Ain't seen nothin' like it 'fore," Webb added, patting the compress gently into place. "Like to ripe you wide open if it hadn't hit the buckle! You got you a bruise black as charcoal an' big as a plate right across your guts, but the skin's only a little broke wheah the plate cut you some. An' if you ain't hurt inside, you're 'bout the luckiest fella I ever thought to see in my lifetime!"

Drew moved a hand, touching the buckle with a forefinger. Then he filled his lungs deeply and felt the answering pinch of pain in the region of the bruise Webb described.

"It sure hurts! But it's better than a hole."

A hole! Kirby! Drew's hand went out to brace himself up, the compress slid down his body, and then Webb was forcing him down again.

"What you tryin' to do, boy? Pass out on us agin? You stay put an' let us work on you! This heah district's no place to linger, an' you can't fork a hoss 'til we git you fixed up some."

Drew caught at the hand which pinned his shoulder. "Will, where's Anse? You got him here too?" He rolled his head, trying to see more of the enclosure in which he lay, but all he faced was a wall of rough stone. Webb was wringing out another compress, preparing to change the dressing.

"Where's Anse?" Drew demanded more loudly, and there was a faint echo of his voice from overhead.

Croff flipped off the cooling compress as Webb applied the fresh one. But Drew was no longer lulled by that warmth.

"He ain't here," replied the Cherokee.

"Where then?" Drew was suddenly silent, no longer wanting an answer.

"Looky heah, Drew"—Webb hung over him, peering intently into his face—"we don't know wheah he is, an' that's Bible-swear truth! We saw you two come out into the valley, but we was busy pickin' off hosses so them devils couldn't make it away 'fore the Yankees caught up with 'em. Then the blue bellies slammed in fast an' hard. They jus' naturally went right over those bushwhackers. Maybe so, they captured two or three, but most of them was finished off right theah.

We took cover, not wantin' to meet up with lead jus' because we might seem to be in bad company. When all the shootin' was over an' you didn't come 'long, me and Injun did some scoutin' 'round.

"We found you down by that crick, an' first—I'm tellin' it to you straight—we thought you was dead. Then Injun, he found your heart was still beatin', so we lugged you up heah an' looked you over. Later, Injun, he went back for a look-see, but he ain't found hide nor hair of Anse—"

"He was hit bad—in the shoulder—" Drew looked pleadingly from one to the other— "when we smashed into that brush he was pushed right out of the saddle, not far from that crick where you found me. Injun, he could still be out there now . . . bleedin'—hurt . . ."

Croff shook his head. "I backtracked all along that way after we found you. There was some blood on the grass, but that could have come from one of the bushwhackers. There was no trace of Anse, anywhere."

"What if he was taken prisoner!" Neither one of them would meet his eyes now, and Drew set his teeth, clamping down on a wild rush of words he wanted to spill, knowing that both men would have been as quick and willing to search for the Texan as they had to bring Drew, himself, in. No one answered him.

But Croff stood up and said quietly: "This is a pretty well-hidden cave. The Yankees probably believe they've swept out this valley. You stay holed up here, and you're safe for a while. Then when you're ready to ride, Sarge, we'll head back south."

He stopped to pick up his carbine by its sling.

"Where're you going?"

"Take a look-see for Yankees. If they got Anse, there's a slim chance we can learn of it and take steps. Leastwise, nosing a little downwind ain't goin' to do a bit of harm." He moved out of the firelight with his usual noiseless tread and was gone.

17

Poor Rebel Soldier . . .

"SERGEANT Rennie reportin', suh, at the General's orders."
Drew came to attention under the regard of those gray-blue eyes, not understanding why he had been summoned to Forrest's headquarters.

"Sergeant, what's all this about bushwhackers?"

Drew repeated the story of their adventure in Tennessee, paring it down to the bald facts.

"That nest was wiped out by the Yankee patrol, suh. Afterward Private Croff found a saddlebag with some papers in it, which was in the remains of their camp. It looks like they'd been picking off couriers from both sides. We sent those in with our first report."

The General nodded. "You stayed near-by for a while after the camp was taken?"

"Well, I was hurt, suh."

He saw that General Forrest was smiling. "Sergeant, that theah story about your belt buckle has had a mightly lot of repeatin' up and down the ranks. You were a lucky young man!"

"Yes, suh!" Drew agreed. "While I was laid up, Privates Croff and Webb took turns on scout, suh. They located some of our men hidin' out—stragglers from the retreat. They also rounded up a few of the bushwhackers' horses and mules."

Forrest nodded. "You returned to our lines with some fifteen men and ten mounts, as well as information. Your losses?"

Drew stared at the wall behind the General's head.

"One man missin', suh."

"You were unable to hear any news of him?"

"No, suh." The old weariness settled back on him. They had hunted—first Croff and Webb—and then he, too, as soon as he was able to sit a saddle. It was Weatherby's fate all over again; the ground might have opened and gulped Kirby down.

"How old are you, Sergeant?"

Drew could not see what his age had to do with Kirby's disappearance, but he answered truthfully: "Nineteen—I had a birthday a week ago, suh."

"And you volunteered when—?"

"In May of '62, suh. I was in Captain Castleman's company when they joined General Morgan—Company D, Second Kentucky. Then I transferred to the scouts under Captain Quirk."

"The big raids . . . you were in Ohio, Rennie? Captured?"

"No, suh. I was one of the lucky ones who made it across the river before the Yankees caught up—"

"At Chickamauga?"

"Yes, suh."

"Cynthiana"—but now Forrest did not wait for Drew's affirmative answer—"and Harrisburg, Franklin . . . It's a long line of battles, ain't it, boy? A long line. And you were nineteen last week. You know, Rennie, the Union Army gives medals to those they think have earned them."

"I've heard tell of that, suh."

The General's hand, brown, strong, went to the officer's hat weighing down a pile of papers on the table. With a quick twist, Forrest ripped off the tassled gold cord which distinguished it, smoothing out the loop of bullion between thumb and forefinger.

"We don't give medals, Sergeant. But I think a good soldier might just be granted a birthday present without any one gittin' too excited about how military that is." He held out out the cord, and Drew took it a bit dazedly.

"Thank you, suh. I'm sure proud . . ."

A wave of Forrest's hand put a period to his thanks.

"A long line of battles," the General repeated, "too long a line—an end to it comin' soon. Did you ever think, boy, of what you were goin' to do after the war?"

"Well, there's the West, suh. Open country out there—"

Forrest's eyes were bright, alert. "Yes, and we might even hold the West. We'll see—we'll have to see. Your report accepted, Sergeant."

It was plainly a dismissal. As Drew saluted, the General laid his hat back on the tallest pile of papers. Busy at the table, he might have already forgotten Drew. But the Kentuckian, pausing outside the door to examine the hat cord once more, knew that he would never forget. No, there were no medals worn in the ragged, thin lines of the shrinking Confederate Army. But his birthday gift—Drew's fist closed about the cord jealously—that was something he would have, always.

Only, nowadays, how long was "always"?

"That's a right smart-lookin' mount, Sarge!" Drew looked at the pair of lounging messengers grinning at him from the front porch of headquarters. He loosened the reins and led the bony animal a step or two before mounting.

Shawnee, nimble-footed as a cat, a horse that had known almost as much about soldiering as his young rider. Then Hannibal, the mule from Cadiz, that had served valiantly through battle and retreat, to die in a Tennessee stream bed. And now this bone-rack of a gray mule with one lop ear, a mind of his own, and a gait which could set one's teeth on edge when you pushed him into any show of speed. The animal's long, melancholy face, his habit of braying mournfully in the moonlight—until Westerners compared him unfavorably with the coyotes of the Plains—had earned him the name Croaker; and he was part of the loot they had brought out of the bushwhackers' camp.

As unlovely as he appeared, Croaker had endurance, steady nerves, and a most un-mulelike willingness to obey orders. He was far from the ideal cavalry mount, but he took his rider there and back, safely. He was sure-footed, with a cat's ability to move at night, and in scout circles he had already made a favorable impression. But he certainly was an unhandsome creature.

"Smart actin's better than smart lookin'," Drew answered the disparagers now. "Do as well yourselves, soldiers, and you'll be satisfied."

Croaker started off at a trot, sniffling, his good ear twitching as if he had heard those unfriendly comments and was storing them up in his memory, to be acted upon in the future.

January and February were behind them now. Now it was

March . . . spring—only it was more like late fall. Or winter, with the night closing in. Drew let Croaker settle to the gait which suited him best. He would visit Boyd and then rejoin Buford's force.

The army, or what was left of it hereabouts, was, as usual, rumbling with rumor. The Union's General Wilson had assembled a massive hammer of a force, veterans who had clashed over and over with Forrest in the field, who had learned that master's tricks. Seventeen thousand mounted cavalrymen, ready to aim straight down through Alabama where the war had not yet touched. Another ten thousand without horses, who formed a backlog of reserves.

In the Carolinas, Johnston, with the last stubborn regiments of the Army of the Tennessee, was playing his old delaying game, trying to stop Sherman from ripping up along the coast. And in Virginia the news was all bad. The world was not spring, but drab winter, the dying winter of the Confederacy.

Wilson's target was Selma and the Confederate arsenal; every man in the army knew that. Somehow Bedford Forrest was going to have to interpose between all the weight of that Yankee hammer and Selma. And he had done the impossible so often, there was still a chance that he *could* bring it off. The General had a free hand and his own particular brand of genius to back it.

Drew's fingers were on the front of his short cavalry jacket, pressing against the coil of gold cord in his shirt pocket. No, the old man wasn't licked yet; he'd give Wilson and every one of those twenty-seven thousand Yankees a good stiff fight when they came poking their long noses over the Alabama border!

"He gave you what?" Boyd sat up straighter. His face was thin and no longer weather-beaten, and he'd lost all of that childish arrogance which had so often irritated his elders. In its place was a certain quiet soberness in which the scout sometimes saw flashes of Sheldon.

Now Drew pulled the cord from his pocket, holding it out for Boyd's inspection. The younger boy ran it through his fingers wonderingly.

"General Forrest's!" From it he looked to the faded weatherworn hat Drew had left on a chair by the door. Boyd caught it up and pulled off the leather string banding its dented crown. Carefully he fitted on Forrest's gift and studied the result critically. Drew laughed.

"Like puttin' a new saddle on Croaker; it doesn't fit."

"Yes, it does," Boyd protested. "That's right where it belongs."

Drew, standing by the window, felt a pinch of concern. He found it difficult nowadays to deny Boyd anything, let alone such a harmless request.

"The first lieutenant comin' along will call me for sportin' a general's feathers on a sergeant's head," he protested. "Nothin' from Cousin Merry yet? Maybe Hansford didn't make it through with my letter. He hasn't come back yet ... But—"

"Think I'd lie to you about that?" Boyd's eyes held some of the old blaze as he turned the hat around in his hands. "And what I told you is the truth. The surgeon said it won't hurt me any to ride with the boys when you pull out. General Buford's ordered to Selma and Dr. Cowan's sister lives there. He has a letter from her sayin' I can rest up at her house if

I need to. But I won't! I haven't coughed once today, that's the honest truth, Drew. And when you go, the Yankees are goin' to move in here. I don't want to go to a Yankee prison, like Anse—"

Drew's shoulders hunched in an involuntary tightening of muscles as he stared straight out of the window at nothing. Boyd had insisted from the first that the Texan must be a prisoner. Drew schooled himself into the old shell, the shell of trying not to let himself care.

"General Buford said I was to ride in one of the head-quarters wagons. He needs an extra driver. That's doin' some-thing useful, not just sittin' around listenin' to a lot of bad news!" The boy's tone was almost raw in protest.

And some of Boyd's argument made sense. After the com-mand moved out he might be picked up by a roving Yankee patrol, while Selma was still so far behind the Confederate lines that it was safe, especially with Forrest moving between it and Wilson.

"Mind you, take things easy! Start coughin' again, and you'll have to stay behind!" Drew warned.

"Drew, are things really so bad for us?"

The scout came away from the window. "Maybe the Gen-eral can hold off Wilson . . . this time. But it can't last. Look at things straight, Boyd. We're short on horses; more'n half the men are dismounted. And more of them desert every day. Men are afraid they'll be sent into the Carolinas to fight Sherman, and they don't want to be so far from home. The women write or get messages through about how hard things are at home. A man can march with an empty belly for him-self and somehow stick it out, but when he hears about his children starvin' he's apt to forget all the rest. We're whittled 'way down, and there's no way under Heaven of gettin' what we need."

"I heard some of the boys talkin' about drawin' back to Texas."

"Sure, we've all heard that big wishin', but that's all it is, just wishin'. The Yankees wouldn't let up even if they crowded us clear back until we're knee-deep in the Rio Grande. It's close to the end now—"

"No, it ain't!" Boyd flared, more than a shade of the old stubbornness back in his voice. "It ain't goin' to be the end as long as one of us can ride and hold a carbine! They can have horses and new boots, their supplies, and all their men. We ain't scared of any Yankee who ever rode down the pike! If you yell at 'em now, they'd beat it back the way they came."

Drew smiled tiredly. "Guess we're on our way now to do some of that yellin'." The end was almost in sight; every trooper in or out of the saddle knew it. Only some, like Boyd, would not admit it. "Remember what I say, Boyd. Take it slow and ride easy!"

Boyd picked up Drew's hat again, holding it in the sunlight coming through the window. The cord was a band of raw gold, gleaming brighter, perhaps, because of the shabbiness of the hat it now graced.

"You don't ride easy with the General," he said softly. "You ride tall and you ride proud!"

Drew took the hat from him. Out of the direct sunbeam, the band still seemed to hold a bit of fire.

"Maybe you do," he agreed soberly.

Now Boyd was smiling in turn. "You carry the General's hatband right up so those blue bellies can get the shine in

their eyes! We'll lam 'em straight back to the Tennessee again
—see if we don't!"

But almost three weeks later the Yankees were not back at
the Tennessee; they were dressing their lines before the horseshoe bend of the defending breastworks of Selma. Everything
which could have gone wrong with Forrest's plans had done
just that. A captured courier had given his enemies the whole
framework of his strategy. Then the cavalry had tried to hold
the blue flood at Bogler's Creek by a tearing frantic battle,
whirling Union sabers against Confederate revolvers in the
hands of veterans. It had been a battle from which Forrest
himself broke free through a lane opened by the action of
his own weapons and the concentrated fury of his escort.

Out of the city had steamed the last train while a stream
of civilian refugees had struggled away on foot, the river
patrolled by pickets of cavalry ordered to extricate every able-
bodied man from the throng and press him into the struggle.
Forrest's orders were plain: Every male able to fight goes into
the works, or into the river!

Now Drew and Boyd were with the Kentuckians, forming
with Forrest's escort a small reserve force behind the center
of that horseshoe of ramparts. Veterans on either flank, and
the militia, trusted by none, in the middle. Thin lines
stretched to the limit, so that each dismounted trooper in
that pitiful fortification was six or even ten feet from his
nearest fellow. And gathering under the afternoon sun a mass
of blue, a vast, endless ocean. . . .

The enemy was dismounted, too, coming in on a charge as
fearless and reckless as any the Confederates had delivered in
the past. With the sharpness of one of their own sabers, they
slashed out a trotting arc of men, cutting at Armstrong's

veterans in the earthworks to be curled back under a withering fire, losing a general, senior officers, and men. But the rebuff did not shake them.

A second Union attack was aimed at the center, and the militia broke. Bugles shrilled in the small reserve, who then pushed up to meet that long tongue of blue licking out confidently toward the city. This time there was no stopping the Yankee advance. The reserve neither broke nor followed the shambling panic-striken flight of the militia, but were pushed back by sheer weight of numbers to the unfinished second line of the city's defenses.

Blue—a full tidal wave of it in front and wedges of blue overlapping the gray flanks and appearing here and there even to the rear—

Having thrown away his rifle, Drew was now firing with both Colts, never sure any of his bullets found their targets. He stood shoulder to shoulder with Boyd in a dip of half-finished earthwork when the bugle called again, and down the ragged line of gray snapped an order unheard before—

"Get out! Save yourselves!"

Boyd fired, then threw his emptied Colt into the face of a tall man whose blue coat bore a sergeant's stripes. His own emptied guns placed in their holsters, Drew caught up the carbine the Yankee had dropped. He gave Boyd a shove.

"Run!"

They dodged in and out of a swirling mass of fighting men, somehow reaching the line of horse holders. Drew found Croaker standing stolidly with dragging reins, got into the saddle, and reached down a hand to aid Boyd up behind him. In the early dusk he saw General Forrest—his own height and the proportions of his charger King Phillip distinguishable even in that melee—gathering about him a nucleus of resistance as they battled toward the city. And Drew headed Croaker in the General's direction.

Boyd pawed at his shoulder as they burst into a street at the bone-shaking gallop which was the mule's fastest gait. A blue-coated trooper sat with his back against the paling of a trim white fence, one lax hand still holding the reins of a horse. Drew pulled Croaker up so Boyd could slip down. As he pulled loose the reins the Yankee slid inertly to the ground.

A squad of blue coats turned the corner a block away, heading for them. Somewhere ahead, the company led by the General was fighting its way through Selma. Drew was driven by the necessity of catching up. The two armies were so mingled now that the wild disorder proved a cover for escaping Confederates.

Twilight was on them as they hit the Burnsville road, coming into the tail end of the command of men from a dozen or more shattered regiments, companies, and divisions, who had consolidated in some order about Forrest and his escort. These were all veterans, men tough enough to fight their way out of the city and lucky enough to find their mounts or others when the order to get out had come. They were part of the striking force Forrest had built up through months and years—tempered with his own particular training and spirit—now peeled down to a final hard core.

In the darkness their advance tangled with a Union outpost, snapping up prisoners before the bewildered Yankees were aware that they, too, were not Wilson's men. And the word passed that a Fourth United States Regulars' scouting detachment was camped not too far away.

"We can take 'em, suh." Drew caught the assurance in that.

"We shall, we certainly shall!" Forrest's drawl had sharpened as if he saw in the prospect of this small engagement a chance to redeem the futile shame of those breaking lines at Selma.

"Not you, suh!"

That protest was picked up, echoed by every man within hearing. Finally the General yielded to their angry demands that he not expose himself to the danger of the night attack.

They moved in around the house, and somehow confidence was restored by following the old familiar pattern of the surprise attack—as if in this small action they were again a part of the assured troops who had fought gunboats from horseback, who had tweaked the Yankees' tails so often.

Drew and Boyd were part of the detachment sent to approach the fire-lighted horse lot, coming from a different angle than the main body of the force. It was the old, old game of letting a dozen do the work of fifty. But before they had reached the rail fence about that enclosure, there was a ripple of spiteful Yankee fire.

"Come on!" The officer outlined against one of the campfires, lurched and caught at the rails as the men he led crawled over or vaulted that obstruction, overrunning the Union defenders with the vehemence of men determined to make up for the failure of the afternoon. It was a sharp skirmish, but one from which they came away with prisoners and a renewed belief in themselves. Though they did not know it then, they had fought the last battle of the war for the depleted regiments of cavalry of the Army of the Tennessee. The aftertaste of Selma had been bitter, but the small, sharp flurry at the Godwin house left them no longer feeling so bitter.

"Where're we goin'?" Boyd pushed his horse up beside Croaker as they swung on through the dark.

"Plantersville, I guess." But something inside Drew added soundlessly: On to the end now.

"We're not finished—" Boyd went on, when Drew interrupted:

"We're finished. We were finished months ago." It was true . . . they had been finished at Franklin, their cause dead, their hopes dead, everything dead except men who had somehow kept on their feet, with weapons in their hands and a dogged determination to keep going. Why? Because most of them could no longer understand any other way of life?

There was that long line of battles General Forrest had named. . . . And marching backward through weeks, months, and years a long line of men, growing more and more shadowy in memory. Among them was Anse—Drew tried not to think about that.

Now, out of the dark there suddenly arose a voice, singing. Others picked up the tune, one of the army songs. Just as Kirby had sung to them on the big retreat, so this unknown voice was singing them on to whatever was awaiting at Plantersville. The end was waiting and they would have to face it, just as they had faced carbine, saber, field gun and everything else the Yankees had brought to bear against them.

Drew joined in and heard Boyd's tenor, high but on key, take up the refrain:

"On the Plains of Manassas the Yankees we met,
We gave them a whipping they'll never forget:

But I ain't got no money, nor nothin' to eat,
I'm afraid that tonight I must sleep in the street."

The Army of the Tennessee hadn't seen the Plains of Manassas, maybe, but they had seen other fields and running Yankees in their time.

Drew found himself slapping the ends of his reins in time to the tune.

"I'm a poor Rebel soldier, and Dixie's my home—"

Croaker brayed loudly and with sorrowful undertone, and Drew heard a laugh, which could only have come from General Forrest, floating back to him through the dawn of a new morning.

18

Texas Spurs

THE soft wind curled languidly in through the open church window, stirring the curly lock which Boyd now and then impatiently pushed away from his eyes . . . was a delicate fingertip touch on Drew's cheek. A subdued shuffle of feet could be heard as the congregation arose. It was Sunday in Gainesville, and a congregation such as could only have gathered there on this particular May 7, 1865. Rusty gray-brown, patched, and with ill-mended tears, which no amount of painstaking effort could ever convert again into more than dimly respectable uniforms, a sprinkling of civilian broadcloth and feminine bonnets. And across the church a smaller block of once hostile blue . . .

As the recessional formed, prayer books were closed to be slipped into pockets or reticules. The presiding celebrate moved down from the altar, his surplice tugged aside by the wandering breeze revealing the worn cavalry boots of a chaplain.

> "For the beauty of the earth,
> For the beauty of the skies,
> For the love which from our birth
> Over and around us lies."

Men's voices, hesitant and rusty at first, then rose confidently over the more decorous hum of the regular church-
goers as old memories were renewed.

"Lord of all, to Thee we raise
This our Hymn of grateful praise."

The hymn swelled, a mighty, powerful wave of sound.
Drew's hard, calloused hands closed on the back of the pew
ahead. Hearing Boyd's voice break, Drew knew that within
them both something had loosened. The apathy which had
held them through these past days was going, and they were
able to feel again.

"Drew—" Boyd's voice quavered and then steadied, "let's
go home . . ."

They had shared the talk at camp, the discussion about
slipping away to join Kirby Smith in Texas, and some had
even gone before the official surrender of Confederate forces
east of the Mississippi three days earlier. But when General
Forrest elected to accept Yankee terms, most of the men
followed his example. Back at camp they were making out
the paroles on the blanks furnished by the Union Command,
but so far no Yankee had appeared in person. The cavalry
were to retain their horses and mules, and whole companies
planned to ride home together to Tennessee and Kentucky.
Drew and Boyd could join one of those.

As they moved toward the church door now three of the
Union soldiers who had attended the service were directly
ahead of them in the aisle. Boyd caught urgently at Drew's
arm.

"Those spurs—look at his spurs!" He pointed to the heels
of the middle Yankee. Sunlight made those ornate disks of

silver very bright. Drew's breath caught, and he took a long stride forward to put his hand on the blue coat's shoulder. The man swung around, startled, to face him.

"Suh, where did you get those spurs?" Drew's tone carried the note of one who expected to be answered promptly —with the truth.

The Yankee had straight black brows which drew together in a frown as he stared back at the Confederate.

"I don't see how that's any business of yours, Reb!"

Drew's hand went to his belt before he remembered that there wasn't any weapon there, and no need for one now. He regained control.

"It's this much my business, suh. Those spurs are Mexican. They were taken from a Mexican officer at Chapultepec, and the last time I saw them they were worn by a very good friend of mine who's been missing since February! I'd like very much indeed to know just how and where you got them."

Lifting one booted foot, the Yankee studied the spurs as if they had somehow changed their appearance. When his eyes came back to meet Drew's his frown was gone.

"Reb, I bought these from a fella in another outfit, 'bout two or three weeks ago. He was on sick leave and was goin' home. I gave him good hard cash for 'em."

"Did he say where he got them?" pressed Drew.

The other shook his head. "He had a pile of stuff—mostly Reb—buckles, spurs, and such. Sold it all around camp 'fore he left."

"What outfit are you?" Boyd asked.

"Trooper, any trouble here?" A Yankee major bore down on them from one side, a Confederate captain from the other.

"No, suh," Drew replied quickly. "I just recognized a pair of spurs this trooper is wearin'. They belonged to a friend of mine who's been missin' for some time. I hoped maybe the trooper knew something about him."

"Well, do you?" the major demanded of his own man.

"No, sir. Bought these in camp from a fella goin' on furlough. I don't know where he got 'em."

"Satisfied, soldier?" the officer asked Drew.

"Yes, suh." Before he could add another word the major was shepherding his men away.

"I'm sorry." The Confederate captain shook his head. "Pity he didn't have any more definite information for you." He glanced at Drew's set face. "But, Sergeant, the news wasn't all bad—"

"No, suh. Only Anse never would have parted with those while he was alive and could prevent it—never in this world!"

"Where was your friend when he was reported missin'?"

"We were on scout in Tennessee, and both of us were wounded. I was found by our men, but he wasn't. There was just a chance he might have been taken prisoner."

"Men'll be comin' back from their prisons now. What's his name and company, Sergeant? I'll ask around."

"Anson Kirby. He was with Gano's Texans under Morgan, and then he transferred with me into General Buford's Scouts. He's about nineteen or twenty, has reddish hair and a scar here—" With a forefinger Drew traced a line from the left corner of his mouth to his left temple. "He was shot in the left shoulder pretty bad when we were separated."

The captain nodded. "I'll keep a lookout. A lot of Texans pass through here on their way home."

"Thank you, suh. Should you have any news, I'd be obliged to hear it. My name's Drew Rennie, suh, and you can address a message care of the Barrett's, Oak Hill. That's in Fayette County, Kentucky."

But the chance of ever receiving any such news was, Drew thought, very improbable. That afternoon when he tried to find Boyd, he, too, was missing and none of the headquarters company knew where the boy had gone.

"Ain't pulled out though," Webb assured. "Said as how you two were plannin' to head north with the Kaintuck boys right after the old man says good-bye. Guess I'll trail 'long with you for a spell. You gotta cross Tennessee to git to Kaintuck."

"Goin' home, Will?"

"Guess so. Heard tell as how they burned out m' old man. Dunno, that theah's sure hard-scrabble ground; we never did make us a good crop on it. Maybe so, we'll try somewheah's else now. Sorta got me an itchin' foot. Maybe won't tie down anywheah for a spell."

"What about you, Injun?" Drew turned to Croff.

"Goin' back to the Nations. Guess they had it hard there too, General Watie and the Union 'Pins' raidin' back and forth. They'll need schools though, and someone to teach 'em—"

"You a teacher, Injun?" Webb was plainly startled.

"Startin' to be one, before the bands started playin' Dixie so loud," Croff said, smiling. "Maybe I've forgotten too much, though. I have to see if I can fit me in behind a desk again."

"Heah's th' kid—"

Drew looked up at Webb's hail. Boyd walked toward them, his saddlebags slung over one shoulder, under his arm the haversack for rations which normally hung from any forager's saddle horn. He dropped them by the fire and held two gleaming objects out to Drew.

"Anse's spurs! How did you get them?"

"Sold m' horse to the sutler at the Yankee camp. Then bought 'em. That trooper gave 'em to me for just what he paid: five dollars hard money. Said as how he could understand why you wanted to have them—"

"But your horse!"

Boyd grinned. "Looky here, Drew, more'n half of this heah Reb army is footin' it home. I guess I can cross two little states without it finishin' me off—leastwise I reckon anyone who has toughened it out with General Forrest can do that much."

Drew turned the spurs around in hands which were a little shaky. "We got Croaker, and we'll take turns ridin'. No, two states ain't too far for a couple of troopers, specially if they have them a good stout mule into the bargain!"

A hot copper sun turned late Kentucky May into August weeks ahead of season. Thunder muttered sullenly beyond the horizon. And a breeze picked up road dust and grit, plastering it to Croaker's sweating hide, their own unwashed skin.

"Better . . . ride . . ." Licking dust from his lips, Drew watched the weaving figure on the other side of the mule with dull concern. They were steadying themselves by a tight grip on the stirrups, and Croaker was supporting and towing them, rather than their steering him.

Boyd's head lifted. "Ride yourself!" He got a ghost of his

old defiance into that, though his voice was hardly more than a harsh croak of whisper. "I ain't givin' in now!"

He leased his stirrup hold, staggering forward a step or two, and would have gone face-down on the turnpike if Drew had not made a big effort to reach him. But the other's weight bore him along, and they both sprawled on the road. Croaker came to a halt, his head hanging until he could have nuzzled Drew's shoulder.

They had made a brave start from Alabama, keeping up with the company they joined until they were close to the Kentucky-Tennessee border. Then a blistered heel had forced Drew into the rider's role for two days, and they had fallen behind. The rations they had drawn had been stretched as far as they would go. Even though there were people along the way willing to feed a hungry soldier, there were too many hungry soldiers. The farther north they traveled there was also a growing number of places where a blue coat might be welcome, but a gray one still signified "enemy."

Drew moved, and raised Boyd's head and shoulders to his knee. If he could summon enough energy to reach the canteen hanging from Croaker's saddle . . . Somehow he did, recklessly spilling a cupful of its contents on Boyd's face, and turning road dust into flecks of mud which freckled the gaunt cheeks.

"Ain't goin' t' ride—" Boyd's eyes opened and he took up the argument again.

"Well," Drew lashed out, "I can't carry you! Or do you expect to be dragged?"

Boyd's face crumpled and he flung up his arms to hide his eyes.

"All right."

With the aid of a sloping bank and an effort which left them both weakly panting, Boyd was mounted and they started their slow crawl once more.

"Drew!"

He raised his head. Boyd had straightened in the saddle and was pointing ahead, though his outstretched hand was shaking. "We made it—there's home!"

Beyond was the green of trees, a whole line of trees curving along a gravel carriage drive. But somehow Drew could not match Boyd's joy. He was tired, so tired that he was aware of nothing really but the aching weariness of his body.

They turned into the drive, the gravel crunching into his holed boots while the tree shadows made a green twilight. Croaker came to a stop, and Drew's eyes raised from the gravel to the line of one step and then another. His gaze finally came to a broad veranda . . . to someone who had been sitting there and who was now on her feet, staring wide-eyed back at the three of them. Then the gravel came up in a wave and he was swallowed up in it and darkness—

The sun, warm through the window, awoke a glint of reflection from the top of the chest of drawers where rested a round cord of bullion with two tassels and a pair of fancy spurs. The wink of light was reflected again from the mirror before which Drew stood.

"Jefferson's shirt has long enough sleeves, but all these billows!" Cousin Merry's tongue clicked against her teeth in exasperation. Her hand was in the middle of Drew's back, gathering up a good pleating of linen, but he still had extra folds of cloth to spare over his ribs. Four days of rest and plenty of food was not sufficient to restore any padding to his frame. "You certainly grew one way, but not the other!"

Boyd, established in the big chair by the window, laughed.

"I could take a few tucks," Drew offered.

"*You* could take a few tucks!" Her astonished face showed in the glass above his shoulder.

"Oh, I'm not too bad with a needle. Did you note those neat patches on my breeches—?"

"I noted nothing about those breeches; they went straight into the fire! Such rags . . ."

"Miss Merry, ma'am—" small Hetty showed an eager face around the corner of the door— "Majuh Forbes and Missus Forbes—they's downstairs."

Drew faced away from the mirror. "Why?" he demanded with almost hostile emphasis.

Meredith Barrett untied the strings of her sewing apron. "Hetty, tell Mam Gusta to set out some of the English biscuits and make tea." Then she turned back to face Drew. "Why, Drew? Rather—why not? They're your kin, and I think that Marianna feels it deeply that you came here and not to Red Springs. Not to go home . . ."

"Home?" There was heat in that. "You, if anyone, know that Red Springs was never really my home. And Forbes is an officer in the Union Army. This is no time for a Reb to camp out in his house. My grandfather wanted the place to be just Aunt Marianna's, didn't he?" He paused by the chest of drawers, his hand going out to the spurs, the gold cord. Three years—in a way a small lifetime—all to be summed up now by a slightly tarnished cord from a general's hat, a pair of spurs a young Texan had jauntily worn.

But it *was* a lifetime. He was not a boy any more, to have to endure his elders making decisions for him. His future was his own, and he had earned the right to that. Drew did not know that his face had hardened, that he suddenly looked a stranger to the woman who was watching him with concern.

"Please, Drew, you mustn't allow yourself to be so bitter—"

"Bitter? About Red Springs, you mean? Lord, I never wanted the place. I hate every brick of it, and I think I always have. But I don't hate Forbes or Aunt Marianna if that's what you're afraid of. It's just that I have no place there any more."

Her mouth tightened. "But you have! You owe it to Marianna to listen to her now. This is important, Drew, more important than you can guess. No, Boyd—" her gesture checked her son as he arose from the chair— "this is none of your affair. Come with me, Drew!"

He picked up a borrowed coat, also much too wide for him, pulled it on over the bunchiness of his shirt, and followed her, swallowing what he knew to be a useless protest.

The parlor was as bright with sun as the upper room had been. As Drew entered a pace or two behind Cousin Merry, the officer in blue strode away from the hearth to meet them. But Aunt Marianna forestalled her husband's greeting, rising suddenly from a chair, her crinoline rustling across the carpet. She held out her hands, and then hesitated, studying Drew's face, looking a little daunted, as if she had expected something she did not find. The assurance she had displayed at their last meeting on the Lexington road was missing.

"Drew?"

He bowed, conscious that he must present an odd figure in

the ill-fitting clothing of Meredith Barrett's long dead husband.

Major Forbes held out his hand. "Welcome home, my boy."

My boy. Consciously or unconsciously the major's tone strove to thrust Drew into the past, or so he believed. The major might almost be considering Drew an unruly schoolboy now safely out of some scrape, welcome indeed if he would settle down quietly into the conventional mold of Oak Hill or Red Springs. But he was no schoolboy, and at that moment the parlor of Oak Hill, for all its luxury and warmth, was a box sealing him in stifling confinement which he could no longer endure. Drew held tight control over that resurgence of his old impatience, knowing that his first instinct had been right: the old life fitted him now no better than his coat. But he answered civilly:

"Thank you, suh."

His proper courtesy apparently reassured his aunt. She came to him, her hands on his shoulders as she stood on tiptoe to kiss his cheek. "Drew, come home with us, dear—please!"

He shook his head. "I don't belong at Red Springs, ma'am. I never did."

"Nonsense!" Major Forbes put the force of a field officer's authority into that denial. "I do not and never did agree with many of Alexander Mattock's decisions. I do so even less when they pertain to your situation, my boy. You have every right to consider Red Springs your home. You must come to us, resume your interrupted education, take your proper place in the family and the community—"

Drew shook his head again. The major paused. He had been studying Drew, and now there was a faint shadow of uneasiness in his own expression. He might be slowly realizing that he was not fronting a repentant schoolboy rescued from a piece of regrettable youthful folly. A veteran was being forced against his will to recognize the stamp of his own experience on another, if much younger, man.

"What are your plans?" he asked in another tone of voice entirely.

"Drew—" Major Forbes waved aside that tentative interruption from Cousin Merry.

"I don't know. But I can't stay here." That much he was sure of, Oak Hill, Red Springs, all of this was no longer necessary to him any more than the outgrown toys of childhood could hold the interest of a man. Once, hurt and seeking for freedom, he had thought of the army as home. Now he knew he had yet to find what he wanted or needed. But there was no reason why he could not go looking, even if he could not give a name to the object of such a search. "I might go west. It's all new out there, a good place to start on my own."

There was a catch of breath from Aunt Marianna. The look she gave Cousin Merry held something of accusation. "You told him!"

"Told me what, ma'am?"

"That your father is alive . . ." She saw his surprise.

"Is that true, suh?" Drew appealed to the major.

Forbes scowled, tugging at the belt supporting his saber. "Yes. We found some letters among your grandfather's papers after his death. Your father wasn't killed; he was in a Mexican prison during the war. When he escaped and returned to Texas, your grandfather had already been there and taken your mother away. Hunt Rennie was too ill to follow immediately. Before he had recovered enough to travel, he was informed his wife was dead, and he was allowed to believe that you died with her—at birth."

"But why?" Alexander Mattock had disliked, even hated his grandson. So why should he have lied to keep Drew with him at Red Springs?

"Because of Murray," Cousin Merry said slowly, sadly. "It was a cruel thing to do, so cruel. Alexander Mattock was a hard man. He couldn't bear opposition; it made him go close to the edge of sanity, I truly believe. I know we are not supposed to speak ill of the dead, but I can't forgive him for what he did to those two. Melanie and Hunt were so young, young and in love. And your Uncle Murray deliberately pushed that quarrel on Hunt. Jefferson was there; he tried to stop it. The duel was *not* Hunt's fault——"

"Uncle Murray and my father fought a duel?" Drew demanded.

"Yes. Murray was badly wounded, and for a time his life was despaired of. Your grandfather swore out a warrant against Hunt for attempted murder! So he and Melanie ran away. They were so pitifully young! Melanie was just sixteen and Hunt two years older, though he seemed a man, having lived such a hard life on the frontier. They went back to Texas, and she was very happy there—I had some letters from her. Yes, she was happy until the War with Mexico began. Then Hunt was reported killed, his father, too. And she was left all alone with distant kin of theirs. So your grandfather went down to fetch her home. I'll always believe he really wanted to punish her for going against his will.

She died—" her voice broke—"she died, because she had no will to live, and *then* he was sorry. But just a little, not enough to blame himself any. Oh, no—it was still all Hunt's wickedness, he said, every bit of it! He was a hard man . . ." Cousin Merry faced Aunt Marianna with her chin up as if daring the other to object what she'd just said.

Drew returned to the news he still found difficult to believe. "So my father's alive, Major. Well, that gives me some place to go—Texas . . ."

"Hunt Rennie's not in Texas." Cousin Merry spoke with such certainty that all three of them gave her their full attention.

"I married Jefferson Barrett six months after Melanie eloped. We went to Europe then for almost two years of traveling. Part of our mail must have been lost. Hunt surely wrote to me! He liked Jefferson in spite of the differences in their ages. If I had only had the chance to tell him the truth about you, Drew. But I never knew he was alive either. You remember Granger Wood, Justin?"

Major Forbes nodded. "He went out to California in '50."

"Yes, and when the war broke out he rode back across the Arizona and New Mexico territories with General Johnston to enlist in the Confederate forces. A month ago he came back here and he called to tell me he saw Hunt in Arizona in '61. He had a horse-and-cattle ranch there, also some mining holdings."

"Drew"—Aunt Marianna caught his arm—"you won't be so foolish as to go out into that horrible wilderness hunting a man who doesn't even know you're alive—who's a perfect stranger to you? You must be sensible. We know that

Father's will was very unjust, and we are not going to abide by its terms—half of Red Springs will be yours."

Gently Drew released himself from her hold. "Maybe Hunt Rennie doesn't know I exist; maybe we won't even like each other if and when we do meet—I don't know. But Red Springs ain't my kind of world any more. And I won't take anything my grandfather grudged givin' me. I may be young, only in another way, I'm old, too. Too old to come under a schoolin' rein again." He glanced across her shoulder, noticing that his speech had registered with the major.

"You're not goin' to start out this very afternoon, are you?" Forbes asked.

Drew relaxed and laughed a little self-consciously, knowing that his uncle had ceded him the victory in this first skirmish.

"No, suh. You know, I brought two things home from the army—and one of them was a pair of Texas spurs. A mighty good man wore those. You'd have to ride proud and tall in the saddle to match him. I told him once I was goin' to see Texas, and he said there was nothing to make a man stay on the range where he had been born. Since I've always wanted to know what kind of a man Hunt Rennie was—is— now maybe I'm goin' to do just that."